"HE'S UNBEATABLE. . . . [PATTERSON] AGAIN PROVES HIMSELF MASTER OF THE HAIR-RAISING THRILLER WITH A CLIMACTIC, DOUBLE-TWIST ENDING."

—*Buffalo News*

"QUICK AND SCARY." —*New York Daily News*

"CHILLING. . . . THIS BOOK IS HARD TO PUT DOWN."

—*Associated Press*

ALONG CAME A SPIDER

"A FIRST-RATE THRILLER—FASTEN YOUR SEAT BELTS AND KEEP THE LIGHTS ON!"

—**Sidney Sheldon**

"THIS READER LOST A GOOD NIGHT'S SLEEP."

—**Ann Rule**

"JAMES PATTERSON DOES EVERYTHING BUT STICK OUR FINGER IN A LIGHT SOCKET TO GIVE US A BUZZ."

—*New York Times*

"WHEN IT COMES TO CONSTRUCTING A HARROWING PLOT, AUTHOR JAMES PATTERSON CAN TURN A SCREW ALL RIGHT. . . . James Patterson is to suspense what Danielle Steel is to romance."

—*New York Daily News*

"HAS TO BE ONE OF THE BEST THRILLERS OF THE YEAR."

—**Clive Cussler**

"TERROR AND SUSPENSE THAT GRAB THE READER AND WON'T LET GO. Just try running away from this one."

—**Ed McBain**

Also by James Patterson

The Thomas Berryman Number
Season of the Machete
See How They Run
The Midnight Club
Along Came a Spider
Kiss the Girls
Hide & Seek
Jack & Jill
Miracle on the 17th Green
(with Peter de Jonge)
Cat & Mouse
When the Wind Blows
Black Friday (formerly Black Market)
Pop Goes the Weasel

JAMES PATTERSON

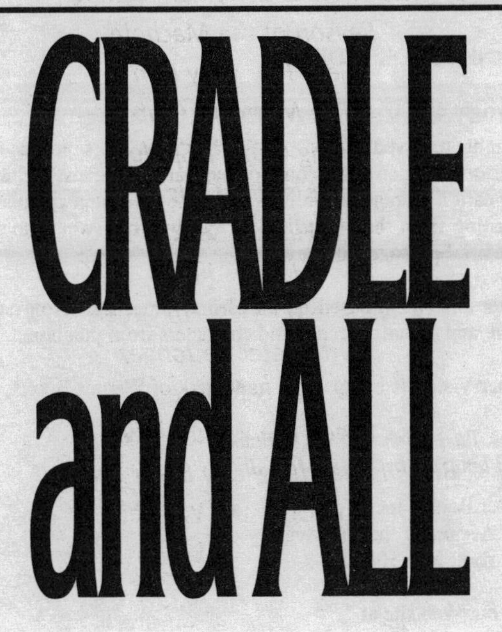

A Time Warner Company

WARNER BOOKS EDITION

Cradle and All is based on an earlier James Patterson novel, *Virgin,* and includes scenes and characters from that book.

Cover illustration by Theo Rudnak
Hand lettering by James Montalbano

Warner Books, Inc.
1271 Avenue of the Americas
New York, NY 10020

Visit our Web site at
www.twbookmark.com

A Time Warner Company

Printed in the United States of America

Originally published in hardcover by Little, Brown and Company
First International Paperback Printing: January 2001
First U.S. Paperback Printing: February 2001

10 9 8 7 6 5 4 3 2 1

PRAISE FOR THE THRILLERS OF JAMES PATTERSON

CRADLE AND ALL

"GIVE JAMES PATTERSON POINTS . . . THE STORY BUILDS IN MOMENTUM RIGHT UP TO THE SHOCKER ENDING. . . . Chills along the way."

—*San Francisco Chronicle*

"GRABS THE READER BY THE PROVERBIAL THROAT."

—*Ft. Lauderdale Sun-Sentinel*

"AN EXTREMELY WELL-WRITTEN THRILLER FOR THE NEW MILLENNIUM. . . . A fast-paced tale driven by well-defined characters, sharp dialogue, and a well-developed plot."

—*San Francisco Examiner*

"SUSPENSEFUL, FAST-PACED, AND IDEAL FOR A QUICK READ."

—*Cincinnati Enquirer*

"ADVENTURE YARN WITH HEART. . . . [HE] KEEPS YOU ENGAGED AND GUESSING."

—*Twin Cities Star-Tribune*

"ROCKS ALONG AT A SNAPPY PACE. . . . Creepy scenes reminiscent of *The Exorcist*."

—*Atlanta Journal-Constitution*

"PATTERSON'S USUAL CLEAN, FAST-PACED PROSE, A CREEPY PLOT, AND A TWISTED ENDING MAKE THIS ONE HARD TO PUT DOWN. RECOMMENDED . . . a good, spooky tale."

—*Library Journal*

"HIS TRADEMARK RAPID-FIRE CHAPTERS . . . A SURPRISE."

—*BookPage*

more . . .

"A TENSE THRILLER . . . LACED WITH THRILLS, CHILLS, TWISTS, AND TURNS. . . . It'll keep you awake, attentive, and on edge."
—*Pittsburgh Post-Gazette*

"EXCITING AND MOVING . . . TACKLES ISSUES OF FAITH WITH ADMIRABLE GUSTO."
—*Publishers Weekly*

"FUN, QUICK . . . A FINE READ."
—*Calgary Sun*

"PATTERSON'S LEGION OF FANS WILL QUEUE UP FOR THIS ONE."
—*Booklist*

POP GOES THE WEASEL

"CROSS IS ONE OF THE BEST PROTAGONISTS OF THE MODERN THRILLER GENRE, AND ONE OF THE MOST LIKABLE. Patterson has a unique gift of making the reader feel Cross's joys and pains."
—*San Francisco Examiner*

"PATTERSON DOES IT AGAIN. THE MAN IS THE MASTER OF THIS GENRE. We fans all have one wish for him: Write even faster."
—Larry King, *USA Today*

"FAST AND FURIOUS. . . . IN THE PATTERSON PANTHEON OF VILLAINS, SHAFER IS QUITE POSSIBLY THE WORST. Best of all, from the perspective of Alex Cross fans, Patterson leaves plenty of room for a sequel."
—*Chicago Tribune*

"HE GIVES CROSS A WORTHY OPPONENT—PROBABLY THE SMARTEST KILLER SPAWNED BY PATTERSON'S WICKED IMAGINATION . . . a worthy addition to the Cross saga."
—*San Francisco Examiner*

"PATTERSON MAINTAINS A FAST PACE THROUGH A COMPLEX PLOT." —*San Antonio Express-News*

"THE BOOK'S SAVAGE TWISTS WILL KEEP YOU ENTHRALLED." —*Woman's Own*

WHEN THE WIND BLOWS

"WHIPS THE PAGES RIGHT BY. . . . It has been more than a decade since I was captivated by a book like I was captivated by this one." —*Denver Rocky Mountain News*

"MEMORABLE . . . A WINNER." —*The Tennessean*

"BRILLIANTLY DRAWN CHARACTERS . . . SKILLED DIALOGUE . . . big, warm feelings . . . reads like a dream."
—*Kirkus Reviews* (starred review)

"ROMANCE, SUSPENSE, ACTION . . . SWIFTLY TOLD. . . . There's magic here, too, leaving readers more than once struck deep in wonder." —*Publishers Weekly*

"FINE WRITING . . . A GREAT STORY . . . WONDERFUL CHARACTERIZATIONS." —*Naples Daily News*

CAT & MOUSE

"A PROTAGONIST WORTHY OF ADMIRATION. ALEX CROSS IS A HERO."
—*Pittsburgh Post-Gazette*

"PATTERSON IS A MASTER AT CREATING SCARY MURDERERS, BUT HIS HERO HAS WHAT IT TAKES TO PURSUE THEM." —*Newark Star-Ledger*

more . . .

"I'VE JUST STARTED JAMES PATTERSON'S *CAT & MOUSE* AND I CAN'T STOP TURNING PAGES."

—**Larry King, *USA Today***

"FAST-PACED . . . THE PROTOTYPE THRILLER FOR TODAY."

—San Diego Union-Tribune

"A RIDE ON A ROLLER-COASTER WHOSE BRAKES HAVE GONE OUT."

—Chicago Tribune

"*CAT & MOUSE* IS A PULSATING GAME. . . . THE ACTION IS FAST AND FURIOUS. . . . The pages turn in a blur. . . . You might just finish this in one sitting. It's that kind of book."

—Denver Rocky Mountain News

JACK & JILL

"CROSS, A BRILLIANT HOMICIDE COP, IS ONE OF THE GREAT CREATIONS OF THRILLER FICTION."

—Dallas Morning News

"FLAWLESS. . . . PATTERSON, AMONG THE BEST NOVELISTS OF CRIME STORIES EVER, HAS REACHED HIS PINNACLE WITH THIS ONE."

—**Larry King, *USA Today***

"FORTUNATELY PATTERSON HAS BROUGHT BACK HOMICIDE DETECTIVE ALEX CROSS. . . . He's the kind of multilayered character that makes any plot twist seem believable."

—People

"Captivating. . . . a fast-paced thriller full of surprising but realistic plot twists. . . . CROSS IS ONE OF THE BEST AND MOST LIKABLE CHARACTERS IN THE MODERN THRILLER GENRE."

—San Francisco Examiner

For Charles and Isabelle Patterson

Special thanks to Maxine Paetro,
who helped me to remodel and
to restore this scary old
beach cottage of a story.

CRADLE and ALL

Prologue

THE WOMEN'S MEDICAL CENTER

Chapter 1

SUNDOWN HAD BLOODIED the horizon over the uneven rooftops of South Boston. Birds were perched on every roof and seemed to be watching the girl walking slowly below.

Kathleen Beavier made her way down a shadowy side street that was as alien to her as the faraway surface of the moon. Actually, she was here in Southie because it was so frozen, so obscure to her. She had on a fatigue jacket, long patterned skirt, and black combat-style boots — the urban streetwear look. The boots rubbed raw circles into her heels, but she welcomed the pain. It was a distraction from the unthinkable thing she had come to do.

This is so spooky, so unreal, so impossible, she thought.

The sixteen-year-old girl paused to catch her breath at the sparsely trafficked intersection of Dorchester and Broadway. She didn't look as if she belonged here. She was too preppy, maybe too pretty. That was her plan, though. She'd never bump into anyone she knew in South Boston.

With badly shaking hands, she pushed her gold wire-rimmed glasses back into her blond hair. She'd washed it earlier with Aveda shampoo and rinsed it with conditioner. It seemed so absurd and ridiculous to have worried about how her damn hair would look.

She squeezed her eyes shut and uttered a long, hopeless cry of confusion and despair.

Kathleen finally forced open her eyes. She blinked into the slashing red rays of the setting sun. Then she scanned her Rolex Lady Datejust wristwatch for the millionth time in the past hour.

God, no. It was already past six. She was late for her doctor's appointment.

She pushed forward into the ruins of Southie. Ahern's funeral parlor loomed in her peripheral vision, then slipped away. She hurried past the crumbling St. Augustine's parish church, past hole-in-the-wall bars, a boarded-up strip of two-storied row houses, a street person peeing against a wall covered with graffiti. She thought of an old rock song, "Aqualung," by Jethro Tull.

She whipped herself forward, as she often did to protect herself against the New England cold. Tears ran from her eyes and dribbled down over her chin.

Hurry, hurry. You have to do this terrible thing. You've come this far.

It was already twenty after the hour when she finally turned the corner onto West Broadway. She instantly recognized the gray brick building wedged in between a twenty-four-hour Laundromat and a pawnshop.

This is the place. This . . . hellhole.

The walls were smeared with lipstick-red and black graffiti: *Abortion = Murder. Abortion is the Unforgivable Sin.* There was a glass door and beside it a tarnished brass plaque: WOMEN'S MEDICAL CENTER, it read.

Sorrow washed over her and she felt faint. She didn't want to go through with it. She wasn't sure that she could. It was all terribly, horribly unfair.

Kathleen pressed her hand to the doorplate. The door opened into a reassuring reception room. Pastel-colored plastic chairs ringed the perimeter. Posters of sweet-faced mothers and chubby babies hung on the walls. Best of all, no one was here at this late hour.

Kathleen took a clipboard left out on a countertop. A sign instructed her to fill out the form as best she could.

Ensconced in a baby blue chair, she printed her medical history in block letters. Her hands were shaking harder now. Her foot, trapped in her trendy combat boot, wouldn't stop tapping.

Kathleen probed her memory for something, anything, that would make sense of this. Nothing did! *This can't be happening to me! I shouldn't be in the Women's Medical Center.*

She had made out with boys, but damn it, damn it, damn it, she knew the difference between kissing and . . . fucking.

She'd never gone all the way with anyone. Never even wanted to. She was too old-fashioned about sex — or maybe just a prude, or maybe just a good girl — but she hadn't done anything wrong. She'd never been touched down there by a boy. Wouldn't she know it if she had? Of course she would.

So how could she be *pregnant?*

She couldn't. It wasn't physically possible. She was a good kid, the best. Everybody's friend at school.

Kathleen Beavier was a virgin. She'd never had sexual intercourse.

But she was pregnant.

Chapter 2

A SUDDEN WAVE of nausea came over Kathleen and nearly knocked her to the floor. She felt dizzy and thought she might throw up in the waiting room.

"Get yourself together," she muttered softly. *You're not the first one to go through this kind of thing. You won't be the last, kiddo.*

She glanced at the clock over the reception desk with no receptionist. It was nearly six-thirty. Where was the receptionist? More important, where was the doctor?

Kathleen wanted to run out of the women's clinic, but she fought off the powerful instinct. She couldn't sit here any longer! She couldn't stand the waiting. Where *was* everybody?

"Let's do this," she said between clenched teeth. "No time like the present."

She stood and walked to a pinewood door directly behind the reception desk. Kathleen took a deep breath, possibly the deepest of her life. She turned the metal handle, and the door opened.

She heard a soft, mellow voice coming from down the hall. *Thank God someone is here after all.*

She followed the sound.

"Hello," Kathleen called out tentatively. "Hello? Anybody? I'm a patient. I'm Kathleen Beavier. Hello?"

The door at the far end of the hall was partially open, and Kathleen heard the pleasing voice inside. She slowly pushed the door open all the way.

"Hello?"

Something was wrong. It didn't feel right to Kathleen. She felt she should leave, but it had taken her so much courage to come here in the first place.

The air was thick, almost viscous. There was a smell of alcohol. But something else, too? Kathleen put her hand to her mouth.

It took her a few seconds to take in the full, horrifying effect of what she saw.

A young, dark-haired woman was hanging from a hook high up on the wall. She wore a white medical coat. Her name tag read DR. HIGGINS. A cord was slipknotted crudely around her neck, which seemed stretched to at least twice its normal length.

The neck and face were congested a brutal dark red. There was petechial hemorrhaging in the eyes, which were frozen in fear. The woman's brown hair cascaded over her shoulders.

Trembling, Kathleen reached out and touched the woman's hand. It was still warm, and damp. *Dr. Higgins. Her doctor.*

This woman had just died!

In a panic, Kathleen jerked her hand away. She wanted to run, but some force held her there. Something so powerful. So awful.

She saw a stethoscope coiled beside a pad of paper. On the pad was written Kathleen's name.

"Oh, nooooooo!" she screamed. There was a gathering in her stomach as fear and guilt and shame overpowered her in one sickening, wrenching movement.

At that instant, she realized she couldn't stand being in this world anymore. The thought was so strange, so overwhelming, it was almost as if it weren't her own.

A tray of instruments glittered near the pad of paper. Kathleen took up a sharp blade. It was ice-cold and menacing in her hand.

She heard a voice — but no one was there. The Voice was deep, commanding. *You know what you have to do, Kathleen. We've talked about it. Go ahead, now. It's the right thing.*

In the space between the pink cuff of her Ralph Lauren oxford cloth shirt and the crease of her left wrist, she sliced. The skin parted.

See how easy it is, Kathleen? It's nothing, really. Just the natural order of things.

Then blood welled up and fell in large drops onto the floor. Tears flowed from her eyes and intermixed with the blood.

One more cut. Just to be sure.

The second cut was harder for her to do. The wristband of her watch covered the best place on her vein, and her left hand was already weak.

She sliced into the vein again.

She sank to her knees, as if in prayer.

Kathleen managed a third slash before everything jumped to black.

She fell unconscious beneath the feet of the hanging doctor, whose mouth now seemed frozen in a knowing smile.

Book One

THE INVESTIGATORS

Chapter 3

GIVEN EVERYTHING THAT HAS happened, it isn't too much of a stretch to say that this is one of the most incredible stories ever, and the strangest I've ever encountered. The weirdest thing of all is that I am part of it. A big part.

I remember how my involvement began, remember every detail as if it happened just moments ago.

I was in my small, hopelessly cluttered, but comfortable office in the Back Bay section of Boston. I was staring off in the general direction of the Hancock and Prudential towers.

The door opened without so much as a tap, and an elderly man stepped inside. He was wearing a gray pin-striped suit, a white-on-white shirt, and a dark blue silk tie. He looked like a successful Beacon Hill lawyer or a businessman.

I knew that he was neither; he was Cardinal John Rooney of the Archdiocese of Boston, one of the most important religious leaders in the world, and a friend of mine.

"Hello, Annie," he said, "nice to see you, even under the circumstances."

"Nice to be seen, Eminence," I said, and I smiled as I rose from my seat. "You didn't have to get all duded up to see me, though. *What* circumstances?"

"Oh, but I did," Rooney said. "I'm traveling incognito, you see. Because of the *circumstances*."

"I see. Nice threads. Very high WASP, which all us Catholics aspire to. Be careful, some chippie might try to pick you up. Come in. Please, sit. It's nearly six. Can I offer you something to drink, Eminence?"

"'John' will do for tonight, Anne. Scotch if you have it. An old man's drink for an old man. Getting older in a hurry."

I fixed the cardinal a scotch, then got a Samuel Adams out of the minifridge for myself.

"I'm honored. I think," I added as I gave him his glass. "Here's to — the circumstances of your visit," I said and raised my beer.

"The perfect toast," Rooney said and took a sip of his drink.

I have a rather complicated history with the Archdiocese of Boston, but most recently, I've worked several times with certain members as a private investigator. One case involved a teacher in Andover. She had been raped by a priest who taught at the same high school. Another case was about a fifteen-year-old who'd shot another boy in their church. None of the cases were happy experiences for either the cardinal or me.

"Do you believe in God, Anne?" Rooney asked as he sat back in one of my comfy, slightly tattered armchairs.

I thought it an odd question, almost impertinent. "Yes, I do. In my own, very unusual way."

"Do you believe in God the Father, Jesus, the Blessed Mother?" the cardinal went on. He was making this very strange meeting even stranger.

I blinked a few times. "Yes. In my way."

Cardinal Rooney then asked, "As a private investigator, are you licensed to carry a gun?"

I opened my desk drawer and showed him one of Smith & Wesson's finest. I didn't feel obliged to tell him that I had never fired it.

"You're hired," he said and knocked back the rest of his drink. "Can you leave for Los Angeles tonight? There's something there I think you should see, Anne."

Chapter 4

I WILL NEVER FORGET Los Angeles and what I found there, what I felt there.

I had first seen the graphic pictures of the terrible disease on CNN, and then on every other TV network. I had watched, cringed in horror, as the children of Los Angeles burst upon Cedars-Sinai Medical Center by the carload, all with aching joints and fever, with symptoms that could kill within days.

When I arrived at Cedars, the scene was more intense than what I had seen on TV. It was so very different to be there in the midst of the suffering and horror. I wanted to turn away from it all, and maybe I should have. Maybe I should have run into the Hollywood Hills and never come out.

The sound of chaos and fear was well over a hundred decibels inside the fabled hospital, which had been turned into a confused mess. The shouting of the emergency-room nurses and doctors, and the wailing of their young patients, ricocheted sharply off beige tile walls.

It was so sad, so ominous. A portent of the future?

A curly-haired boy of four or so in yellow pj's was waiting to be intubated. I winked at him, and the boy managed to wink back. On another table, an adolescent girl was curled up in a fetal position around her stuffed sandy-haired bear. She was crying deep, heartrending sobs as doctors tried to straighten her contorted limbs. Other children were banked in a holding pattern along the perimeter of the room. Policemen, their radios squawking loudly, manned the doorways as best they could. They restrained desperate parents from their babies. The long linoleum hallway was packed wall to wall with feverish children tossing and turning on blankets laid across the bare floor.

Each room off the corridor had been turned into a dormitory of tragically sick kids. Their families seemed eerily related by the flimsy, blue paper gowns and the masks they all wore. Each new image was indelibly stamped into my mind, and then into my soul.

The doctor walking beside me was named Lewis Lavine, and he was the hospital's director of pediatrics. He was tall and somewhat gawky, and his black pompadour made him look even taller, but I found him heroic in his own way. Dr. Lavine had the presence of a rock in a sea of chaos. He was giving me the grand tour when clearly he had no time for it.

The same deeply mysterious plague had just broken out in Boston. Before I left for L.A., I saw the devastation at St. Catherine's, a very large hospital run by the Church.

The archdiocese had sent me to L.A. on a fact-finding mission. I was their investigator.

"You know what it is, don't you?" I asked Lavine as we walked hurriedly down the hall.

"Yes, of course," he told me, but seemed reluctant to go further, to actually give a name to the horror. Then he spoke gravely. "It's basically poliomyelitis, only this time the virus is faster, even deadlier, and it seems to have appeared out of nowhere."

I nodded. "It's the same in Boston. I talked for over an hour with Dr. Albert Sassoon at St. Catherine's. He's a terrific doctor, but he's baffled, too. It's polio — the second coming of the dreaded disease."

Polio had once been a killer plague that attacked more than six hundred fifty thousand people, mostly children. It killed some twenty percent of the infected, receding from the rest like a lethal tide, leaving behind deformed limbs and crippled spines, bodies that would never heal. Dr. Salk's and the Sabin vaccines had eradicated polio, ostensibly for good. There had been only a handful of cases in this country since 1957. But this present, mysterious epidemic had a much higher fatality rate than the polio of old.

"All of these children were vaccinated?" I asked.

Lavine sighed. "Most of them. It doesn't seem to matter. We're looking at the Son of Polio," he said. "The old menace with a new, more potent kick. It rushed past the old vaccine without blinking. Some of the World Health people think a broken sewer line contaminated a water source, and that's how it spread. But in Los Angeles we don't know how the hell it originated. Here. In Boston. Or wherever it breaks out next. And we certainly don't know how to stop it."

As if to emphasize his point, he looked around at the sick children — the dying children. Many of them wouldn't be going home, and that was so sad, so incomprehensible.

"No, Doctor, neither do the doctors in Boston. They don't know how this could have happened. But it did. What the hell is going on?"

Chapter 5

Rome, one week earlier.

FATHER NICHOLAS ROSETTI had never been so focused yet so devoid of original and illuminating thought in his life. He knew all about the "mysteries," the tragedies in Los Angeles, in Boston, and elsewhere. Sadly, he knew much more, so much more that his mind was threatening to implode. He thought that he knew *why* the diseases and plagues were happening. *He knew the unthinkable.*

Nicholas Rosetti's workman's build spoke of years of hard labor and outdoor life. He dressed simply, but well. His smile was disarming and self-assured, even when he was feeling almost total panic. He was darkly handsome, and that was inconvenient for a priest.

He had been born of poor, simple parents, but Nicholas was very smart, and he was ambitious. He understood how powerful the Church still was, but more important, how powerful it could be. He knew, he just *knew,* that one day he would be a cardinal.

But an odd and unexpected thing happened to him once he was ordained a priest: Nicholas Rosetti started to believe; he was given the divine gift of faith. From that moment on, he promised God that he would dedicate his life while here on Earth to serving the Church and its people. He was almost too good to be true — but he was consistent. That was how he eventually came to the attention of the Holy See, and then Pope Pius himself. It was known that Father Rosetti was as smart as any priest in Rome, but he was loyal, a genuinely good man, and he actually *believed.*

As he walked he found himself staring up at the familiar, shimmering gold domes, the two-thousand-pound crosses and needle spires of St. Peter's Basilica. He was looking for answers, but finding none. His already brisk pace accelerated.

As he struck out across the familiar, swarming St. Peter's Square — that majestic piazza with the Bernini colonnades — he could still hear the recent words of His Holiness Pope Pius XIII. The words kept ringing above the din of the Roman streets crowded with tourists, peddlers, and honking cars.

Nicholas, Pope Pius had said, speaking to him as a true confidant, *you are the chief investigator of miracles all over the world. I want you to investigate a miracle for me. Actually, two miracles. You can tell no one. You will be alone.*

Nicholas Rosetti strode quickly past the four magnificent candelabra built at the base of the Egyptian obelisk that had once towered center ring in Nero's Circus. His mind was still fixed on the words of the man whose spiritual authority and leadership spanned the globe.

Eighty-one years ago a message was left at Fatima, Portugal, by Our Blessed Lady. As you know, the "secret" of Fatima has never been revealed. Circumstances dictate that I must now tell you of the extraordinary message. I must tell you this secret, but you can tell no one. . . . It's vitally important, Nicholas. It has to do with the polio outbreak in America, the famines in Asia and Africa, so much more. . . . Everything is connected. You'll see for yourself soon enough.

Rosetti had already come to the Porta Sant'Anna. He was about to leave the 109-acre papal state called Vatican City. *And will I also be leaving its protection?* he wondered. *Am I truly alone now?*

As he turned down the ancient, crumbling Via di Porta Angelica, the priest felt a curious surge of dizziness. It was disorienting, a kind of swooping vertigo.

He felt that he was being . . . *watched.*

Shooting pains engulfed his heart, like knives piercing into his broad chest. His vision dimmed and was reduced to a narrow pinprick of light.

"Oh, God," he whispered. "What's happening to me? What's happening?"

Suddenly he heard a voice — deep and powerful. *There is no God, you fool. There never has been. Never! There is no way a human fool could ever know God.*

He tried to steady himself, grabbed on to a lamppost as a tide of nausea swept over him. But it wasn't like a wave of food poisoning. It was far worse.

"A man is sick," someone shouted in Italian. "A man is very sick!"

Nicholas Rosetti gasped hoarsely. Excruciating pain

lanced suddenly down his left arm and entered his leg. He had the thought: *I'm being skewered.*

He again heard the Voice deep inside his head. *You are going to die, and that's the end for you. You'll cease to exist in a few seconds. Your life meant nothing.*

Could he be having a heart attack? No, he was too young for this to happen! Only thirty-six. He was as healthy as a horse. He'd been in excellent health just days before. Hours before! He'd jogged five miles along the Tiber that morning.

Your exercise, your jogging, is a joke! You see that now, don't you, fool?

He fell to the cold stone pavement. The sky seemed to be fading in and out. Colors swam before his eyes. Faces looked down at him, blurred in his sight. They were grotesque, changing shape.

He thought of the incredible revelation he'd received — just moments before, inside the gold-domed Apostolic Palace — in the papal apartment itself.

I must tell you the secret, Pius had said. *I have no choice. Listen to me. Listen closely. Father Rosetti, Our Lady of Fatima promised the world a divine child. It's happening now. You must find the virgin mother, Nicholas. Only she can stop the diseases, the plagues around the world. You must find her.*

"Please, help me," Nicholas Rosetti gasped as he lay in the street. "I can't die now. I know the secret."

"We all know it," whispered someone in the crowd gathered over him.

"We all know the secret," they said in chorus. They smiled. *"We all know!"*

And he saw now that they were devils — every one of them. The streets were filled with grotesque, snarling devils. They looked like werewolves, vicious, hateful beasts up on their hind legs.

He heard the Voice again.

You're going to an early grave with your precious secret, Nicholas. You're going straight to the Kingdom of Hell.

Chapter 6

Newport, Rhode Island.

KATHLEEN BEAVIER NERVOUSLY scratched at the ragged red and purplish scar on her wrist. The sixteen-year-old remembered when she had cut herself in Boston, but she put it out of her mind now. She tried to anyway. Months had passed, but of course she couldn't forget.

She glanced at the *Boston Globe* sitting on the breakfast table beside her. The headline was about a mysterious outbreak of polio in Boston. The whole world seemed to be going crazy lately. Or maybe she was just projecting her own feelings and fears.

Suddenly, she had the sense that there was something wrong with the air circulating in the house. It was thick and nasty. It seemed almost evil to her.

Stop it. Just stop it, Kathleen commanded herself.

She had thoughts like this all the time now. Heard voices. Had crazy ideas. But at least Kathleen knew they were crazy. Ever since South Boston, she'd known that she might be crazy. But who wouldn't be a little nuts under the circumstances? She turned the newspaper over. No need for bad news right now.

A figure moved across her vision.

"I don't want any breakfast," she said to the housekeeper, Mrs. Walsh.

"Don't talk to me like that, Kathy," Mrs. W. scolded mildly. She put out a tempting little tray of goodies: fresh fruit, cereals, hot breads. The breakfast table on the veranda looked out over the rocky shoreline behind the Beavier house in Newport, Rhode Island.

Kathleen finally smiled. And despite her wish to be obdurate, to starve herself, to just say no, she stuck her spoon into the muesli cereal.

"Blech," she said.

"You're very, very welcome," said Mrs. Walsh, who'd been the Beaviers' housekeeper since before Kathleen was born.

The girl played with the cereal and the mandarin orange sections and the seven-grain toast on her tray. She sipped her chamomile tea and found it just about perfect, exactly as she liked it. Then she extricated herself from napkin and chair and slowly moved away.

"Be careful, Kathleen," Mrs. Walsh called after her.

It made the girl smile. Careful? Wasn't it a little late for that?

Chapter 7

SUPPORTING HER PROTRUDING stomach with her left hand, Kathleen negotiated a steep flight of bleached wooden stairs outside the house. Her one guiltless pleasure lately was the beach, and it lay directly ahead.

She could cry on the beach. She could scream all she wanted to and her voice would be drowned out by the crashing waves. She could act crazy if she wanted to. And she very much wanted to. She was eight months pregnant and that was just one of the things that made no sense to her. The doctor who was supposed to abort the child had either committed suicide or been murdered — the police still didn't know. Kathleen too might have died that night in South Boston if another patient hadn't arrived and found her bleeding on the floor.

Kathleen sighed loudly as she reached the beach. Her swollen feet were bursting out of her high-top Nike sneakers. She would have untied the laces but she couldn't see her feet, let alone reach them.

How had this happened to her? *How? Why?*

Wading through the ocean's low tide, she put her hand on her huge tum. She made the gesture pregnant women everywhere make: She rubbed a soothing circle on the swollen globe.

She wanted to hate it, but no matter how angry she was that she was trapped in this body, the baby was hers. And she couldn't be angry at the baby. Her baby hadn't done anything wrong.

She stood with her face to the early-morning wind and watched a crack drill team of sandpipers on tiny match-stick legs scrambling in and out of the frothy surf.

The gray-and-white birds watched her right back.

Was it her vivid imagination? Or another of the weird things that had been happening to her since her old life was taken over by this new one?

She sighed. Gently stroked her belly again. A thought about the polio epidemic jumped into her head. She forced it out.

Give it up, she thought to herself. *Enjoy the morning before your parents get up.* The nervous, embarrassed looks everybody gave her made her ill.

Kathleen walked away from the water and up toward the dunes. As she brushed her way through the high, yellow grass something darted out and stood directly in her path.

A red squirrel stared at her with frozen, gleaming eyes. She was certain the squirrel was staring.

"What's up with you?" she asked it.

As she glanced up toward her elegant, white-framed

Victorian home, she noticed a second red squirrel. It was staring at her from a branch of a tree.

And a big gray fellow standing upright like a tiny bear over near the stairs. *Watching?*

Then Kathleen heard a screeching voice above her head. Looking up, she saw flapping white wings. Six or seven circling gulls. Swooping. Kiting. Sailing over the gray beach like rudderless ships.

Were these birds keeping an eye on her too?

Watching?

Kathleen heard a whirring, the buzzing of insects, in the waving dune grass.

A cloud of blackflies appeared just above the grass.

Watching?

She started to cough; she waved both hands in front of her face.

Down the beach, two usually friendly golden retrievers began to bark.

Other neighborhood dogs took up the howling, yelping, whining, baying.

Kathleen's heartbeat quickened.

The squirrels.

The screeching gulls.

The buzzing insects.

The thick cloud of blackflies.

The howling dogs.

They all seemed to be gathering in a tightening ring around her. They hated her, didn't they? *Am I going crazy?*

"Stop it! Stop it! Stop it!" she screamed. "Just fucking *stop it!*"

Cradling her swollen stomach with both hands, Kathleen hurried back to her house. Her chest heaved with great choking sobs.

She slammed the front door behind her and ran into the parlor. She was breathing heavily as she stood before the huge window and watched the morning sun continue its climb over the ocean.

She hadn't imagined any of it. She knew that she hadn't.

They *were* all watching her.

Chapter 8

THE HIGHWAY SIGN up ahead read NEWPORT, R.I. 30 MILES. I had traveled from Los Angeles to Boston, and now I was on my way to my third destination in two days.

My windshield wipers cleared a half-moon tunnel over the slick, gray interstate highway. I felt lost, a little confused, and very tired. I couldn't stop seeing those poor children at Cedars-Sinai Medical Center.

The late-afternoon rainstorm pounded ominously on the roof of my sturdy, nine-year-old BMW, but I kissed off the warning. I punched on the window defroster, then concentrated on the blurred white stripes that sliced the interstate into curving, sliding, equal parts.

I was hitting over seventy, trying to distance myself from rafts of dying young Angelenos — even as I sped toward Newport and the very strange assignment I'd recently accepted from the Archdiocese of Boston.

What could the polio epidemics in L.A. and Boston have to do with a young girl in Newport? And why had the Church taken me on to investigate? Agreed to my $300-a-day fee without any attempt at negotiating?

I couldn't make sense of it and that bothered the hell out of me. I thought back to a conversation that morning with Cardinal Rooney. His voice on the telephone had been as persuasive as ever. "The situation is also being investigated by the Vatican," he'd told me. "They're sending their investigator. I don't care, Anne. I want you in Newport."

I liked the cardinal. Seven years before, when I'd told him why I was quitting my order and why I could no longer be a nun, he'd been sympathetic and accepting. I'd never forgotten that. I felt that I owed him.

I went to Harvard, and not long after that I picked up my master's in psychology. My thesis, "Firewalking: The Journey from Ages Twelve to Twenty," became a book that was credited with having an impact on the practice of adolescent psychotherapy. I'd gotten into police work to earn my way through school, and I liked it more than I could have imagined. I spent three and a half years with the Boston Police Department and enjoyed everything except the old boy network at the top. So I left the force and got a license as a private investigator. I'd done the right thing to leave the Dominican Order. I was pretty sure that once my habit was in mothballs, I would see my last of the Archdiocese of Boston.

I was wrong.

The cardinal had kept me in his active file. Very active. He sent me a note every time I was mentioned in a newspaper piece. He hired me to work on a few delicate cases. Cardinal Rooney wasn't just smart; he was clever. I should have known that he was keeping tabs on me for a reason. Apparently, that reason had arrived.

My drive from Boston to Newport had already taken two hours, and during that time I went over and over everything Rooney had said to me. "There's a sixteen-year-old girl in Newport," he confided. "She's a virgin, Anne. And she's pregnant. I need for you to check her out."

I respected the cardinal, but I couldn't contain myself. "It's got to be a hoax," I sputtered. "This is the twentieth century. This is America! I doubt there are any sixteen-year-old virgins *left*."

He laughed and admitted that that was his first reaction too.

"And now?" I asked.

"Anne," the cardinal said, "humor me this one time. You know the younger generation a lot better than I do. If this girl Kathleen Beavier is on the level in any way, you'll know. If it's total bunk, you'll know that too. Do what you do — *investigate*."

"And let the pieces fall where they will? You have no problem with that, Eminence?"

"Absolutely none. You have free rein on this. Just make sure you don't get hit by any falling pieces."

It was the second time that Rooney had alluded to danger, but an excited chill came over me. I exited the highway and cruised into the town of Newport. I couldn't wait to meet Kathleen Beavier. I was trying hard not to be biased against her, but I couldn't help it.

The truth was, I just didn't believe in virgin births anymore.

Chapter 9

I WAS MET at the front door by the Beavier housekeeper, who briefly introduced me to Mrs. Beavier and then showed me to my "room at the cottage." Apparently, I would be staying the night.

It was only 62 degrees in the room, but I'd already worked up a little sweat thinking about Kathleen Beavier. I'd arrived at the large manor house called Sun Cottage at four-thirty. Now I stood at a large bay window in my bedroom suite. I was looking out at an unbeatable ocean view. I was cogitating, one of my favorite pastimes, when there was a knock at the door.

"Yes? Who is it, please?"

A soft mumble came from the hallway. "It's Mrs. Walsh. Come to draw you a bath, Ms. Fitzgerald. Is that all right?"

"That would be . . . wonderful," I said, trying to conceal my surprise. "Please, come in."

Mrs. Walsh, a slight woman with a curly snow white

cap of hair, stood in the doorway. She nodded, then scurried to the adjoining bathroom. I watched through the open door in mild amazement as she sprinkled bath oil under the torrent streaming from the shiny brass taps.

"Your bath is nearly ready," the housekeeper said, ducking her head, then brushing past me. *My bath is nearly ready. Wow. Okay, I can handle this. I think.*

I thanked her and entered the handsome bathroom. Mrs. Walsh seemed a little strange to me, a little high-strung, but that was okay.

I drank in the stunning details of the room: the Victorian towel racks, the wood-paneled glass cabinets overflowing with thick bath sheets, the old footed tub, and a magnificent pier glass mirror.

I dropped my blouse and khaki trousers to the floor and stared at my image in the glass.

I had entered the novitiate at fourteen, before my body matured. I was a novice at the Dominican convent in Boston. The mirrors built into the walls of St. Mary's were blacked out with paint. My only looking glass was four inches square. For a couple of years, I wore a full habit, complete with wimple and oxford shoes. Even when I was alone, I put on and removed my plain cotton underwear under my voluminous nightgown. My hair was covered day and night. Mortification of the senses, it was called.

I understood now that I had entered St. Mary's as an alternative to staying in our house in Dorchester. I was the next to youngest of eleven Fitzgerald children. My mother was a cleaning lady and a functioning alcoholic. My father was an insurance salesman and a functioning alcoholic also.

I learned about St. Mary's from a sympathetic sister at my grammar school, and then I escaped to the convent. At St. Mary's I was "the tough one from Dorchester," which served me pretty well. The sisters were good to me, actually loved me better than my parents had, and they tried to save me. Who knows, maybe they succeeded.

I would have been shocked back then if I could've peeked into my future. Seen my grown-up-woman's body. I stared into the steamy pier glass, still awed, amazed, and amused that I'd emerged from my nun-y duckling feathers with what could pass as a model's body. Well, almost. Well, in my dreams.

I gathered the hair off my neck with one hand, then slowly released the thick, glossy sheaf of it, watching as it swung gracefully around my shoulders. My post-adolescent narcissism satisfied, I smiled to myself and settled into the hot, fragrant bath.

"I could get used to this," I muttered.

I had a moment of pure hedonistic pleasure before a chill invaded me, and I remembered exactly where I was. I wasn't a pampered society babe at Two Bunch Palms or the Canyon Ranch spa. I was in the Beavier house in Newport, Rhode Island.

I was here to investigate a virgin birth, which seemed to me, at best, a physical impossibility.

Chapter 10

AROUND FIVE O'CLOCK, I peeked into a very large, softly sunlit library room, feeling like an intruder in someone else's dream. I heard a woman's voice before I saw anyone. "Good evening, Ms. Fitzgerald."

Carolyn Beavier was standing in front of a wall of leaded, floor-to-ceiling windows that looked out on a lawn that rolled all the way down to the ocean. I'd met her briefly when I arrived. She'd been courteous but formal and restrained. She was in her late forties, with an elegant oval face, prominent cheekbones. Her streaked blond hair was held back by a simple velvet band. She fit very well in the world of Newport, Greenwich, and Palm Beach.

She introduced me to her husband, Charles, a silver-haired man who had the sharp, angled look of a corporate warrior. He was dressed in a charcoal gray business suit, crisp white shirt with French cuffs, gold cuff links, and a striped silk tie.

He acknowledged me politely, then bent over a handsome writing desk, snapped closed the latches of a black briefcase. Carolyn dropped into a sofa covered in a muted floral chintz, and invited me to sit in a nearby striped Regency chair.

Charles Beavier said, "You've got impressive credentials, Ms. Fitzgerald. Degree in adolescent psychology. Experience with disturbed children at McLean Hospital in Belmont. And of course, *Everything You Ever Wanted to Know About Teenage Girls but Were Afraid to Ask.*"

It was a small dig but I said nothing, just gave him a steady, cordial look. Since Cardinal Rooney hadn't included my experience in police work as part of my background, I decided not to add it to my résumé now.

"Sorry," Charles Beavier said then. "That was uncalled-for. I'm sure that *Firewalking* is a valuable book."

"We're under a lot of stress," Carolyn broke in.

"I understand," I said.

"No offense, but you really can't understand the strain," Charles Beavier said roughly. "When we learned Kathy was pregnant, I wanted to strangle her —" His voice caught in his throat.

Carolyn finished for him. "It wasn't just the pregnancy. It was that Kathleen hadn't told us. Then, as you know, she tried to kill herself. I wish she'd tried to kill me instead."

"Stop it," Charles Beavier said. "It's not your fault, Cee."

But his wife continued. "I wish Kathleen and I were closer. I wish I'd made more time for her. I wish, I wish." Her eyes slid off to the side. I sensed that Carolyn Beavier wasn't a carpool–field hockey kind of mom. I could imagine the Newport–Boston–New York social whirl she led; the life of a society woman married to a corporate chieftain.

"Kathleen and I do love each other," she added softly, "but we're not close enough. Especially now. We've never really been friends."

"I don't like it when you talk this way," Charles Beavier interrupted. "You didn't get her pregnant, Cee. You didn't slit her wrists in an abortion clinic in Southie."

He sounded very tough, unpleasantly so. Then, surprisingly, he choked, and tears rolled down his face.

What a scene. I reached out a hand impulsively — and impulsively he squeezed it. Then he took his hand back from mine and pressed his eyes with a folded white handkerchief.

"Sorry," he said. "We *are* under a lot of stress."

"Will you both take it easy on yourselves," I said. "Please. I'm not here to judge anyone. I'm not a judgmental person. I'm here to help Kathleen, if I can. And to represent the archdiocese."

I lifted the prettiest teacup I'd ever held. Sprigs of violets danced on white porcelain banded with gold.

Carolyn Beavier smiled weakly. "I'm certain you'll get along with her. She's considerate and loving. She's a very nice young woman."

I nodded. "I'm sure she is."

Charles sat down beside his wife on the sofa and took her hand. "I'll start at the beginning. As much as we know about the beginning," he said in a grave tone.

Stopping and starting as he sorted through the details, Charles Beavier tried to explain. The first days had been incredibly difficult for the family. That had been the worst time. They had always trusted Kathleen. The pregnancy had been a jolting surprise, the dramatic, nearly tragic kicker of her attempted suicide. It was when they were nursing their daughter back to health that Kathleen revealed that she was still a virgin.

"A virgin birth? Give me a break. How were we supposed to believe that?" Charles Beavier asked. "If she was lying, it was a scandal that would stain her reputation forever. If she was telling the truth, then she was a medical freak —"

"— or the mother of our Savior," Carolyn said softly.

Her words hung in the air as I turned the concept around in my mind.

The silence was broken by another voice that came from behind us, in the doorway to the library.

"I'd like to try and answer Ms. Fitzgerald's questions."

Chapter 11

A TEENAGE GIRL stood beside a huge glass-fronted bookcase overflowing with jacketless hardback novels and histories of another age.

She was blond and unusually pretty, her long hair hanging in a thick braid down the middle of her back. She wore a long plaid dress that reminded me of the singer Sarah McLachlan, and high-top sneakers. She had a henna tattoo on one arm. She was thin-featured, except for the shockingly swollen belly of a woman eight months pregnant.

I knew, of course, that this had to be Kathleen.

I searched her face for signs of depression, worry, fear, but couldn't find any of that. Not at first glance, anyway. She was spanking-clean, and her clothes were chosen not just to contain her shape, but because they looked good. She sure didn't appear to be a troubled kid who'd tried to kill herself a few months back.

"I was told you were coming." She smiled quite wonderfully, and bravely, I couldn't help thinking. "I'm Kathleen, as you can probably tell by this." She patted her huge stomach.

"Hello, Kathleen," I said.

I was clutching the arms of the chair so hard I was sure I was leaving nail marks. I couldn't take my eyes away from the young girl's face.

The lovely face of Kathleen Beavier reminded me of the Blessed Virgin Mary. There was no mistaking it.

Chapter 12

Maam Cross, Ireland.

A WEEK HAD PASSED since the brutal and mysterious attack on Nicholas Rosetti in Rome, just outside the Vatican gates. He looked so much older now; he felt so much older.

He felt . . . that someone was watching him, and he thought he knew who it was, and what it wanted. His only defense was his iron will to serve his Church at any cost to himself.

His recent affliction had frightened and frustrated him, and the doctors who attended his mysterious illness had no explanation. Tests revealed nothing. *Nothing!* Meaning what? That the attack had all been in his mind? He'd been deathly ill for five days. Then the shooting pains and high fever, the blackouts, left him as quickly as they had appeared.

So am I well now?

Am I cured?

Am I sane?

Father Rosetti drove his small rented car over the Irish hills, around sudden twists in the roads, with grave determination. He hardly noticed the beauty of the furrowed fields and pastures that flanked the country roads, nor their curious emptiness now that the spring lambs had been sent to slaughter.

His 225-kilometer trek from Dublin's O'Connell Street to Maam Cross in Galway was ending. But he knew his real journey had only just begun.

As he got closer to Maam Cross, his fear and anxiety about another physical attack increased. He desperately wanted to control the fears but found that he couldn't.

Why did he feel he was being watched? He could see no one on the roads.

And he hadn't heard the deep, terrifying voice in a couple of days.

He asked directions at the petrol station just inside the almost-medieval village of Maam Cross. A toothless mechanic in a greasy cap and blackened workman's clothes directed him farther west. He proceeded in that direction.

Stone gateposts marked the beginning of a long curving drive. Elm branches moved overhead, sending shifting shadows across the car's windscreen. The parkland on both sides of the drive looked lonely, unnaturally so.

He gave a sigh of relief when he saw that the road wound to a halt at the forecourt of a handsome and secure-looking stone manse.

The Holy Trinity School for Girls.

Yes, this was the place.

The girl was here. The virgin Colleen.

If he could believe that.

Abandoning his English Ford at the entrance, he made

his way up the broad stone steps. He could hear a class of girls through an open, latticed window, the sweetly monotonous chant of Latin conjugation. *Amo, amas, amat . . .*

He found himself reciting the known facts of his investigation. A litany of impossible ideas connected to an outrageous prophecy made decades ago at Fatima in Portugal.

A virgin here in the Republic of Ireland, site of Pope John Paul's mysterious visit in 1979.

A virgin eight months gone with child.

A fourteen-year-old schoolgirl named Colleen Deirdre Galaher.

A secret that Rome and the church in Ireland were struggling to keep under containment.

And *that* was just the start of things, just the beginning.

Father Rosetti absently lifted the heavy ring knocker on the school's front door. His heart was racing, and he felt weighted down with fear. Was he being watched? Followed? If so, by whom?

At least the Voice was leaving him alone.

A tall, flat-chested girl presently appeared at the doorway. The Holy Trinity student wore a puffy white blouse, a gray pleated skirt, conservative black shoes. She seemed to be expecting him. She curtsied, then silently led Rosetti upstairs to the office of the Reverend Mother.

Still afraid of another attack, he gripped the slight wooden banister as if he were an old man. It was constantly on his mind now — being struck down with terrible crippling pain — then dying, simply ceasing to be.

The school's principal was expecting him, waiting upstairs in her small, dank office.

"It isn't often we're receiving visitors . . . much less

from Rome," Sister Katherine Dominica said with a benedictory smile that made Rosetti distrust her. She was surely conflicted about her student Colleen Galaher, and concerned about the purpose of the visitor from Rome, of all places. But Sister Katherine would not ask leading or probing questions. As a provincial Irish nun, she knew her place.

"This term, Colleen has been studying her lessons at home," the nun told Rosetti. "The other students — and especially their parents — haven't been kind to her about this unusual situation."

"Unusual? Yes, it certainly is that," Rosetti agreed.

He forced a smile and offered words that were sincere. "I'm originally from a small town, Sister. People can be cruel. I think I understand what's happened here."

"I'll take you to see Colleen." The nun then nodded curtly and said, "She's here today, *at your request.*"

"My request. And the Vatican's," he reminded the solemn-faced nun.

Chapter 13

SO THIS WAS the girl that Pope Pius had wanted him to see.

Nicholas Rosetti's badly bruised heart lurched wildly the moment he saw the fourteen-year-old. His head ached terribly. The shock to him was that a month ago, even two weeks ago, he had been stable, strong.

My God, my God, my God.

The girl standing before him had skin as white as milk with a light sprinkling of freckles across her nose and a ragged haircut. It looked as if the ends of her curling red hair had been chewed off. She was dressed in a tattered beige raincoat, clean but too thin for the weather. The hem of a red flannel dress hung beneath it. Under the dress, she had on blue jeans. Boy's wool socks, elastic long since sprung, drooped over ancient school shoes with rips along the toes.

And yet, his heart continued to beat wildly. Why?

On a desk were a couple of schoolbooks, but also a paperback — *Omnivores,* by Lydia Millet. He thought he'd better find out about the book. What was *Omnivores?*

Is this the one? Dear God in Heaven, she is so young, so small.

The bulging stomach seemed a brutal thing for this poor waif of a girl to bear.

"Please sit down," he said. "Please, Colleen. You don't have to stand because I'm here. I'm just a simple priest."

A sister brought in tea and scones, then Nicholas Rosetti began the formalistic interview of the Congregation of Sacred Rites. It was the first test. The first of many, if she was the one.

A young child, fourteen years old, who very innocently ascribes her mysterious condition to the will of God the Father, Nicholas Rosetti would enter in his notes later that night. *She is just a child, though. My prayers are with Colleen Galaher. To my eyes, her features seem luminous, as if lit by a glow from within. She seems without guile, an honest young Irish girl. A ninth-grader. Imagine that.*

I am struck powerfully with this notion: Colleen is precisely the age of Mary of Nazareth when she bore Jesus!

He studied the girl as they talked; he couldn't take his eyes away. Suddenly, Rosetti was struck by a wave of feeling so primitive and hideous, his mind reeled.

He heard the Voice, but there were no words, just laughter. Awful, hideous laughter that the priest couldn't stop.

He braced for another physical attack, but this feeling was different, he realized. He gripped the edge of the desk and watched the skin under his fingernails go white.

"Are you all right, Father?" asked Colleen. Her voice was sweet, melting with genuine concern.

"Quite all right," said Father Rosetti. But he wasn't.

The Voice spoke: *She's so young, so small, so tight.*

He was sexually aroused. He was violently tumescent, and he was awash with guilt and shame. He was powerfully tempted to have sex with this young pregnant girl. He wanted her more than any woman he had ever seen in his life.

Take her right here on the floor. You can have her, Nicholas. You won't be her first, though.

Father Rosetti almost fell in his rush to leave the library. As he ran from the convent school, he was shivering uncontrollably.

He's seen the young Virgin, the Voice taunted, *and he likes what he's seen.*

Chapter 14

Newport, Rhode Island.

I STOOD AT the top of the wooden steps leading down to the beach and watched Kathleen Beavier below.

She was tossing small flat stones into the surf, and I could tell she was athletic by the way she threw the rocks. She had an air of confidence, and it seemed so odd, so sad and wrong, that she'd tried to kill herself not long ago.

I draped an old blue cashmere sweater around my shoulders and walked down toward the girl.

Kathleen seemed to accept me so far. She waved, complimented me on the way I'd twisted up my hair, and told me that the watercolor blue of my sweater was a real "wow."

Kathleen looked like most girls her age, though she was prettier, and pregnant, of course. She wore a tan hooded sweater, wide-legged cargo pants, chunky boots, a wool beanie. I'd been noticing her favorite brands: Roxy, Blue Asphalt, Union Bay. She wore makeup, but not too much.

She gave me an enthusiastic guided tour of the picturesque Beavier estate, which was once a working farm. There were still antique outbuildings dotting the grounds. The cottage was a beautiful structure, with four imposing wings added on to an impressive Victorian shell. The house had twenty-four rooms, eight full baths.

"It's pretty awesome," I said.

"It's not exactly a humble stable in Bethlehem," Kathleen said. She smiled at me. "I thought someone should break the ice."

I laughed. "Consider it broken. You know that I'm a private investigator."

"Do you get to carry a gun?" she asked.

"Everybody asks me that lately. I have a gun, yes."

We walked at the frothy hem of the sea, skirting the foam as it surged toward our sneakers. I said, "Maybe we should talk about what I know about you, and what I don't."

She took a deep breath. "Okay. If we have to."

"We have to," I said, hoping I sounded nonchalant. "All I know for sure is this: You're pregnant, and you say you're a virgin."

"Strange, but true. And you know I tried to kill myself."

I nodded. "I also know that the Archdiocese of Boston is concerned about your condition. I know they're trying to keep the story quiet, which is understandable. But why did they become involved in the first place?"

Kathleen rolled her eyes, which were bright blue and very pretty. "Okay. First of all, though, one minor correction. You said the Church was concerned; I'd say they're terrified. The almighty cardinal came here himself. He couldn't look into my eyes. That's very strange. *I* think it is, anyway.

"After I tried to end 'IT' and then to end me, my mother finally listened to me. She didn't believe me at first, naturally, but then she got it big-time. I didn't expect her to say, 'Mother of God!' Literally! But that's what she said."

The girl was funny; I had to hand it to her. She was a charmer. "So she called the local church?"

"Yeah. If it had been up to Dad, he would have sent me to Switzerland, put the baby up for adoption . . ."

Kathleen turned somber. She took off her beanie, rolled it in her hands. I couldn't help running diagnostics on her as she talked. Was she bipolar? One symptom of manic-depressive tendencies was megalomania or delusions of grandeur. The belief that one was going to be the mother of God could certainly fit under that category.

Kathleen rubbed at the still-livid scar on her wrist, then wrinkled up her face.

"Things got pretty wild around here after that. I was examined by a high-priced gynecologist they flew in from Boston. Then I was cross-examined by theologians at Harvard University, of all places. After that, all these different priests began to come to the house. And now you! Anyway, you seem much nicer than the others. They must have made a mistake when they chose you. Or you're sneaky?"

"I'm very sneaky. Kathleen, please start at the beginning. I've heard the story in bits and pieces. There's something about a day last January. Eight months ago. You'd gone out with a boy after a school dance? Who was he? What was that all about?"

Kathleen's blue eyes hooded over suddenly, a door seemed to slam shut on the newly formed trust between us.

"I'm sorry," she said. She shook her head. "I can't tell you about that. Don't go there. I'll talk about anything else."

Tears filled her eyes and she had to cover her face with her hands. I wondered if she was conning me. It was impossible to tell.

"I'm so afraid," she whispered at last. "I feel so alone and afraid. People think I'm either a liar or a saint. I'm neither. I'm just me! I'm still just me!"

She leaned against me and I took the badly shaking girl in my arms. I could feel her emotions, her fears, her terrible loneliness. I had seen it before, but never quite like this. What had happened to Kathleen Beavier?

Chapter 15

I WAS AGITATED after my talk with Kathleen. I liked her. Period. My objectivity was weakening already. I spent the remainder of the early evening interviewing the staff of five who worked at the house. I tried to do my job as if it were any other. The staff idolized Kathleen and none of them thought she was a liar. They *believed* in her.

I watched the evening news in my room and saw more about the polio outbreak, but also about a famine in India and a plague in Asia. What was happening around the world? I noticed I was hugging myself as I watched Peter Jennings report the news.

Just past seven-thirty, I checked in with Cardinal Rooney. I told him I was making progress but that there was nothing earth-shattering to report so far. That was when he dropped *his* little bombshell. He was sending a priest from Boston to stay at the Beavier house.

"I'm sending Father Justin O'Carroll," the cardinal told me. "You know Justin." *Yes, I know Justin O'Carroll.*

I had a late dinner with the family that night around nine, but my mood kept wandering all through the meal. Kathleen had gotten under my skin the second I saw her, and she defied easy classification. Now Justin O'Carroll was coming. God give me strength.

Around ten o'clock, I took a walk alone on the grounds. My mind was in overdrive, and I knew I would have trouble sleeping if I went up to my room.

This is a hoax. It has to be. Now how do I prove it?

And what will that do to Kathleen?

She had warned me to be careful walking around outside, and I thought that odd advice. The place was beautiful, and extremely well lit. I thought that I could handle any danger I found here.

Chapter 16

THE NIGHT AIR was cold and felt brittle to me. I had hoped that the roar of the waves would soothe me, but instead the sound called up a touch of melancholia that caught me off guard.

I had been trying to think of something other than the young girl. And as iron files are attracted to a magnet, so were my thoughts drawn straight to Justin O'Carroll. *Damn, damn, damn. Why is Rooney sending him?*

I hadn't thought about Justin for months, but now that I did I remembered everything all too well. I had been a Dominican nun for only two years, and I felt I'd made the right choice. But then something completely unexpected happened. I met Father Justin O'Carroll, originally from County Cork, Ireland. And damn it, I fell in love with him.

I first saw him when he was a caseworker for Catholic Charities in South Boston. He was wearing a plaid flannel shirt, jeans, work boots. I didn't even know he was a priest. I was attached as a social worker to Cardinal Rooney's office, the main archdiocesan office, on Commonwealth Avenue.

Justin was handsome; not quite Daniel Day-Lewis good-looking, but close enough to make the comparison. All of the laywomen at the chancery thought so, too. He had the most intense royal blue eyes and thick black curls. Some days he banded those curls into a ponytail and then he was virtually irresistible.

But I had resisted physical temptation before. I knew where it led: eleven kids and a lifetime of alcoholism. Even when I was a nun, attractive men had sometimes come on to me: fathers of my classmates and men on the street who couldn't tell I was a nun in my street clothes. But there was something so compelling about Justin; an unmistakable strength that intrigued me; self-reliance and individuality; a seeming indifference toward the rude ways of the world. He was a rebel with a cause: He was devoted to the poor, and especially to children.

Justin was worldly-wise, too. He could speak intelligently on a variety of subjects ranging from Irish sociology to classical music and art to American politics and pop culture, even baseball. He loved Mozart, and he really loved U2 and the Cranberries, and I had caught him humming and singing selections from both musical worlds. He was classically educated and had a quiet, sensitive temperament. But he was a *priest;* I was a *nun.* And the two of us simply couldn't be together.

Down on the beach near the Beavier house, I took a seat on a log of driftwood and stared out to sea. Pictures were flowing into my mind, filling in spaces I'd forgotten were there.

I remembered how dumb and giddy I'd felt when I was around him and how dumb and guilty that made me feel. To be honest, I'd never experienced anything like it before. Naturally, Justin and I never discussed this for the first year of our acquaintance. Then I went to an international conference in Washington, D.C., a trip that lasted two weeks.

One night during my second week, I got a midnight phone call. It was Justin.

"What's wrong? Did something happen?" I asked.

"The only thing that's wrong that I can think of," I heard a dreamy, faraway voice say, "is that you're in Washington, I'm here in Boston, and I'm missing you terribly."

I felt my heart seize up in my chest. I was tempted to hang up the phone. But before I was forced to find an answer, Justin was brushing past the awkward silence.

"You can't imagine how hard it was for me to make this call. I picked up the receiver and hung it up again at least a dozen times. I feel like a total fool, Anne, but I seemed to have no choice about it. *I had to call you.*"

What to say? The word *flustered* had been invented for moments like this. Could I possibly tell Justin that I'd been missing him too? That constant thoughts of him had been destroying my concentration all week? All month? All year?

No. I could not. I would not.

I said, rather inconsiderately, "I'll be back in Boston next Monday." And then I said I had to get some sleep, and hung up on him. What willpower, what confusion, what disingenuousness.

I thought about *us* for the rest of my time in Washington. I was extremely negative. When I got back, I asked for, and received, an immediate transfer out of Boston. I had taken vows; I had made a solemn commitment; I couldn't go back on those now.

Justin seemed to understand my decision. He didn't write to me or phone me at my new school in Andover. Slowly, my faith and some of my commitment returned.

Then one afternoon he was waiting for me outside the private high school where I taught.

"I had to see you again," he said in the quietest voice. "I'm sorry, Anne. I almost feel as if I have no choice anymore. No free will."

"Well," I said, and smiled. "It's good to see you too. But you do have free will. And so do I."

We went for a long walk through the streets of the village. I tried to talk reasonably, logically, calmly. It seems so ironic when I think of my impassioned lecture to him that day. Then suddenly this positively gorgeous man I wanted to love held me by the shoulders, and I was looking up into those stormy blue eyes of his. We were standing outside a place called the Pewter Pot. I'll never forget it.

"Justin," I whispered, "please don't."

"I love you, Anne," he said, still holding me. It was the only time I had ever heard those words.

"I don't want to see you again," I told him. "I'm sorry. I'm deeply sorry." Then I went back to my car and drove home, trembling and sobbing uncontrollably the whole way.

Months later, I heard that Justin had been transferred to the Holy See in Rome. Not too long after that, I was at Harvard, no longer a nun. As Kurt Vonnegut wrote over and over in one of his novels, *So it goes.*

Now, on a cold, windy, deserted beach in Newport, I knew that I wanted to see Justin again. I wanted to tell him about Kathleen Beavier, and how she had affected me. I wanted to talk to Justin O'Carroll, and I had no idea why the urge was suddenly so overwhelming.

But maybe I did have an idea.

Soon, I was going to be thirty years old.

I was still a virgin myself.

Chapter 17

THERE WAS A VISITOR sitting in an armchair in the large Beavier library. I knew who he was and why he was here. He was head of obstetrics at Mount Sinai Hospital. Still, I was introduced to Dr. Neil Shapiro, who'd been brought from New York to examine Kathleen. *A Jewish doctor,* I thought. Well, does that represent some kind of acid test to the Church?

Shapiro was an ordinary-looking man with thinning gray hair and a solid appearance that seemed to have been shaken by his trip to Newport. He talked rapidly about missed flight connections and a weird feeling of vertigo when he entered the city limits.

I sat beside Carolyn Beavier on the chintz-covered sofa and accepted a mug of coffee. My mind chewed on several ironies of Shapiro's visit, but then I gave my full attention to the doctor.

"I understand that Kathleen has been examined previously, but I've been asked to see her anyway. Of course, a home gynecological exam limits severely what I'm going to be able to tell you," Shapiro said in professional tones. "I'll be using a hand-held sonograph, for one thing. And since the Church wouldn't permit amniocentesis —"

"Kathleen's child may be a holy child," I interjected, playing devil's advocate. "It would be unconscionable to take even a one-in-a-thousand chance with its safety, don't you think?"

"Not my call, of course," Shapiro said, and smiled thinly. "So, how *is* our patient?"

"I'm sure she'll be fine," Carolyn Beavier said with a stiff upper lip. Perhaps she and Kathleen did love each other, but they obviously weren't close. They seemed to spend as little time together as possible.

"She wasn't delighted to hear that you were coming," I admitted to Dr. Shapiro. "I can't say that I blame her. I'll go check on her."

I climbed the narrow stairs to Kathleen's third-floor room. Kathleen was sitting up in bed. Copies of *Jump, Moxiegirl,* and *Teen People* were spread out on her quilt. Neo-swing music was playing loudly on the radio. The expression on her face plainly showed that she was very close to reaching her limits. I understood completely and I empathized.

"Why should I let him examine me?" she said reasonably. "Dr. Shapiro isn't even my doctor. He's another stranger poking into my private parts! I feel like I'm in an episode from *The X-Files.* It's a total invasion of privacy."

"I understand, I really do."

"Good," she said. "It's settled then. *C'est fini.* No stranger's giving me a pelvic exam."

"However," I said, "Dr. Shapiro is a doctor with no ax

to grind. He doesn't know you. He's not a Roman Catholic. The public will find him believable. And that, Kathy, will make life easier for you and your parents, and a whole lot easier for your child."

Kathleen nodded her head. "Fine," she said. Her lips were quivering with exasperation, though. I thought she was going to cry, but she managed to hold back the tears. She was strong.

I helped her out of the oversize metallic knit cardigan and flea market–style skirt she had been wearing all day. I had thought her mother would be there with her, but Carolyn had politely declined.

Kathleen's breasts were swollen and her belly was huge. She looked about ready to burst. I couldn't wait to hear what Dr. Shapiro had to say about her condition.

Chapter 18

"SAFE TO COME IN?" Shapiro said half-jokingly.

"As long as you don't touch me," Kathleen said from her bed. I don't think she was joking.

Dr. Shapiro apologized for the intrusion, then sat in a rocker near the window. His eyes drifted up to posters on the wall: Justin Timberlake from the group 'N Sync; David Boreanaz from TV's *Buffy the Vampire Slayer;* Matt Damon and Ben Affleck. Affleck had a gold star affixed to his forehead.

Very calmly, almost casually, Dr. Shapiro asked Kathleen a number of questions regarding her weight, sleep patterns, digestion, whether she was feverish, and where she was swollen.

He removed a few things from his doctor's bag. He took Kathleen's blood pressure and her temperature. Then he measured her abdomen from pubis to the top of the downward slope. He took a peculiar-looking stethoscope out of his bag. It was a six-inch-square plastic box with a speaker on one side.

"This is called a Doppler stethoscope," he told her. "It's like a mini-ultrasound machine. We can listen to the baby's heart."

He pressed the Doppler on Kathleen's abdomen, which he'd slicked with gel, and kept moving the instrument around until he got the strongest sound.

Kathleen was entranced — and so was I.

The sound that emerged from the little box was engaging, mysterious, and very real. It was the rapid beating of a tiny heart.

"Would you mind removing your panties, Kathleen?" the doctor said, but it was clear he wasn't asking her permission now. "And scoot down to the end of the bed. Thanks, now bend up your legs."

She took off her underwear and leaned back. Then she closed her eyes.

"Kathleen," he said, "you've never had sex with a boy?"

"Right," she said. Her eyes remained shut. "Never. Not in this lifetime, anyway."

"But you've had dates?"

"Of course. Who hasn't?"

"And you've been kissed and so on?"

"And so on?" Kathleen repeated.

Dr. Shapiro paused. I sensed him trying to rephrase the question in a tactful way. "You know that a boy doesn't have to put his penis all the way inside you in order for you to conceive?"

Her eyes flashed opened. "No one has ever touched me

down there," said Kathleen, emotion choking her throat. "No *penis* has touched me down there."

"All right, Kathleen, thank you."

"You're absolutely not welcome."

Shapiro signaled to me to assist him. I felt he was being a bit presumptuous, but I helped anyway. He pulled a stool out from under Kathleen's vanity, then brought it to the end of the bed.

"Hold this for me, will you?" he said. He took a slim flashlight from his jacket pocket and handed it to me.

Instinctively, I angled the light so that he could see Kathleen's exposed genitalia. He placed his hand on her outer thigh, giving her a reassuring pat. He tugged on latex surgical gloves.

"I can't use a speculum, obviously," he said, "if her hymen is intact."

With gloved fingers he spread Kathleen's labia majora, then her labia minora.

"There," he said to me, "the hymen ring."

The enclosed membrane was soft pink with a vertical squiggle of an opening at its center. The opening was tiny, too small to admit anything larger than a matchstick.

Dr. Shapiro looked stunned.

"I've never seen this before," he mumbled.

He had to steady himself before he spoke again. "We're all done, Kathy. You can put your legs down now and get dressed."

He snapped off his rubber gloves.

"She's definitely pregnant," said the expert from New York, the other paid gun in the room. "And this young lady's hymen is definitely intact."

Chapter 19

COLLEEN DEIRDRE GALAHER was alone in her small room, bundled in woolen blankets to keep away the cold of the night. Outside of the village of Maam Cross, less than a dozen people knew about her condition and few of them paid it much heed.

The Virgin Colleen had already been dismissed as either a fraud or a head case by the conservative Church in Ireland. The Vatican would have liked the same anonymity for Kathleen Beavier, but it was more difficult for the Vatican to hide things in America, the wild, wild West.

Colleen was awake, and, as she did every night, she prayed to God and the Blessed Virgin that her baby would be born healthy.

"Just let the child be healthy," she whispered, "that's all I ask. Please let my baby lead a good, healthy life. That's all, Lord."

Colleen continued to repeat the prayer over and over as

the wind whipped across the flatlands outside, through the trees, and up against her house.

"Dear God, I don't know why that priest came from Rome. I don't even care. I only pray that my baby will be blessed and born in your grace, and *live* in your holy grace."

It was such a simple prayer, and the Irish girl said it beautifully, because it came from her heart.

Over and over and over — until she finally fell asleep.

Outside, someone watched over the house, the girl, and the child growing inside the girl.

Chapter 20

JOHN CARDINAL ROONEY KNEW that what he was considering was unusual and dangerous, to say the least. He couldn't help that. Not anymore. He'd had lengthy conversations with Dr. Shapiro and Anne Fitzgerald. Then he'd spoken with Charles and Carolyn Beavier.

Finally, he'd gone to St. Catherine's Hospital and wandered through the wards, which were overflowing with sick and dying children. It was his walk among the poor, afflicted children that finally made up his mind. He saw, and felt, a connection between the polio outbreak . . . and Kathleen Beavier.

He worriedly rubbed his hands together. The glass of Glenlivet wasn't helping at all. Perhaps it was because it was so infernally cold that day in Boston.

Dying children, a virgin birth, he mused. *My God, how can this be?*

All across the city, thin plumes of gray-blue smoke rose determinedly and blended with the high, subtly warring skies. All day the story of a possible virgin birth had been building. He wondered how the rumor had started. Who was the leak?

Finally, late on Sunday evening, he wrote out a terse statement from his office high over Commonwealth Avenue.

> In response to the interest in the pregnancy of Kathleen Beavier, there will be a press conference on Monday. The conference will be held at Sun Cottage, the Beavier home in Newport. Kathleen Beavier will be present to answer questions.
>
> Admittance will be by invitation only.
>
> Until Monday, God bless all of you. You remain in my prayers.

He sat back, read it over twice, and reconsidered going public. A voice deep inside him said, *Yes, you should.* He wondered if the voice was his own, or his God's. Or someone else's.

Chapter 21

AT 9:39 P.M. thirty-year-old *New York Daily News* reporter Les Porter was home in his fourth-floor walk-up apartment on the West Side. He booted up his PC, and while his live-in lover prodded the lamb roast with a long steel fork, he checked his E-mail. He had a feeling the story was breaking tonight. His gut said it was.

The instant he saw the "Heads up!" message from his source in Rome, Porter forgot everything else: the smell of the roast; Renata's amusing anecdote about her day at work in the gallery; their cat, Annette Funicello, arching her back, passing her furry tail right under his nose.

"Git," he said, pushing the cat off the keyboard. "I'm working here."

He appended a note and forwarded the E-mail to Tom McGoey, international news editor in New York. Then he grabbed the cordless, flapped open his overstuffed Filofax on the lacquer telephone table. He punched buttons and finally connected with Boston. He had a confirmation in

Rome; now he needed one from Cardinal Rooney's office. The contact there was Father Justin O'Carroll. O'Carroll was clever, and worldly. For a priest.

"Father O'Carroll, can you give me any other confirmation on the story? Anything? Anyone you can send me to? I have two confirmations now. I'd like to have one more. It's in the best interests of all of us to get this absolutely right."

Porter cupped his hand over the telephone. He sensed that this was it. "Renata, turn it down. Please." He glared meaningfully until the soundtrack of *Les Mis* was a mere thumping murmur.

"All right, Father. Yes, yes. I understand your problems completely. Now please listen to what I'm saying. I'm going to talk with our international news editor right now. He'll have to clear this with the managing editor. You will stay near your telephone? Yes, I honestly do understand. I know how sensitive this story is. Now please, stay by your phone. The *News* will do an honest and fair job with this."

He was already halfway out of his apartment, heading downtown to the *Daily News* offices on 42nd Street.

Fifteen minutes after he flew out of his apartment house door and onto the street, Porter was at his desk in the newsroom — his command center. He pointed and clicked on the address book in his office manager program. He watched names and phone numbers scroll down his computer terminal. He pressed a key that connected his phone line to one James Lapinsky's, a stringer in Boston. Lapinsky was in bed and, from the ragged sound of his voice, asleep when Porter told him he had to beat it over to Commonwealth Avenue, to the archdiocesan office.

"Of course right now, Jim. I'm sorry about your headache. I'm sorry it's Sunday night. I need a face-to-face confirmation. This is urgent. Father Justin O'Carroll will tell you the whole thing from their point of view. He's Irish-Irish and has a quick tongue. He's reluctant to take any kind of stand, but he knows the story is coming out one way or the other. He's Rooney's mouthpiece, so it's official. Sorry to foul up your evening. You nelly," he muttered, clicking off the phone.

While he waited for Lapinsky to do his damn job, he took off down the hall to McGoey's glass-walled box-shaped office. He rapped, entered, closed the door behind him.

Then he told a perpetually snarly Thomas "the Colonel" McGoey the story that had just been confirmed by Father Justin O'Carroll of the Boston Archdiocese office.

When he'd heard everything Porter had to tell him, McGoey picked up his hotline to the managing editor, Joseph Denyeau. In his own way, McGoey pitched like crazy, but he told it straight.

When he hung up a minute later, the editor turned to young, frightfully ambitious Porter.

"Frankly, Denyeau doesn't know what the hell to make of it either. Just coming out of the cardinal's office, it's a story. The fact that they won't deny the rumor helps our case. He wants to see some copy, Les."

At 11:45, the computer-generated layout of the day's paper showed that there were additional news stories coming for pages one, nineteen, and thirty-two.

At 11:59, the head union printer at the printing plant in Jersey City pressed the starter button. The midnight edition began to roll.

At 12:16 the monster presses were screaming. Several hundred thousand copies would reach homes in the metropolitan area alone, by breakfast.

Les Porter left the News Building a little after twelve-thirty with a fresh newspaper under his arm. The paper was still as warm as a loaf of freshly baked bread. No — hell, this paper was *hot.*

Renata was waiting for him in the familiar surroundings of the Café des Artistes bar, two blocks up the street from their apartment. Les unfolded the newspaper and scanned it in the dim yellow light.

He slid it between Renata and her Smirnoff with a twist. Renata let out a soft "Wow" when she read the headline over her lover's byline:

CATHOLIC CHURCH CLOSELY WATCHES

A VIRGIN PREGNANCY IN NEWPORT

"A divine child. A divine fucking American child," Les Porter muttered in the buzzing Café des Artistes. "You heard it first here."

Chapter 22

Rome, the Vatican.

HIS HOLINESS POPE Pius XIII lay in his bed with one leg twisted under him. His skin was a sheet of running sores. He was in pain, and he was badly frightened.

Of the polio epidemics in America.

Of the famines and floods in Asia and Mexico.

Of the pregnant virgin girls.

Of his own mortal body and what was happening to it.

He could still breathe. He could still swallow. But he couldn't move or speak. He was virtually helpless in his own bed. He couldn't even press one of the buttons on the buzzer system for help.

And the pope found that for the first time in his life — he could not pray.

He knew that he would be found in his spartan bedchamber the next morning. The camerlengo would confirm his death in the presence of the master of papal liturgical celebrations and a worried knot of other high-ranking Vatican officials. He wondered, *Will I be standing then in God's holy light? Or will I be kept here, a prisoner of my own mind and body?*

He sensed he was not alone. He believed the Devil was with him this very moment and had been for what seemed an eternity, mocking his frailty and hurling a storm of grotesque images against the soft tissues of his brain.

He felt no fear for himself, only for the void his passing would create. His terror was for the people.

And for the virgins, the *two* young girls who had no idea that their destinies were crisscrossing.

He stared at the wooden crucifix on the wall opposite his bed and wondered in all humility how he had failed God. How he'd been so easily defeated. He wondered if he would even be forgiven. Or if he was about to go to Hell.

He reached out his mind to the young investigator, Father Nicholas Rosetti. Had he told him of the miracle at Fatima? He was no longer sure. But he found the memory of that day long ago in an untouched niche of his ravaged mind.

The details were still as intact as they'd been for more than eighty years.

The pope remembered October 13, 1917. This had happened, and was reported in *The Times* of London and in the *New York Times*.

One hundred ten thousand witnesses from all over Europe and as far as the United States had collected on the hilltops of Portugal. They had stood in the downpour, waiting for the three small children. He had been there himself.

The torrent of rain had been mercilessly flooding the desolate sheep pasture since before dawn. Thousands of dark umbrellas shrouded the crowd against the chill, numbing rain. The smells of gamy, half-cooked lamb, chicken, and onions thickened the air.

A miracle was expected, and at that time people still believed in miracles.

At five past one in the afternoon the three children finally appeared. They were wide-eyed and trembling, inside a tight procession of severe-looking nuns and priests. Behind them came more priests in dripping soutanes, holding flickering red torches and gold crosses.

The children — Francisco, Jacinta, and their cousin Lucia — suddenly began to point toward the whipping, black skies.

This was their sixth and last appearance.

"Put down your umbrellas and she will stop the rain!" ten-year-old Lucia cried out.

The little peasant girl's urgent command passed through the swelling crowd.

"Please, madame, your parasol."

"*Senhor,* your umbrella, please."

At 1:18 P.M., October 13, 1917, the black thunderclouds that had cloaked the sky since dawn suddenly separated.

The sprawling festival of people stared upward with open mouths and widening eyes.

A golden glow fanned out at the cloud edges. The sun then appeared with blinding brilliance.

"Look! The sun has come out!"

"Our Lady is here!"

Thousands knelt in the thick mud. And as it would soon be reported in the *New York Times* and everywhere else, the afternoon sun began to tremble and spin at a terrifying speed toward the earth.

Brilliant light rained down on the transfixed crowd as they watched it spiral back up to the sky.

"Please pray to Our Lady," begged little Lucia. "She says the world war will end soon! She says the Devil will be stopped this time *as a sign!*"

The horde of men and women surrounding the three children pounded their breasts and began to scream. "I see her! She is so beautiful! The Mother of God has come back to Earth here at Fatima!"

His Holiness Pope Pius XIII cherished the memory. He had been right there as a young boy. He'd been sitting on the shoulders of his father. He had been too young to truly understand.

But it had happened.

The Lady had spoken to him. The Lady had appeared. *And she had foretold everything that was happening now — all of it!*

The seizure ripped through the cerebrum of the most revered man in Christendom, canceling all but one regretful thought: He would never know which virgin bore the divine child.

Chapter 23

I AM A PRIEST. I'm here on important Church business.

Father Justin O'Carroll stood in a patch of bright sunshine at the foot of the Beavier driveway and tried to catch his breath. This was going to be a challenge.

I am a priest.

His face was crinkled up, but the thin smile had more to do with the harsh glare than happy anticipation. He would be seeing Anne Fitzgerald here at the house, and he wasn't sure that he wanted to. It had taken him a long time to get over Anne. He didn't want to relive the heartbreaking experience.

He was a believer in fate, however, and here he was, in close proximity to Anne again. He knew she would be at the house, since he was at least partly responsible for her being here. He'd recommended her to the cardinal, who agreed immediately. John Rooney said that Anne was tough, perhaps even cynical at this stage of her life, and that was what was needed in Newport.

The last time he'd seen her, Justin had absolutely believed he would never see her again. He could still recall her anger when he'd shown up at the girls' school where she worked. She was right to be mad, but God, had she let him have it with both barrels.

Anne is a trial, he thought to himself. A trial he had earned. Perhaps he'd been selfish before. This time, he wasn't going to inflict his feelings on her.

"Jesus, God," he muttered suddenly. "There she is."

He watched a lithe, strikingly attractive young woman coming over the dunes toward the main house. He wasn't quite ready for it, but there she was. He had the same thought he always did: He still loved this woman. Only now he was sensible enough not to show it.

Anne's surefooted stride was achingly familiar to him, as was the way her thick black hair whipped around in the breeze. She seemed to be walking in slow motion — there could be no other logical reason why it took an eternity for her to reach him.

He felt his insides shift. No amount of rehearsing and girding himself had prepared him for this actual moment.

Finally, they stood facing each other in front of the Beavier house. Somehow, the impressive and dramatic locale seemed appropriate for their meeting.

Anne stared at him, wordless, perhaps furious with him for having surprised her again. He could have called, he knew. Given her a warning.

"Hello, Anne," Justin said. He was uncharacteristically tongue-tied. "I'm archdiocese staff too. Part of all this intrigue."

At last, she murmured a quiet "Hello, Justin." That was all. She apparently didn't have anything else to say.

He stared into her brown eyes a little longer than he ought to. She looked better, wiser, prettier than she ever had. It made his heart physically ache to see her again.

"I'm sorry about just coming like this," he offered, "but you don't just say no to the cardinal."

"I know, Justin. I'm here for the same reason."

He stood rooted to the driveway, blood pounding in his forehead, watching her features for some small sign of her feelings. Would she tell him she was glad to see him? Or would she turn and walk away? Or suddenly begin to shout?

When her smile finally came, he felt as if he'd been blessed.

Anne held out her slender hand to him. Formal, yet with the warmth of friendship. "I'm glad to see you, Justin. We've got a great deal to do here. Kathleen Beavier is an amazing young woman. But I *don't* believe she's going to be the mother of God."

Chapter 24

LES PORTER WAS WIRED in the best way he could imagine. The *Daily News* reporter stubbed out his second cigarette that morning and put the ashtray back on the nightstand. From his wide double bed in the Newport Goat Island Sheraton, Les had a pretty neat view of the gently arching Jamestown Bridge.

"What hath God and the *News* wrought?" he muttered under his breath. There was a traffic jam from hell on the bridge — and he used that term advisedly.

Who were these people rushing to Newport? Believers? Curiosity seekers? Ambulance chasers? All of the above?

The virgin-birth story had certainly caught fire in a hurry. Fox, Hearst Entertainment, and Warner Brothers had all tried to nail him down for film rights only a split second after he'd signed on with UTA. His new agents, Richard and Howie, had licked their collective chops and assured him that the Kathleen Beavier story was going to do huge things for him. He'd already known that. This was front-page material out into the indefinite future.

First, speculation before the birth, with all of its ingredients of mystery, controversy, religion, and sex — or the possibility thereof.

And then the spectacle of the birth itself.

Was it a hoax?

Or was it for real?

And then what?

Personally, he thought Kathleen was the other side of Tawana Brawley, but from his point of view it didn't matter if the Beavier girl was a virgin or a clever fraud.

He'd broken the story, but he couldn't own it. He could, however, put his fingerprints all over it. And that's what he meant to do.

Les Porter dressed quickly in cords and lamb's wool and an Irish oilskin jacket. His clothes cost more than the maintenance in his co-op apartment. He'd always had a thing for good clothes. Only now, for the first time, the expense was justified. Cameras were going to be pointed *at him* today.

His rental car was waiting outside the Sheraton, and as he pulled out of the parking lot he found himself doing something he couldn't remember having done for fifteen or twenty years.

Les Porter, graduate of Regis High School and Manhattan College, quietly said the Lord's Prayer. It wasn't that he believed in the virgin. It was just that . . . with all of his bravado, he couldn't quite *not* believe.

Chapter 25

THE CROWDS HAD STARTED to gather early around the Beavier cottage. The Newport police were there in numbers, and I spent half an hour out on the barricades talking to them. Most of the cops were highly skeptical and cynical of the so-called virgin birth. Same as me.

One of the more verbose of the patrolmen told me, "This is just rich people turning adversity to their advantage." It was a funny line, but I think the cop was dead serious, and maybe dead right.

As the hour of the press conference approached, reporters and a few family friends were allowed onto the grounds of the estate. I talked to several of the Beaviers' friends and relatives, but no one could shed any more light on the mystery.

I was working hard at this but not getting very far. The people I talked to were strictly divided between believers and aggressive skeptics.

I saw three teenage girls being refused admittance to the grounds and raising a pretty big stink about it. They were dressed in the familiar urban-female style and looked as if they might be friends of Kathleen's. I hurried over to them.

"Can I help you girls?" I asked across the wooden barricades set up by the Newport police.

"Who are *you*?" one of the girls asked defiantly. She had on carpenter's jeans, work boots, a camouflage-patterned parka. All three of the girls had WWJD fabric bracelets on their wrists. I knew that the WWJD acronym could mean either "What Would Jesus Do?" or "We Want Jack Daniel's." Or both.

"Who am I? Well, right now, I'm the one on the inside of these barricades. Are you friends of Kathleen's?"

"We used to be. Before *this,*" said the group's designated spokesperson.

"Before her parents cut her off from everybody," said a tall blonde. "Her parents, and that evil witch Mrs. Walsh."

"We're her New England–style ya-yas," said the third girl. I assumed that had to do with the book *Divine Secrets of the Ya-Ya Sisterhood,* which I happened to love.

"All right. Well, come on in and join the party of the year."

I opened a space for them, and my new cop friends figured it had to be all right with the Beaviers.

"Where is she being *held?*" the ringleader of the girls asked.

"Down in the cellar. Actually there's a *lower* cellar that's particularly dingy and ice-cold," I said. "I'm Anne. I'm part of the establishment around here, but at least I have a sense of humor. And I did get you ladies in here."

"Sara," said the tall blonde.

"Francesca," said the roly-poly one who looked Italian.

"Chuck," said the ringleader.

"Okay," I said to them. "Let's go see your friend."

Chapter 26

KATHLEEN COULDN'T BELIEVE that I'd broken the rules and brought her friends to the house, but she lit up wonderfully when she saw them grouped at the bedroom door.

"It's just your ya-yas, darlin'," Chuck drawled, and then they were all hugging one another in the bedroom.

I left the girls alone for several minutes, but then I figured we had broken enough house rules and it was time to get them out again.

"Thank you, thank you, thank you, Anne," Kathleen said at the door, and she hugged me tightly. "Did I say thank you? Well, thank you very much. I owe you one."

We passed Mrs. Walsh in the hall, and she gave us the *look*.

I took Sara, Francesca, and Chuck down the back stairs to the pantry and I talked to them on the way.

"So why were the three of you banned from the house?" I asked.

"The Beaviers are *incredibly uptight* assholes," Francesca spoke up. "They are the worst. Carolyn treats Kathy like one of those porcelain dolls all over the formal living room."

"Rooms," Chuck corrected. "Living rooms. Plural."

"And?" I asked.

"We, uh — we helped Kathy with the abortion attempt. We went and checked out the clinic for her. We set it all up."

"But she went there all by herself. Why did you let her go alone?"

Chuck got angry. Her eyes were dark, tiny beads. "She told us her appointment was the *next* day. We would have gone with her. Are you kidding?"

When we got down to the pantry, I stopped walking and looked at the girls. I could tell that they were comfortable with me — up to a point.

"So who *are* you?" Sara asked.

I hesitated, then said, "I'm somebody trying to make some sense out of this."

"Yeah, well, join the crowd. This is beyond all our comprehension. It *can't* be happening," Sara said. "Ergo, it isn't."

I nodded. "So you don't believe Kathleen is a virgin?"

They began to whisper among themselves.

"No, actually, we do. Kathleen never lies. Never, ever. She has this personal-code-of-honor thing. No lies."

"What about the mystery man in all of this?" I asked. "Do you know who he is?" I held my breath.

Francesca blurted, "His name is Jamie Jordan the third,

and he *isn't* the F.F. That's fucking father, by the way. Though he *says* he is. He's a total asshole, and he definitely isn't the father of the new Jesus."

All three girls agreed.

And now, I had a name: James Jordan III.

Chapter 27

THE GIRLS HAD BEEN in the house — *those hideous, wicked, scurrilous girls! Blasphemers one and all!* The housekeeper, Mrs. Walsh, thought she heard Kathleen speaking loudly in her room once they had left. *Talking to whom?* she wondered.

Curious, she dropped the clean white linens on the fruitwood sleigh bed in the guest room. Then she slipped out into the dimly lit hallway and tiptoed toward Kathleen's room. Her ears pricked up under her cap of white hair.

Ida Walsh couldn't clearly make out the words, but it certainly sounded as if Kathleen was talking to someone. But who? She hadn't seen anyone come upstairs after the blasphemers left.

Was Kathleen saying her prayers before the important meeting with the news people? Of course she had to be frightened. Even though she was pregnant with a child, Kathleen was still nearly a baby herself.

Ida Walsh took a cautious step closer to the girl's room.

She hooked her hand around the doorjamb, and as quietly as possible the sixty-year-old woman levered herself into Kathleen's room.

"Sweet Sacred Heart of Jesus," Ida Walsh gasped. Her hands flew to her mouth. She couldn't believe her eyes, or her ears.

The housekeeper actually fell backward. Her right hand fumbled at her breasts, searching vainly for the crucifix that always hung from the chain around her neck.

It was gone! The crucifix wasn't there anymore! How could it be gone!

Suddenly she couldn't see! She'd been struck blind.

She couldn't hear! Not a sound! She was deaf!

She opened her mouth and bellowed wordlessly. She couldn't speak! She thought she had been struck deaf and dumb or had actually died. She collapsed to the carpeted floor, moaning and clutching at her eyes.

Then, in a horrible flash of cognition, she *knew.* She'd done this to herself. She was like Lot's wife, who had looked back at Sodom and was turned into a pillar of salt.

She had defied GOD!

In the split second before she'd been stricken, she had seen Kathleen Beavier talking to someone. Talking out loud. Gesturing with great animation. And then — Kathleen had uttered the most vile curses.

She'd heard a second voice — and it was very deep — a man's voice. It kept calling Kathleen "Whore! Satan's whore!" And she had better admit it, the man's voice commanded. She should tell everyone at the big press conference.

Only there was no one else in Kathleen's bedroom. No one Ida Walsh could see.

And in the young girl's mirror, the housekeeper was sure that she'd glimpsed rising, licking, gold-and-crimson flames. She had seen the terrifying flames of Hell.

"Mother of God, save me," she whispered as she convulsed on the floor like a mad person. She had just seen Hell with her own eyes, and she believed with all her heart that she'd heard the Devil himself speaking to Kathleen.

Chapter 28

A WET GRAY MIST and patches of fog washed over Sun Cottage as Kathleen was led down the long flight of wooden back-porch steps. The sky overhead was ash gray, streaked with long purple slashes. It was quite epic-looking. From below, the lamps in the living room windows could be seen glowing warm and yellow, the homey way house lights look on late fall and winter nights.

Keenly aware of the weather as I was, I thought of the strange happenings around the world: outbreaks of sickness, deadly plagues, a famine. It was all very scary, and I kept searching for a connection to the virgin birth. The Apocalypse? I couldn't swallow that. Still, I couldn't keep the images of chaos and evil out of my head.

I saw Kathleen cover her eyes as hundreds of cameras flashed out across the darkening lawn. What an incredible photo opportunity this was.

Her family and friends formed a tightly protective wall

two-deep around her as she approached the imposing wedge of microphones that had been set up on a twenty-foot-long banquet table.

On the opposite side of the table were a hundred or more news reporters, some of them recognizable faces, and behind them was a blinding gallery of lights. Video-cameras stared with insolent red eyes, and I could see scores of satellite dishes set up on top of news trucks parked along the road.

A half-dozen news choppers chattered noisily overhead. I worried about the possibility of a helicopter crash.

Reporters and cameramen jostled and pushed for better positions.

And finally, right up in front, there was Justin. He was here because the cardinal had big plans for him. But why else? Why now? Why had he and I been brought together again? I couldn't help thinking that there had to be a reason. I wanted everything to be logical and clear and sane — but would it happen that way?

Kathleen stared out into the noisy, unreal scene and she shivered. I felt for her.

More cameras flashed and popped wickedly in her eyes. She blinked rapidly; her eyes teared up.

She began unconsciously to grab and squeeze handfuls of her tunic top, the only thing she could fit into comfortably these days. I knew what she was thinking, because she'd told me: What did these important men and women think of her? They weren't stupid, and they were paid to be skeptical. Did the news people think she was a terrible liar? A freak? A fraud? What could she possibly say that would make them believe her?

Tall and imposing in his courtly red clerical robes, John Cardinal Rooney finally stepped up to the microphones.

The press conference had begun. The world had to be told *something*.

Chapter 29

"THANK YOU one and all for coming here on such short notice," said the cardinal in his pleasant man-of-the-people tone. He smiled engagingly over the shifting, restless crowd, seeming to look each and every person in the eye.

He wouldn't let anyone know how worried he was, or how scared, or, especially, how his feelings about related, apocalyptic events occurring all over the world during the past several weeks would affect the gathering.

"Will you please join me in a brief silent prayer?" He folded his hands and bowed his head. Many, even those who'd never been to a Catholic church, lowered their heads.

After the silent moment, the archbishop of Boston opened the news conference for background-information questions.

An attractive woman in a tan Burberry raincoat began. "Terry Mayer, *Chicago Sun-Times.* It seems to me and many others I speak to that the Church is going through an extinguishing period." The reporter spoke with a pleasant Midwestern accent. "We hear rumors that a schism is possible between the conservatives and the liberals. Is there any connection between these political difficulties and what is happening here today?"

Cardinal Rooney was already shaking his head before Terry Mayer completed the question.

"I don't want to sound apologetic, but there really shouldn't be such disappointment and concern when the leaders of the Church struggle. The Church *is* human. That is its flaw. But that is also its strength, *and* its beauty.

"As to Church politics and Kathleen Beavier, there is absolutely no connection. The birth of this child has nothing to do with Church politics."

Cardinal Rooney's deep voice hung over the crowd. He sounded both serious and wise, and he certainly seemed truthful and sincere.

He answered several more questions before he finally acknowledged the reporter from the *New York Daily News.*

"Les Porter, the *New York Daily News.* Cardinal Rooney, could Kathleen Beavier please give us some of the background information from her unique perspective? There is a lot of conjecture right now. We want to hear from Kathleen herself."

The cardinal nodded thoughtfully, then he gestured for Kathleen to come forward. "Yes, Kathleen will speak to you. She wants to be heard."

Chapter 30

KATHLEEN FELT NUMB and unreal. For a few seconds her mind went completely blank as she stared out at the reporters.

Then she saw her three girlfriends — Sara, Francesca, Chuck — and that made it a little better, or worse. She wasn't quite sure. Of anything.

"I've never spoken to a large, august group like this," she finally managed to say. Her voice boomed across the lawn, surprising her with its volume.

She turned to Anne, who gave her a smile and a wink of encouragement. "And so," Kathleen continued, "I'm not very good at this. To be honest, I did some practicing in the house before and I was terrible."

Kathleen finally smiled at her own obvious discomfort. So far, the reporters seemed taken with her honesty and simplicity.

"Last spring," Kathleen went on, "I discovered that I was pregnant, although I was — am — still a virgin. I was frightened and confused, of course, and I finally worked up the necessary courage to tell my parents. They took me to our family doctor, who said I definitely was pregnant, and a virgin.

"There were more tests by doctors in Boston, then at Harvard University. There were a lot of suspicious questions by all sorts of priests, and finally Rome became involved. Last week, another doctor flew here from New York. Once again, he verified that I'm intact. That's all there is to say. That's all there is so far. I'm eight months pregnant now. I'm healthy. The child is very healthy. I see him once a month — on the sonogram."

A reporter's voice floated up out of the crowd. "Ms. Beavier, you just said 'That's all there is to say.' With all respect to you, why should we accept that? Many of us think there might be much more to this."

Kathleen hesitated. She *felt* like telling them everything.

And then she heard the Voice: *Yes. Do it. Tell them everything! Tell them!*

"Well, there is something that happened to me back in January," Kathleen whispered. Her breathiness was a rumble amplified by the sound equipment.

"Will you tell us what it is, Kathleen?"

Tell them the truth about your fucking child! Yes, yes, yes — do it now!

"I'm sorry." Kathleen shook her head, her satin-blond hair shimmering in the overcast atmosphere. "There are some things that I can't tell you about yet. I'm sorry. For now, you have to accept certain things *on faith.*"

Kathleen suddenly choked up as the picture-taking accelerated. She felt cold and frightened, and so alone in front of all the microphones. She didn't want to cry, but she couldn't tell them the truth. She wasn't able to do it.

"I really don't mean to be this way. I'm sorry," she said.

Suddenly, Kathleen appeared distracted. She leaned forward.

Something was happening near a dark stand of pine trees that stood tall, like giant sentries, behind the mass of reporters.

Kathleen's heart began to pound rapidly. The child moved inside — violently. A strange heat rushed through her and she was terribly afraid.

She heard the Voice again — *Tell them! Tell the truth, bitch! Tell them whose child it is!*

Kathleen shook her head, then raised her voice above the crowd, above the *other* voice.

"She's here. She's here now!"

The reporters looked back to where the young girl was pointing.

"Our Lady has come."

Kathleen's soft blue eyes glazed over. They became distant and peaceful. Her face was beaming.

Every camera moved in for a close-up of the young girl. They all wanted to capture the innocence and rapture of her expression.

"Can't you all see her?" Kathleen whispered to them. Tears rolled down her cheeks. She began to tremble violently. She looked as if she were about to faint.

"Can't you see her? Oh, please God, why me? Why me alone? She's here now and none of you can see her. She's here, I promise you. Oh, God, she's so beautiful! Can't any of you see?"

Chapter 31

PEOPLE HAD ALWAYS NEEDED to believe in something, but especially now. They wanted to have faith, but maybe they no longer knew how to go about it. That night I sat in the den of the Beavier house with Justin, Cardinal Rooney, the Beaviers, and Kathleen. We watched the reports come in from all over the world.

It was the most amazing thing I have ever experienced. I kept remembering the old TV show *You Are There* and thinking, *Yes, I am.*

A thunderous and resonant chant occurred and seemed to spread spontaneously around the globe: *"A miracle! A miracle!"*

An eighty-year-old Italian laborer danced and spun his wife across the magnificent consecrated piazza of St. Peter's in Rome. She looked twenty again in his arms. A newspaper photographer captured the couple's magical dance.

Six-foot-wide gold bells began to toll across the majestic basilica's cobblestone piazza. The ageless chimes of the bells held a new and special meaning for the more than ten thousand faithful gathered in the vast shadows cast by the world's largest church.

A long ribbon of Germans trailed out of the wafflelike exterior of Berlin's famous cathedral, the Kaiser-Wilhelm-Gedächtniskirche. The line extended far down the glittering Kurfürstendamm.

At St. Patrick's Cathedral in New York, John Cardinal O'Connor celebrated an unscheduled High Mass at nine o'clock. Nearly six thousand New Yorkers crowded into the Gothic cathedral. Cardinal O'Connor knew there was a somber message to be delivered, a message of caution.

But the congregation didn't seem to want to hear it.

In Dublin and Cork, white-and-yellow papal flags flew from the general post office on O'Connell Street, from all the restaurant and pub roofs, from the portal of the famous Gresham House.

At Cathédrale Notre-Dame de Paris, the south tower's great thirteen-ton bell sent out the holy message to the Left Bank's La Sorbonne, the Marché aux Fleurs, and Les Halles. Below the great towers in the Place du Paris, the people watchers, the lovers, the street entertainers, and the *clochards* actually stopped for a solemn moment. The crowd offered a prayer for the young American girl. And the French were especially proud of her, for Kathleen was related to them by blood.

At midnight, smoke wafted upward from a small chimney in the papal palace near the chapel. Great ceremonial cannons exploded across Bernini's magnificent elliptical piazza in front of St. Peter's in Rome. "We have a pope," cried the people in ecstasy.

High up in a top-floor window of the gold-domed Apostolic Palace, a tiny figure in a white silk cassock and skullcap finally appeared. The Holy Father, the new pope, Benedict XVI, extended his cloaked arms out over the people.

People in the crowd began to wave to the distant papal figure. "Papa, Papa," they chorused. "Tell us of the virgin."

Chapter 32

THAT NIGHT AROUND DINNERTIME, two nuns from the school and the parish priest came out to Colleen's house. She saw the priest's old Volkswagen bus coming through the fields and she went and hid in the attic.

There was a musty-smelling pile of old clothes, bed sheets, and a rag rug in one corner of the room. It was dark there, even with the overhead lightbulb on.

Colleen burrowed underneath the clothes and made sure she was completely covered up. She could see nothing, smell very little except the clothes and the mothballs her mother had once sprinkled among them. But Colleen heard everything.

They were in the house now, downstairs, talking among themselves, then calling her name.

"Colleen, Colleen, it's Sister Katherine."

"It's Father Flannery. Are you here, Colleen?"

Finally they were upstairs and in the bedroom with her mother.

Ma wouldn't help them find her, even if she could. She rarely made sense to anyone anymore. Her memory was gone too. Colleen was virtually alone in the house these days — except for the baby, of course.

She cradled her belly carefully with both hands.

"Hello, sweet baby. Don't be afraid. No one is going to hurt you, baby. No one is going to bother us.

"It's just the two of us, sweet baby. It's just the two of us, but we'll be good. You'll see, sweet baby. It's just the two of us."

Chapter 33

Ireland.

THAT SAME NIGHT, Father Nicholas Rosetti took a commuter plane to Shannon Airport. He knew where he had to go now. He had to see the *second* girl. There were two virgins: One in Ireland. One in America.

He was pleased that, because she lived in such a small and distant village, the story of Colleen Galaher hadn't spread. He wished the same thing were true in America, but that story was spreading like wildfire. Rosetti wondered why. What did it mean? What did it tell him? What did it say about the two girls?

He tried to relax. He hoped the damnable Voice wouldn't come again.

He wrote several pages of notes about Colleen. He tried to sleep after that, but couldn't. Around him, other passengers slept peacefully, and he couldn't help envying them.

With his seat reclined, Nicholas Rosetti leaned back and reread his notes on Colleen Galaher. He was becoming obsessive, wasn't he? Suddenly the small commuter plane began to buck and shake. He was reminded of his attack in Rome. *What was happening now? What in the name of God?*

Rosetti looked around him. Everyone was suddenly awake. The passengers were afraid.

And then the engine of the Beech 1900 seemed to explode. It was as if a small bomb had gone off inside his head.

For a moment, he believed the plane might have struck another aircraft. Instinctively, he covered his head with his arms. The man beside him clutched at him. "We're going down! We're going to die!" he screamed.

The shrieking in the cabin was the audible manifestation of terror. Time became elastic. The plane was coasting downward with a sickening, unrelenting pull.

This can't be happening. It's too much; it just can't be. My plane can't be going down.

But the plane *was* going down! It had gone into a spiraling descent in a wide circle to the right. This meant that the pilot couldn't see where the plane was heading. Moisture was whipping past the window like shreds of gauze. A shroud of clouds enveloped the plane.

The screaming of the passengers got louder and louder.

"Brace, brace," came the voice of the captain.

Rosetti leaned over and grabbed his ankles as hard as he could. He prayed furiously. *In nomine Patris, et Filii, et Spiritus Sancti . . .* The faces of his mother, his sister, and his older brother flashed before him. And then he saw the face of the virgin Colleen, strikingly, terrifyingly real, as if she were right there.

He waited to hear the dreaded Voice, but it never came.

The small aircraft dipped steeply to the right, then it crashed through the trees. The plane hit the ground with a furious crunch of metal. Another deafening explosion . . . Rosetti's rib cage smashed down on his knees as the craft cartwheeled, shattered, flung pieces of itself across the ground.

Then every particle of sound — both human and mechanical — stopped. It just *stopped.*

He opened his eyes into the black chaos of the plane.

With a sudden earsplitting rush, flames shot back over his head.

I'm going to be burned to death. All of these people are going to die. Am I in Hell?

Breathing hard, he unbuckled his seatbelt with wet and trembling fingers. And he fell to the ceiling!

Confused, Nicholas Rosetti rolled and tumbled. He found his feet, picked his way over fallen luggage and soft, wet objects, instinctively heading toward the opening that had been the emergency door.

Beyond the wreckage, sunlight streamed across the brilliant emerald green of the cornfield.

This couldn't have happened. But it had. People were lying dead everywhere.

He hesitated, then looked back at the flames. The heat was building, unrelenting.

"Is anyone alive?" he shouted back into the furnace.

When there was no answer but the hiss of melting plastics, he jumped through the hole of crackling flames and onto solid earth. He had no other choice. He ran on rubbery legs toward the center of the field. His breath tore at his burning lungs as he waited for another explosion.

Turning, he saw the largest section of the cabin lying on its back, consumed in a huge, blackening ball of fire.

It is Hell, isn't it? A gateway straight to Hell.

The surrounding air smelled of polycarbons and charred flesh. It was like nothing he had ever experienced.

The only movement from inside the plane was the wave of the heated molecules of air.

Rosetti wiped his forehead with the back of his arm and watched the fire from fifty yards away. He alone had walked away from the disaster. Why him?

He had a brief, shameful burst of exhilaration — he had survived!

But this feeling was quickly replaced by overwhelming grief.

He fell to his knees to pray for the souls of the dead. He remembered the pontiff's solemn words so recently spoken in Rome: *You will be alone.* They washed over him like a benediction.

He stumbled to his feet. He urged himself to think, to plan. *Think, think.* If there was a cornfield, there would be a farmhouse. There would be a town.

His shirt and pants were smudged but intact. He still had his shoes. He looked as if he'd slept rough, but otherwise he had not a scratch on him anywhere.

You will be alone.

Nicholas Rosetti straightened the fall of his jacket and set off toward a hedgerow that marked the edge of a road. The next thoughts came to him fully formed.

Something or someone is trying to kill me.

And something or someone wants me alive.

Chapter 34

THE YOUNG GIRL heard a nearby *thumping* in the dark, and her eyes flashed open. Her heart thundered. A man was in her bedroom! She could see his full figure in profile.

"Did you miss me?" he asked and laughed. His voice was deep and full. He loomed over her, casting moon-shadows across her bed.

"Not for a second," she answered, matching his sassy tone. But her heart was galloping. She wanted him deep inside her.

His coarse woolen pants dropped to his feet, sending coins scattering and rolling. His erection, silky and hard, gleamed in the faint white rays of moonlight.

She reached out a hand and touched him. He brought it to her mouth and she took him in.

"Oh — God," he sighed, and laughed again. He with-drew from her, and in a swift movement threw back the sheets and stretched his muscular body along her milky warmth. He ran his callused hand across her swollen belly in slow, sweeping strokes.

"You're a devil," she said, "and I want you again. I can't get enough of you."

Another man standing beside the bed replaced the first. He fumbled fretfully in his leather bag. He had a present for her, a gold ring with a glinting crimson stone in the center.

"You didn't have to do that. *You're* my present, my gift," she said. "Touch me," she said. "Please. You're such an angel."

His touch was like velvet. He knowingly stroked the slick creases of her sex until she begged him to finish her. . . .

A third man pushed aside the second. The mattress sagged under the weight of this man. "You've got the softest skin, you know?" he said. "You're a miracle."

"I know it. That's the truth."

He pressed himself into the divine wet spot she presented to him, holding her breasts, crying into her hair in his ecstasy.

When he had finished with her, a fourth one went to her. He smelled of seawater and unwashed wool and pine needles. He was only fourteen and he loved her too. He ejaculated on her thigh, and again when he entered her.

A huge man came next and roughly dragged the boy out of her embrace. Then he lowered his aching limbs down beside her. "Warm me, my love," he said. "It's very cold tonight."

He was the one, the leader, the most experienced, by far the best lover. He was wearing sheepskin and tweed and a complex essence of musk and spices and tobacco that she found endlessly compelling. His voice was deep and smooth and sounded like a cello, and when he said her name, tears filled her eyes.

She went to her knees beside him, tipped her breasts to his mouth, and he sucked each of them. Then she mounted him, rode him until her cries were tearing from her throat in a delicious ecstasy streaming out of the open window and into the cold night air.

"Why do you disobey me?" He suddenly roared out a question.

Kathleen Beavier woke with a violent start. She was sweaty, panting as if she'd been running for her life. She'd also been crying.

She could still hear the Voice — tormenting, taunting.

She was wet everywhere. Her bed was wrinkled and soaking, as if she hadn't changed it in weeks. She could almost hear the trailing end of a voice. There was a funny smell on the sheets.

But she was entirely alone. It was just as it had been every night for months.

At the very instant that Kathleen Beavier woke up, Colleen Galaher also bolted straight up in bed, and screamed. Afterimages flickered and popped like huge bubbles in front of her eyes. The flannel sheets were tangled around her bare feet. How had that happened?

She began to cry, hysterically.

Chapter 35

Ireland.

OF COURSE, THERE WERE some people who knew about Colleen. The locals knew, but they kept it to themselves. It was their problem, their bloody business. No one else's.

The village boys and girls of Maam Cross were cruel, without pity or remorse or reason. They called Colleen "the little whore of Liffey Glade." They also painted their opinion of her in fierce red letters on the newly white-washed walls of the McDonald's in town: *Colleen sucks fairie dicks!*

When she came to town, she had to pass that horrible, obscene sign. It made her sick to her stomach.

Today, she was doing the shopping. Her father was dead from cancer. Her mother had been crippled for many years. She and her mother made do on their allotment from state and church.

DONAL MACCORMACK, FAMILY GROCER was third in a row of newly repainted one-story storefronts at the village crossroads. Since the infusion of billions of pounds to renovate Ireland, fresh paint was in evidence everywhere. The buildings were contrasting bright colors: marigold, violet, persimmon, lake blue. Signs were gilded in order to attract tourists.

Colleen thought life was better now in Ireland than it had ever been, but small-mindedness and antiquated values clung to the people like tar to a wooden spoon.

She wrapped the thin cloth coat she'd bought three years ago at Dunnes in Galway more tightly around her bulging belly. She glanced up the tangerine-color exterior of the grocery store to the slate roof. Beside the satellite dish, a chimney pot puffed smoke into the dank fall skies.

She skipped her eyes down again, across the bloody half-torso of a calf that hung in the market's window. *Disgusting! Gross!*

Then she sighed and went in to do her shopping. Enjoying the unaccustomed luxury of the electric-heated neighborhood store, Colleen placed a half-dozen eggs, flour, salted herring, praties, milk, honey, and a hunk of farmer cheese in a basket.

As she put her rumpled bank notes on the counter, she felt terribly conscious of the female clerk's probing eyes. So distracted, Colleen left the store and stepped directly into the path of Michael Colm Sheedy.

"Oh, bloody excuse me, *missus.*" Michael feigned a polite smile and pulled off his Donegal tweed cap. His shaven head glistened.

A black stone of an earring dotted his earlobe. He wore a zip-up hoodie and long baggy trousers, but not because he was wearing his dad's clobber. Gangsta clothing was the style of these boys, who emulated big-city-gangster behavior.

"Well, would you believe this!" The sixteen-year-old clapped both hands onto his wiry hips. "It's wee Colleen Galaher with her awful big, awful shameful belly right outta *The X-Files.* Still pregnant with the son of God? Is that Himself down there?"

Colleen's eyes quickly moved from Michael to the others in his group, who'd all changed out of their school uniforms of gray trousers and blue school blazers. John O'Sullivan, Finton Cleary, Liam McInnie, and Michael's girl, Ginny Anne Drury.

They were lolling in front of the Sweet Shop. Billie Piper's hit tune "Because We Want To" was playing in the background.

They were waiting for her.

Colleen stumbled backward, almost dropping the groceries. "Please, Michael, my mother is very sick. I have to go now."

"Aye, Colleen. This won't take but a minute, darlin'. We'd just like a bit of group discussion here. What we're wanting to know is, Did God take you to the cinema first, or did he just fuck ye in the backseat of his car?"

Colleen gasped. "You shouldn't be talking bad like that, Michael."

Suddenly Michael Sheedy lifted tiny Colleen and her shopping bundles right off the sidewalk, up toward the red sun just sinking over the village roofs.

Colleen's face had turned pale. Tears slipped out of her bright green eyes. "Oh, dear God, no, Michael Sheedy!"

" '*Oh, dear God, no, Michael Sheedy!*' " the boy mimicked in a high-pitched, mocking voice.

As his lads fell into laughter, the head bullyboy passed Colleen down the line.

"Quick think, Johno. Don't drop the ball now, the *god-head.*"

Johno O'Sullivan, nearly twenty-five stones in weight and only sixteen years of age, nearly did drop Colleen. He was okay at football but not so good with his hands.

At the last juggling second, he shuffled her along to Liam McInnie, Michael's chief lieutenant, flatterer, and imitator. Liam wore a swastika tattoo on his right hand.

"Please, Liam," Colleen cried out. "Ginny Anne, please! Make them stop! I didn't hurt anyone. I'm pregnant!"

The freckled Irish farmboy held Colleen up above his head. He screamed out a loud Croke Park football cheer. The others howled with laughter.

"Pregnant with a little bastard, ye mean. Aye, ye little whore, Colleen! Never give me a proper date! But then, you were screwin' the Lord on High."

At that moment, the most peculiar thing happened on the desolate main street of Maam Cross, the strangest thing ever in the ancient Druid village.

Out of thin air came a brown-and-yellow thrush at the speed of a bullet. The small bird screeched once and then caromed hard off Liam McInnie's head.

The Irish boy instinctively put Colleen down. His hands flew to his face to cover his stricken eyes.

"Bloody fucker!" Liam McInnie screamed in pain as the bird dived again. "Oh, you bloody fucker! My eyes! Oh, Jaysus! My eyes!"

Colleen looked back once as she slipped away from the terrifying scene. Liam was clasping his eyes. Blood was coursing down his face. Ragged strips of red flesh hung from the boy's cheek.

The bird was nowhere to be seen. It had disappeared as quickly as it had come.

The bird was an angel, Colleen thought. It truly was. Heaven must have sent it to stop Liam McInnie and his mean, awful friends.

Chapter 36

New York City.

NICHOLAS ROSETTI AWOKE with a start. His mind was still focused on the incredible secret; he'd been thinking of it all night. He thought that he knew why he was being attacked, though no one of sound mind would believe him.

He blinked away the violent and morbid images until he got a fix on his actual location. He was in a hotel room in midtown Manhattan, a city he'd never visited before and one he had disliked intensely from the moment he entered it.

Turning his head, he took in faded ivory wallpaper, mahogany furniture, and the heavy swags of drapery striped rose and pink and beige now blocking out the light on Broadway, north of Times Square.

He listened absently to the whine of a police siren above the soft hum of the air-control unit.

He ordered tea and an assortment of rolls from room

service. Then he showered, cleansing himself at last of night sweat.

He dressed in black pants and a gray wool turtleneck sweater. Placing the teacup on the desk by the window overlooking the street, he unbuckled the black satchel.

The bag held all of his work on the investigation. He smoothed out an old newspaper clipping. The yellowed paper was dated October 14, 1917, and the headline was as stark and powerful as the event itself: MIRACLE AT FATIMA.

The reporter for the *New York Times* had written these words:

> *To the astonished minds and eyes of this baffled and terrified crowd whose attitude goes back to biblical times — who, pale with fear, with bared heads, dared to look up at the sky — the sun clearly trembled violently. The sun made abrupt lateral movements never seen before. The sun did a macabre dance across the sky today as the Mother of God supposedly "spoke" to three small children.*

There had been a terrifying warning at Fatima. Even the *New York Times* admitted as much.

And the secret had been kept since that time — for almost eighty-two years!

The most recent evidence and documentation sat at the top of his bulging bag: a nineteen-page deposition on his meeting with fourteen-year-old Colleen Galaher in Maam Cross.

Next came a packet of two- and three-day-old newspaper clippings. Pieces from the *Times* of London, the *Los Angeles Times,* the *Observer,* the *Irish Press,* and others. Tales of viruses out of control, plagues, strange unexplainable deaths.

Rosetti felt his neck stiffen. Tension was returning in waves. He was afraid again. He couldn't hide, not even in New York City.

Pope Pius had told him the secret of Fatima. *No, please!* Rosetti prayed. *I am not worthy!*

But he knew the secret was true. He was a believer, and he believed.

There were two virgins, thousands of miles apart.

One girl would bear the Son of God, the Savior.

The other girl would bear the Son of Satan.

Book Two

KATHLEEN AND COLLEEN

Chapter 37

New York City.

IN THE AFTERNOON, Nicholas Rosetti slogged through bottomless despair as he walked down New York's crowded Eighth Avenue. He was in Hell, wasn't he?

He pushed against the rush-hour pedestrian traffic, wincing at the frequent touch of strangers. He was a mass of tics and nerves, he knew. He jumped at every sound, imagined or real.

Soldier of Christ, he thought. *No, just soldier. Soldier!*

He pushed onward, mourning the recent death of His Holiness Pope Pius, a good pope, a grave loss to many millions. And he felt the loss more than any of them. He'd been charged with a mission that he'd had the grandiosity to accept.

And now he was alone. He was definitely in Hell. These New York people were all damned. He could see it in their eyes. He could feel evil and desolation everywhere he walked.

The *New York Daily News* under his door that morning had caused his desperation and despair to overflow. On the front page, where it most surely didn't belong, was a story about Kathleen Beavier.

It was a grievous error for this news to be released. It was typical of America, wasn't it? Everything was a circus here. There were no secrets. Kathleen was rich and American — so she was news. Colleen was Irish and poor — so where was the story? He wished that none of it had been made public.

News — that was his mission for the day. He had made several calls to Rome, and then calls had been made to him back to New York. He arrived at a West Side studio owned by ABC Television at six o'clock. He was escorted to a small viewing room, and then, mercifully, he was left alone.

Bracing himself, he slumped lower and lower in the screening-room chair. He forced himself to watch . . . the news.

All of it was very bad . . . and very scary.

The unreleased footage, all of it shot within the past week, portrayed the ongoing drama of a terrifying five-month drought in the Indian state of Rajasthan.

The first jumpy tape image was a wide traveling shot flashing through a grotesquely impoverished village, Sirsa. In a husky, authoritative voice, the news anchor described the conditions depicted on the screen.

"In much of modern-day India, life is not as you or I have seen it portrayed in movies about the British East India Company or the Bengal Lancers. The state of Rajasthan, in particular, is sometimes called the Great Indian Desert because of its vast arid plains and its relentless siroccos and simooms; a seething hellhole with an average daily temperature of one hundred fifteen degrees."

Hellhole, Rosetti thought. *How very precise.*

"This Indian state, with a population of more than forty-four million, is the worst drought and famine area in the world. From April until July, a feverish white-hot sun bakes the scorched land and the people like a demonic torch. Dust accumulates for miles. Hot, suffocating winds blow dust and meal chaff as far north as New Delhi.

"Villages are like smoking furnaces. The great, motionless sand dunes make you feel that ancient, primordial evil presences are there in the Indian desert.

"As of September seventh of this year, the terrible drought has persisted for two full months, longer than ever before. This entire Indian state has become a smoldering pyre for its dead.

"Six hundred thousand men, women, and children have died here since April! Over six thousand more die each day!

"If there is a hell on earth, then it is here in doomed Rajasthan."

The time is close at hand, Rosetti thought. Too close. He could feel the danger everywhere, and it was real, not his imagination.

Everywhere, there were clear signs of the Beast's presence.

Gehenna.

Six hundred thousand dead! That was nothing to the Beast.

He began to enumerate: The drought in the state of Rajasthan, the unspeakable famine in India. The slaughter in Rwanda; genocide so brutal and senseless it could have been inspired only by evil. AIDS, with a death grip on China, most of Africa, and now Spain and Sicily. The new polio was crippling the West Coast and breaking out in New England as well. A burgeoning hemorrhagic plague resembling Ebola had suddenly appeared in southern France, flowering near the miraculous shrine of Lourdes.

The Enemy had come as foretold.

Lucifer's army was here — fallen angels, legions of them.

It was their time.

Chapter 38

Newport, Rhode Island.

I WAS ACUTELY AWARE of Justin's closeness as we walked on the seaside footpath. I was also aware of what a handsome couple we made, because several people passing us gave us a sideways look. If they only knew the story, our story. I had been a nun, and Justin was still a priest.

But we weren't a couple. Far from it. It was as if there were a thick wall of electric current between us, simultaneously attracting and repelling.

Three times in the past two days we had taken walks or drives together. Ostensibly to discuss Kathleen Beavier. Justin was the cardinal's point man and he was very serious, and good at the job. I couldn't tell if he believed in Kathleen, but he was intellectually open to all possibilities.

Of course, there was much more than that between us. And I kept thinking, *I'm not a nun anymore. I can think about Justin O'Carroll any way that I want.*

As we walked, I told him a brief, harmless history of Cliff Walk, the slender, three-and-a-half-mile trail that fit like a choker around Newport's graceful southeastern shore.

"William Backhouse Astor once walked here with his lady, the 'Queen of the Four Hundred,'" I said, showing off my grasp of trivia. "John Kennedy supposedly courted Jacqueline on Cliff Walk while he was in the Navy and she was Newport's debutante of the year."

Now, Justin and I walked along the same historic path. But there was a substantive difference. We weren't lovers and never would be. Except for a brush of his hand three days ago in a café, we never touched. Honestly, I wanted to hold him more than anything in the world, but knew I wouldn't.

Why had we been brought together like this again? *Smashed together* was more like it. It proved to me that God was a sadist.

We continued along a long, winding stretch of Cliff Walk overgrown with blackberry bushes and flanked by historic Newport mansions and their high fences. It was so perfect. We passed behind Millionaires' Row, the place where, locals swore, Henry James coined the phrase *white elephants.* Here was the Breakers; Stanford White's Rosecliff; Beechwood; Richard Hunt's obsessive Marble House.

"You know, Annie," Justin finally said, "sometimes I think that you have a strange image of yourself. You seem very open, very free and easy. And yet you hold yourself off from people."

I stopped in the footpath and looked at him. What he'd said hurt me, true or not. "I don't know what you mean. I have lots of friends. I like my life a lot. Do you mean that because I'm not married I can't be fulfilled?"

He smiled thinly. He didn't want to fight.

"I didn't mean it the way it sounded, Anne."

"What, then?"

"Ah, Annie. All I mean is that you have a beautiful and very special passion for life. I've watched you in Boston. Here in Newport. You are in magnificent communication with Kathleen already. But you *are* closed off to yourself. Oh, hell, I'll keep my big mouth shut. And walk. And take in the gilded fantasies of turn-of-the-century America. It is beautiful here. I'll give you that."

Justin was afraid to look at me now. When he did, he saw the big glistening tears flowing down my cheeks.

He'd hurt me, hurt me badly. Struck close to home, and he had no right to do that.

I suddenly broke away from his side. I couldn't stay here. I began to run up the vine-strewn path, not knowing where I was going, except that I knew I had to go away from Justin O'Carroll.

Chapter 39

KATHLEEN WAS GOING STIR-CRAZY in her parents' house. She desperately wanted to be with her friends — Sara, Fran, and the irrepressible Chuck. She felt hemmed in by the walls and by the heaving bulk of her own flesh.

She came carefully down the back stairs, holding tightly to the thin banister. Every single tread creaked under her weight.

It was still hard to get used to the physical changes in her body. Her breasts were bigger than her mother's. Her fingers and ankles were swollen. Her eyes were puffy and red-rimmed. And it was infuriating not to be able to wear any of her normal clothes.

When this was over, would the old Kathleen reappear? God only knew.

Until the baby came, the only pleasure she had was the beach. Thank God for the beach!

Miraculously, Kathleen got to the pantry without being

heard. In particular, she didn't want to have to face Mrs. Walsh right now. For the past few weeks, her old friend just wasn't herself. She seemed to disapprove of everything that Kathleen did or said.

Beyond the pantry, the mudroom was deserted. An assortment of footwear was lined up under a bench. Kathleen stepped into a pair of Docksiders. Her father's yellow cardigan was hanging from a hook and Kathleen buttoned it over her jumper.

Minutes later she was at the shoreline, listening to and watching the hypnotic breaking of the waves. God, what a day. It had to be seventy and so far the fall had been incredibly mild. She took off the sweater and slung it over one arm.

An idea occurred to her, and she absolutely loved it. Something she had once read about water and weightlessness and that it was good to take the weight of gravity off the baby. She stepped out of her Docksiders, then her sweater and jumper, and moved into the ocean.

This was so daring of her, but so right. The water was warm on the surface and felt unbelievably good slapping up against her swollen legs. She thought the wavelets were like puppies licking her feet.

Kathleen waded in several more feet, still only yards from shore. She felt in a trance now, as if she weren't completely herself. Did she dare? Yes, she did. She took a breath and bent her knees so that the water came up almost to her chin. It felt so wonderful.

"Oh, this is heaven."

The waves lifted her a little, then put her down. She sighed. Then she laughed out loud. Here was the weightlessness she craved. She felt light, no longer the lumbering elephant she'd become. She hadn't been this comfortable in months; she hadn't been so at peace with herself.

The next wave had a long, sweet pull, and it hauled her away from the beach. She went with the gentle flow. She put her arms out and her head back and floated for a moment or two. The changing of colors in the sky was fascinating. Blue to pink to purple to indigo . . .

Kathleen lost track of time. How long had she been floating? With effort, she rolled over on her stomach and got a fix on her position. She was already out much farther than she'd thought. How could it have happened? *It couldn't have! Something was wrong. How had she gotten way out here?*

Frightened now, she began to stroke the water, to swim toward land.

It seemed that every yard she advanced was taken away by the outward pull of the tide.

Don't panic, she told herself.

Just keep your eyes on the house and swim.

She wondered how she could have been so stupid. She knew about tides, had known about them her whole life! Something very weird had happened. *It was as if she had lost time. Was she crazy?*

Her arms were aching. She had a stitch in both sides and the cold was leaching out the strength in her body. She wanted to call out for help, but there was no one out there, no one at all who could hear her. As if the ocean were a big powerful man with his arms around her waist, Kathleen was pulled, then dragged down beneath the waves. She was frightened by the sea's grip.

Don't be afraid, she heard. It was the Voice, but it was almost soothing.

No! She gulped water, then managed to find the surface again. She screamed a long, wordless scream.

Just go with the sea, Kathy. The sea is the universe and it is eternal. Be the sea!

She pawed at the air, futilely, as splintered images flickered before her. Her friends, her mom, her dad, her baby —

The next wave dragged her under again. A sharp pain in her lungs increased unbearably before it was quenched by the sea.

She was drowning, and so was her baby.

Chapter 40

I STOPPED RUNNING when my shoes finally hit pavement out on lovely, tree-tented Bellevue Avenue.

What is the matter with me? What is the matter?

I mopped the ridiculous tears from my cheeks with the Kleenex tissues I kept up the sleeve of my sweater, then stood beside the towering black iron gates of one of the mansions and watched a bright yellow tour bus from Batavia, New York, loading pilgrims.

After a while, I managed to get a grip on myself.

I knew exactly why I'd run away from Justin. No big secret for the ages there. I was still in love with him, wasn't I? And now I was angry with him too. *I wasn't cut off from life.*

He was. He was the Irish Catholic priest. He acted so smart and worldly, but how much had he really experienced?

Having caught my breath, I wandered down behind the houses to a walkway that led to the beach. I was obsessing as I played "can't catch me" with the creamy lip of the ocean. Maybe I really did love Justin. I thought about him constantly. He wanted me to be married, to be a mother. Maybe he'd expressed a selfless thought. Or he was just reminding me of what I already knew.

I wandered the beach, cycling and recycling these thoughts until twilight streaked the sky in ever-darkening bands of blue, from a pale aqua over the ocean to a deep, star-studded indigo in the great upended bowl of a sky. I cast my eyes around to get my bearings. Something on the beach pinned my attention.

A form lying motionless on the sand.

The form of a young woman.

"Kathleen!" I screamed.

Chapter 41

I CHARGED FORWARD, calling out, *"Kathleen!"*

When I reached her, I threw myself onto the sand beside her. I rolled her gently onto her back. Kathleen was unconscious, but thank God she was still breathing. Why was she on the beach? How had she gotten this soaking wet? Had she been swimming?

"My God, Kathy! Oh, my God."

She was too heavy to carry, and we were alone on the darkening beach. What had happened to Kathleen? Had she hurt herself on purpose again? What about the baby?

She was still breathing all right. I called her name again. Tried to think in straight lines. I considered my options. There were two.

Stay with her.

Run as fast as I could for help.

"Okay, Kathy. Kathy . . . It's okay."

I tapped her lightly on the cheek.

Kathleen's skin was very cool to my touch. Had she

taken an overdose of something before she went in the water? I couldn't know, but it was never far from my mind that she'd attempted suicide once before. Kathleen moaned and moved her legs.

And that's when my heart nearly stopped. I muttered, "Oh, my God! Kathy!"

I screamed her name over and over again.

I saw the streaks of blood along her thighs.

Something was terribly wrong.

When I turned my head, I saw Justin running full speed toward us.

"Justin," I called out. "Kathleen's losing the child!"

Chapter 42

WE ARRIVED AT the hospital with the ambulance's sirens wailing. A half-dozen doctors and nurses came stampeding out to meet us. I was wrapped in Justin's windbreaker and an EMS blanket. I'd gotten soaking wet trying to help Kathleen. I looked ridiculous, but I didn't care.

Every available obstetrician at Newport Hospital was called in to observe Kathleen. She was conscious. She was also calm, although no one else was.

There was a medical consensus: The baby was in trouble. Deliver the child by C-section before it was too late.

Kathleen absolutely refused. "The baby will be fine," she said. "Leave us both alone."

Her own physician, Dr. Armstrong, begged her to let the doctors intercede. Her parents pleaded with her, tears streaming down their faces. If the baby was taken now, it would have a chance. If she waited, it could die. But it was no small thing to force a competent young woman to have a cesarean section.

"Anne — tell them. I've seen the Lady. She told me not to be afraid."

I blanched visibly at her suggestion. Medically, a C-section was the right course to take. Kathy would live and the baby would have a good chance of survival. It was the only sane thing to do.

But then, of course, the delivery would not be a miracle. The birth would bypass the birth canal. And the Church would never claim the child was a miracle.

"Kathleen," I said, "I want you to listen to everyone — give the doctors their due — and then do what you believe is best."

It was a night of living hell, and I don't say that lightly. We stayed at the hospital for hours. One of the nurses brought me dry clothes from her locker.

Finally exhausted, I slumped in a chair. I was starting to doze off when I became aware of someone shaking me. Carolyn Beavier was sobbing. She threw her arms around me.

"She's fine, Kathleen's fine," she said. "And the baby's fine. The bleeding has stopped and there's no sign of damage. Kathleen is still carrying her baby. It's truly a miracle!"

I was told it wasn't exactly a miracle, but it was extraordinary enough to stun the medical staff at Newport Hospital. The only person who wasn't surprised, or impressed, was Kathleen herself.

"Thank you for having faith in me," Kathleen said. "You were the only one who did. You're the special one, Anne. That's why you're here. You and Father Justin. You're my special protectors."

I stayed in the hospital room with Kathleen until Justin

peeked in, around one in the morning. He gestured for me to come out into the hall. Kathleen was sleeping, so I did.

When I got into the hallway, I saw that Justin was pale, his eyes wide. I was concerned for him. "What's the matter? Are you okay?" I asked.

"Something quite unbelievable has happened here at the hospital," he said in a hushed whisper. "Anne, there's been a case of polio. It's as if it followed Kathleen here."

Chapter 43

Ireland.

COLLEEN GALAHER THOUGHT that if she had to stay within the claustrophobic confines of her home any longer, her mind would explode into the tiniest pieces, never to be put back together again. She made sure her ma was comfortable in her room, then she sneaked from the house and saddled the horse.

She rode down the hill on horseback, her hand wrapped in the mane of her mother's horse, Gray Lady. She sang one of her favorite Boyzone songs to herself, pausing midverse to wave at the gypsies in the lower field. She wanted to be a simple schoolgirl again; she wanted her life back.

The gypsies were not the dusky Romany types from Central Europe, but rather descendants of displaced Irish people who'd lost their holdings during the Great Famine in 1845. For generations they'd moved from county to county, mending things, racing their sulkies at fairs, and, some said, doing thievery or worse.

They were scorned as she was scorned. It wasn't fair; it wasn't right.

She remembered now with shame how she, too, had scorned the gypsies. Then, six months ago, something had happened that changed her mind.

As today, she'd been passing the field on her way to the idyllic spot widely known around Maam Cross as Liffey Glade. A woman with flaming red hair, a purple velvet skirt, and an old Harris tweed jacket had beckoned to her.

The gypsy woman walked toward her — her eyes gone huge. She crossed herself and began to pray, clutching her rosary as if it were a lifeline attached to Heaven itself.

Colleen had been shocked by the display, afraid and curiously bold. Yet moments later, she'd accepted the gypsy's invitation to join her for tea inside the caravan. The woman's name was Margot, and her caravan was a marvel of organization. There were neat shelves layered with tools, hatboxes covered in shelf paper, racks of clothing hanging according to color, and, surprisingly, an expensive new television set, battery-operated.

Beside the TV was a shrine to the Holy Virgin. She was a beautiful porcelain Madonna, her hand raised in blessing, a shawl of blue and white lined with real gold draped over her flowing hair.

"You've seen her in the flesh as well as the spirit," said Margot. "I know you have. Isn't it true?"

Colleen had turned to her, dumbfounded. What did this strange woman know?

"You love children, Colleen," Margot then said, her

voice humble and reverent. And she'd looked pointedly at Colleen's stomach, which had just barely begun to swell.

"I know your secret, little girl. You are just like her. Your secret will change the world."

Chapter 44

I KNOW YOUR SECRET, little girl.

Colleen took a long, slow ride that day toward the north side of town. The large hospital for the county was there and she wanted to visit before it was her time.

She tied Gray Lady to an old oak in a lush field near the hospital. Then she walked across the back lawns and entered the small lobby. Colleen had been at St. Brendan's before to visit sick relatives, but she didn't remember ever coming by herself.

She felt grown-up and maybe a little brazen as she slowly made her way up the winding staircase to the second floor. Colleen knew where she wanted to go — the maternity ward. It was to the left once she entered the main corridor on the second floor.

She pushed open the swinging doors and was immediately met by a nurse. The woman saw her condition and smiled in recognition. "Hello, dear."

"Just taking a walk," Colleen said. It wasn't actually a lie.

A woman was moaning loudly inside one of the rooms, and then the woman began to scream.

Almost immediately, and seemingly in sympathy, a second woman down the hall let out a piercing scream.

Colleen leaned against the wall and tried to compose herself. *My God, it sounds so awful. Will I be able to do this when the time comes?*

She listened to the two women as they continued to moan and scream.

One of them called out for her husband, then almost in the same breath she cursed him.

I'll be alone, Colleen thought. *I have to be so brave.*

She had thought the pre-visit to the hospital would be a good idea, but it didn't seem to be. She was clearly more anxious now than she'd been.

She turned down the corridor in the opposite direction. What was down here? More birthing rooms? More women in terrible pain?

But then Colleen noticed the glass window, and she saw the tiny babies inside. Some were crying, but most were sleeping or just looking around, checking out the world.

Colleen began to smile for what seemed the first time in months, and she knew she would be all right. She wasn't going to be alone anymore. She would have her baby.

Chapter 45

WHEN SHE WAS JUST half a kilometer away from home, Colleen could smell the cool sweet air of Liffey Glade. She looked forward to entering the grotto-like clearing that had been a natural shrine long before the Christians, even before the Druids. It was to Liffey Glade that Colleen came when she wanted to be alone.

A brisk-flowing clear stream bubbled through the grotto on its way to Loch Corrib. The pine and spruce trees hunched over the water.

Nine months earlier, on January 23, in Liffey Glade Colleen had undergone what she now considered a mystical experience. Before that night, she had been known around Maam Cross as a quiet and well-mannered scholarship student at Holy Trinity.

Colleen was liked at school, but she was never fully accepted by most of her schoolmates. She was appreciated best by the sisters at the convent school, who perhaps saw themselves in the quiet and reflective girl who was usually near the top of her classes.

She felt herself lucky to be of service to others, and that was why she'd come to her decision. She would become a nun.

Then, in a moment in Liffey Glade, everything changed. Colleen Galaher became the bride of Christ not just in spirit, but in body as well.

This particular early October afternoon, Colleen carefully rode Gray Lady down across the sodden cow pastures behind their cottage. At Liffey Glade she tethered the horse to a tree and pushed her way through wet, rustling branches. The girl knelt on the soft carpet of pine needles and duff in the private little outdoor chapel.

Colleen lowered her head of gleaming dark red hair.

"Dear Father in Heaven, I am your humblest servant. I know you can feel my sadness, and my love for you. Father, I am so lonely now. I am so terribly lonely these nine months."

But Colleen Galaher was not alone.

She was being watched — always watched.

Chapter 46

I WAS GETTING CLOSER to accepting the fact that Kathleen Beavier's baby was special in some way, and that troubled me more than I could say. It definitely worried me that I was starting to believe that Kathleen could be telling the truth, that my objectivity might be fading. I had gone from "This is a fraud" to "There just might be some truth here."

For just about the first time since coming to Sun Cottage, I had a few hours to myself. Kathleen was catnapping in the sunroom. Mrs. Walsh was baking furiously in the kitchen when I went in to get a pot of tea. Carolyn and Charles Beavier had gone to town to shop. Justin was off somewhere taking a run.

I'd looked forward to an investigation of the Beavier library. As big as the libraries in some small towns, it was a place where I could do serious research. There were history books, biographies, yards of reading materials on sailing, seashells, gardening, birds, and finance.

And there was a section right by the fireplace that was full of books on religion. Many of these were so recently purchased at Barnes and Noble, and the Maryknoll Bookshop that there were still sales slips tucked between the pages.

A fire crackled in the grate. I poured myself a cup of tea, then placed a stack of books about the Virgin Mary on a mahogany end table beside a cozy rose-colored wing chair. Since I'd already read just about everything available on Mary, this was a review for me. I ran my hands across the spines of *Our Lady in the Gospels, Our Lady of Fatima, Woman's Mysteries: Ancient and Modern,* before cracking open a wonderful book written in the late seventies called *Alone of All Her Sex.* I couldn't read this book without falling in love with Mary all over again.

"The Virgin, sublime model of chastity," the author wrote, "remained for me the most holy being I could ever contemplate, and so potent was her spell that for some years I could not enter a church without pain at all the safety and beauty of the salvation I had forsaken. I remember visiting Notre-Dame in Paris and standing in the nave, tears starting in my eyes."

I thought it was so true. This was the way faith worked, the way it had felt to me. It was the power of the Blessed Mother Mary that so many women understood. Further in her book, Marina Warner wrote that the Virgin "is one of the few female figures to have attained the stature of myth." She quoted Henry Adams, who had written, "The study of Our Lady leads directly back to Eve, and lays bare the whole subject of sex."

Quite an interesting dichotomy, I thought. The Virgin — who many and increasing millions feel should be elevated to the level of her Son — and Eve, who was tempted by the serpent, ate the fruit of the forbidden tree, and was cast out of the Garden of Eden. Eve had accepted Satan. Our Lady would crush him.

I forgot the time as I contemplated the literature, looking for clues to the situation in Newport. There was pitifully little in the Bible about Mary, only six slight references, and there wasn't that much historical evidence about her either.

Two major theories, based on what scholars loosely called Christian tradition, were usually accepted in theological circles. The first was that Mary herself was conceived immaculately, inside the womb of her mother — she had been born without original sin. The second accepted theory was that when Mary died, perhaps in the ancient city of Ephesus in western Asia Minor, her body and soul ascended directly into Heaven. This was called the Assumption of the Blessed Virgin Mary.

I was still, after all these years, amazed that Mary was the least known, by far the most mysterious, of all major biblical figures. And why?

I didn't have to phone any feminist for the answer. Mary was a woman, a mother. The Scripture writers were men.

Some things had changed since the birth of Christ. This modern blessed event surrounding Kathleen Beavier, *if it was that,* would be the most completely documented birth in almost two thousand years. There would undoubtedly be books and films.

And — I hoped it wasn't too vain of me to hope — I would be standing at the foot of the birthing bed.

Maybe then I would know the whole truth about the virgin Kathleen.

Chapter 47

I STILL HAD PLENTY of work to do and I finally had a little time to do it. I grabbed my ancient pea coat from the hall closet and walked quickly outside to my car. Within minutes I was sweeping past Newport's famous Bellevue Avenue, heading west on Memorial Boulevard.

I drove the mile-and-a-half length of Sachuest Point, where Kathleen had apparently parked with a boy nearly nine months before, in January. The mysterious and perhaps mystical evening of January 23.

Now that I was away from Sun Cottage, my latent feelings of doubt rose up again. I was actually more confused about Kathleen than ever. When it came right down to it, nothing made complete sense; everything required some faith on my part. Faith. It always came down to that.

Cardinal Rooney seemed to accept the virgin facts, and I knew he wasn't easily fooled. The cardinal was a sarcastically brilliant, cynical, and tough-minded priest of the old school. And Rooney believed in Kathleen Beavier.

He seemed to believe a holy child was about to be born. Justin believed as well, and he was nobody's fool.

Why? What made them so sure about her? What did they know? What was I here in Newport to find out? What mystery still had to unravel?

Next, there was Kathleen herself. She was a virgin, and she was pregnant. That much I knew for sure. Kathleen said that she'd seen the Blessed Virgin, and I — tough-minded and cynical myself — felt emotionally convinced that she was telling the truth, at least the truth as she knew it.

No facts, just feelings, but I was swept up in them as I drove through Newport.

Here was another fact: Kathleen had tried to kill herself and had failed. If she was pregnant with the Holy Child, why had she tried to take her life and that of the baby? Or should I be looking at the other side of that coin? How was it that help had showed up in an abortion clinic that was supposed to be closed for the night? Another patient arriving late. Help that had saved Kathleen's life.

No one had known Kathleen was going to be there on that day, not even her three best friends. They thought she was going the next day. That was the plan.

Finally, there was an important historical perspective to consider. Christianity was based on a belief in miracles. Christians all over the world believed in the Virgin Birth, and that Jesus Christ, the Son of God, had become man. Was it truth or was it myth?

I wanted a *fact.* I was starving for one measly, crummy fact to prove what I was starting to believe.

As I continued down Memorial Boulevard, I saw a

gold-and-blue sign pointing to the left, just past Spring Street: ROGERS HIGH SCHOOL.

I hit the turn signal. There was someone at the school who might give me what I wanted: a little light on this fantastic puzzle. Kathleen's date on the night of January 23.

Jamie Jordan.

He was a cold hard *fact.*

Chapter 48

I POINTED THE CAR down the tunnel of colorful maple trees called School Street and stepped down on the gas pedal.

It was 2:57 by my watch. I was just in time for the end of the school day.

An electric bell rang out and the clamor of boisterous youth filled the crisp fall air. A mob of students stampeded out of the school's eight swinging glass front doors. Car horns blared, and a bloated, faded brown football wobbled out away from the sedate, Colonial-style school building.

I stared into the swarm of shaggy-haired kids, trying to pick out one teenage boy from the many.

I scanned the crowd several times. My eyes finally settled on a tall muscular boy with a bright shock of blond hair falling across his eyes.

He was swaggering, shoving, engaged in physical repartee with a fellow male student who was no match for him.

I knew it was him. I'd seen a picture in Kathleen's room, and it couldn't be anyone else. James Jordan was a big boy, more like a man. I figured he was probably six-two and close to two hundred pounds. He was good-looking to be sure, but somehow I couldn't see him with Kathleen.

I had an inkling of fear, the thought that maybe it was nuts to force a confrontation, but I pressed on. It's called counterphobia, I knew, and not generally advisable in my trade.

"Hi, excuse me," I said, interrupting his horseplay with his pals. "Are you James Jordan?"

He stopped, turned, gave me a slow, cool, appraising smile.

"I guess that means that you are," I said. I forced a smile I didn't feel as he tapped out a cigarette from a red-and-white pack.

"My name is Anne Fitzgerald. I'm a friend of Kathleen's."

Jordan lit up a cigarette, then shot a look at his buddies, who'd begun to clump around him. They were sniggering and giving me the once-over, trying to be as unsubtle as possible about it.

"Yeah, I'm Jamie. And you're a friend of Kathy's? What kind of friend?"

"I'd like to talk with you for just a few minutes."

I kept my eyes steadily on James Jordan. I didn't move a muscle. I didn't show any fear, or doubt that he would talk to me.

His curiosity about me won out over the don't-give-a-shit posturing. I knew it would. It's what I do for a living.

Chapter 49

HIS FRIENDS WERE SHIFTING their feet like a herd of prickly young bulls. They were standing too close to me, violating the invisible margin of space I try to keep with strangers. They knew it, too.

"Who are you? You from *Hard Copy* or something?" one of them asked.

"No," I said coolly. "Not a tabloid reporter, just a friend."

"Okay," Jamie said after a few long seconds. "Let's walk and talk, friend. You've got five minutes to get my full attention."

"Oh, thank you, thank you," I said, then finally smiled.

And so did Jordan. I could tell that he liked me, and also that he considered himself good with women, even an older one like me.

There was a side street at the end of the block and on it were pretty little houses with Jeeps and the like parked in the driveways, bikes and skateboards on the walks. Jordan was a head taller than me and as thick-chested as a lumberjack. Nothing had ever unsettled this boy, or at least that's what he wanted me to believe.

"Okay," he said as we rounded the corner. "You have my attention anyway. Who the hell are you? Really? And what do you want? You aren't Kathy's friend. That much I know."

"Jamie, you don't know shit," I said. "And that's a fact."

I told him who I was but very little about my actual assignment. I also gave off an indisputable don't-mess-with-me attitude. Machismo could cut both ways.

"This past January," I continued, "you went out with Kathleen Beavier. That's an established fact too. The two of you dated at least once."

He shook his head. "I knew this shit was coming. You guys are so predictable. You're another one writing a book, right? So write this! I went out with Kathy Beavier *once*. One date. Plus a few trips to get a Big Mac or something after school."

"How come there was only one date?"

"How come only one date? Well, we can't spread the boy around too thin, can we?" Jordan said.

He was too smug to be real. I couldn't help thinking that this kid was a heartpounder of the Brad Pitt school. He and Kathy would have made quite a striking couple, but still, I couldn't see her with him. She might have had a slight infatuation, but she didn't like cocky people.

"Could you be straight with me for one minute? Back

on January twenty-third, you took Kathy to a formal dance at her school. Then *something* happened. Kathy told me that much. What happened?"

A look of anger flashed across his face. I saw what he would look like as a grown man, and I didn't like it. "Listen, goddammit, isn't it obvious as the nose on your pretty face? She won't tell because we made it after the dance. Everybody knows that Kathy was like a dead fish in the sack, I'll admit, but that doesn't make her the blessed virgin!"

His scowl was intimidating. I wanted to throw up my hands and say, "Thanks. See ya." But I couldn't walk away. Not yet.

"A medical expert from New York came here the night before last, a doctor with no reason to lie. Jamie, I was standing right there when he examined her. Kathleen is *still* a virgin. She never *made it* with anyone! Not you, not anybody else."

"Hey, bullshit!" he screamed at me. "I had her!" He grabbed himself between his long legs. "With this."

I must have telegraphed my disbelief, because he scowled again. Then, before I could move away, he shoved me hard.

I went down on the ground. I clapped my hand to my chest. I was more embarrassed than scared. The kid had decked me! My side where I'd landed hurt.

But I got right up. I shoved the bully. Then I shoved him again.

"You're a real tough guy, right? How tough are you?" I yelled at him. I kept coming at him. "Answer my questions! What happened that night at Sachuest Point? Something happened. I can see it in your lying, coward's eyes. I can see right through you."

Suddenly, he whirled and hurried away. I wanted to chase after him, but I knew it wouldn't do any good.

He was lying to me — I was sure of it.

But if that was true, then Kathleen was not.

Chapter 50

ALL I WANTED was the simple, unvarnished truth, but isn't that what we all are searching for? That night I sat in an old painted pine rocker beside Kathleen's pretty canopied bed. The moon had just floated up over the ocean like a big yellow balloon, but tonight it failed to move me with its beauty or serenity.

My head was still ringing from my brief, disturbing interview with Jamie Jordan. I was mistrustful of just about everything. I needed to know what terrible thing had happened between Jordan and Kathleen at Sachuest Point.

Kathleen was weak and exhausted. I could see it on her face. The darkened bedroom was lit only by a small lamp on the nightstand. I turned on the radio/CD player on the white lacquered bookshelf. Music enveloped us and I recognized Jewel. A popular love ballad Kathleen liked.

"You don't go for that sentimental stuff, do you?" Kathleen asked.

"The idea is for you to go to sleep," I told her. I went

back to my chair and rocked quietly. As bad as my talk had gone with Jamie Jordan, it would have been worth it if I'd learned something useful. Why wouldn't either of them talk about that night?

"Kathy, I have to ask you a question," I finally said.

She was staring off into space, seemingly oblivious to what I'd said.

"That day on the beach when I started bleeding," she finally said, "I was terrified. I've never been so scared in my life. I love this baby," she admitted to me for the first time. "I can't lose it now."

And that admission moved me. I rocked silently for long minutes, just trying to get a grip on my emotions.

"Do you trust me, Kathy?"

Kathleen smiled her incredibly innocent smile, an absolutely charismatic look that she has.

"I trust you. Of course I do. You're very honest, open."

I took a deep breath. Kathleen could knock the wind out of me just about anytime she wanted to with a few little words. How was it that she could affect me like this? Was it why I was starting to believe in her?

"Kathy, please tell me about Jamie Jordan. I went to see him today at Rogers High School. I spoke with Jamie. He said that —"

"He said we did it. He tells that to people because he thinks that's what they expect to hear from him. Honestly, I feel so sorry for Jamie. His whole macho fantasy is so sad."

I could tell that Kathleen was trying to mask her hurt. She clutched an ancient rag doll to her breasts, looking even younger than sixteen years.

"We didn't have sex, Anne. Jamie took me to go parking out on Sachuest Point, but I wouldn't do anything with him. He was like an ugly animal forcing himself on me. I wouldn't do it. I didn't do anything with Jamie. That's everything there is to tell right now," she said.

I'm sure I had a blank expression on my face, but my brain was whirring.

"Don't you believe me?" Kathleen asked. "Please believe me, Anne. If no one believes — what will happen to me? What will happen to my baby?"

I shushed her, then got up and smoothed her hair, tucked her covers up under her chin. She'd said she was innocent, repeatedly, but it nagged at me that she always added, "That's all I can say right now."

I wanted to believe that Kathleen was being honest because I cared about her so much. But . . . I couldn't. Something important had happened to Kathleen that night at Sachuest Point. I had been sent to Newport to find out what it was.

So far, I hadn't succeeded.

Chapter 51

Upstate New York.

ST. JOHN OF THE CROSS was nestled deep within forested hills, ninety miles north of New York City, along the Hudson River. As his car bumped up the rutted drive, Nicholas Rosetti had never been more afraid for his life, or his soul. The compound, made up of a castlelike estate building and a dozen sandstone cottages, was a rest home for alcoholic, deranged, and melancholy priests from the Archdiocese of New York.

But there was someone here who offered some hope to Father Rosetti. If there was any help in this world, it would come from Monsignor Bernard Stingley. This was Rosetti's final stop before he traveled to Newport to see the second virgin.

Inside the almost medieval estate, Rosetti was met by a slender, crew-cut monk who led the visiting priest down stone-block corridors. Their footsteps and voices echoed like pistol shots in an underground tunnel.

At the end of a third or fourth hallway the monk

knocked, then swung open a dark oaken door. A robed priest was standing at the window. Rosetti felt his heart expand when he saw him.

Then he heard the Voice — laughing, cackling obscenely. *You stupid, stupid fool. This vain old man can't help you. No one can help you.*

Monsignor Bernard Stingley was his former mentor and confessor at the Lateran in Rome. Silenced for the past half-dozen years, the elderly priest was a great biblical scholar, and he was renowned for his writings on the Apocalypse.

"Nicholas." Stingley came forward and embraced the much younger Vatican priest. "I can't believe it's you. It's so good to see you."

"Bernard," Nicholas said into the rough cloth of the older man's robes. It was an uneasy embrace, and when he stepped back, he was alarmed by the worried lines crossing the silver-haired priest's thin, pinched face.

"Are you well?" he asked.

"It is not *my* health you should be thinking about," the older man answered.

Once again, the Voice laughed loudly inside Rosetti's head. He tried to ignore it, but couldn't.

Nicholas Rosetti carefully closed the door behind him and took in the book-lined walls of the room. Shelves on the longest wall held Stingley's collection of Chinese, Greek, and Far Eastern statues, all of them depicting a Christlike figure. There was an unmade daybed in one corner. A plain wooden crucifix hung above it. Beneath one of two casement windows was a cluttered worktable.

The two sat down at the table overlooking the Hudson River, which ran like a wide glass highway far below.

They exchanged condolences about the passing of the late Pope Pius.

Then Stingley said, “I think I know why you’ve come, Nicholas. I have a bad feeling. I’ve had it for several weeks, actually.”

Nicholas Rosetti didn’t doubt that. The drums must have begun beating loudly the day he left Rome. The Vatican community was small, almost incestuous. He stared into Stingley’s familiar steel-blue eyes. Clearly, more small talk would be unwarranted and inappropriate.

“Monsignor, I *know* that you know the secret of Fatima. Pius told me you’ve actually read the words. The message of the Virgin: the promise *and* the warning.”

The monsignor didn’t speak yet. His eyes showed nothing. He merely listened.

Rosetti continued, but suddenly he wasn’t so sure about his old friend. “You were with Pius much of the time he was ill. Back in ’ninety. He spoke of Fatima, and you were there. You heard it all. And now I know what you know.”

Distress flashed across Monsignor Stingley’s face. “Pius had no right. No right to ask you.”

“It’s too late for recriminations or regrets. I know about the two virgins. One good. One so evil.”

“Then you know *nothing!*” Stingley’s voice rose. “There is so much more. God doesn’t create in black and white. It’s not so easy. The truth has little to do with the human logic systems.”

As Stingley spoke, Rosetti felt the small room at St. John’s begin to spin, jerking him back to the spinning sidewalk in Rome and the hot knives lancing into his heart. The swirling sidewalk became the Beech plane spiraling down, cartwheeling into the trees, splintering metal and bones. It was more than a memory or a hallucination. He felt the heat crackling around him and the sharp odor of burning flesh.

The vision was a warning. *Leave this place! Leave now!*

But he would not.

He couldn't!

Why was he being warned, though? Why had he been spared?

He heard his own voice as if it came from far away.

"Please, I need to know how to prepare myself. The search for the true virgin. What do you mean, *I know nothing?* I want you to tell me exactly how it's going to be. I fear that my descent into Hell has already begun."

Chapter 52

IT HAS, NICHOLAS. You have that much figured out correctly. You're already lost! Your soul is forfeited!

The Voice screamed laughter inside Rosetti's head. It seemed like hundreds of voices, and the pain was unbearable, as if his skull were being ripped apart.

The old priest rose up suddenly, overturning a large oak chair with a resounding crash.

"They're *here!* You've brought them here!" His eyes widened with fear. "The legions are here! They're everywhere! I can *see* the unholy bastards! Now they're waiting to be turned loose."

Father Rosetti tried to go to his former mentor, but his arms and legs wouldn't move. They felt as if they were weighed down by stones.

What in God's name was wrong with him? Was he having a stroke? Was this another attack? Could he possibly survive again?

Nicholas watched in horror as the same force struck Stingley. The priest flailed his arms, trying to swat away an invisible presence. He stumbled toward the overflowing book cabinets. He drew in a deep, raw breath. Then Monsignor Stingley's entire body sagged.

When he spoke, his voice was low and hoarse, as if he were having trouble getting out the words.

"At first there will be the loss of control," he said, swinging his head back and forth at an exaggerated speed. "You will find that you have *no free choices* left.

"No freedom of thought.

"No freedom of action.

"That's only the beginning!"

That's nothing! Rosetti heard the Voice inside his head. *Get to the good parts.*

"Next you will feel a physical decaying of your body, your mind, your soul, Nicholas. You will lose all hope. And that foul, rotting hopelessness, that abject feeling of pointlessness and futility, is the most defeating of all human experiences."

This is a smart man, Nicholas. For a priest. Listen to him!

"When it happens, when there is nothing for you except that abysmal black hopelessness, then you know you have crossed the threshold into Hell."

Monsignor Stingley stood at the window, his back arched horribly, the light breaking around him, blinding the Vatican priest. He passed his hand several times across his chest as if trying to relieve a constriction there, and then he spoke again.

"I should beseech God the Father to have infinite

mercy on you. But that would mean deceiving you with false hope!"

Rosetti wanted to speak, to ask for the monsignor's blessing, when the old man suddenly cried out. Bernard Stingley's face was as white as bone. His lips, the edges of his ears, and his fingertips were a shocking shade of blue.

A deep rasping breath came from his mouth as he pressed his hand hard against his sternum. Frothy white mucus spilled from his mouth and nose.

He screamed, "There are *legions* of devils, fallen angels everywhere. Look beyond the two virgins, Father. Look beyond the virgins! The legions are right before your eyes."

Rosetti tried to go to him, but he couldn't rise from his chair.

He watched as the old man's skinny legs buckled and he fell to his knees. His eyes rolled upward and foam continued to boil over his lips and down the knob of his chin. He fought wildly against unseen forces.

With extraordinary effort, Nicholas Rosetti lurched from his seat. He was forced down to the floor. He crawled on his hands and knees to where Bernard Stingley had fallen.

"Monsignor, no! Dear God, no! Get away from him! Take me!"

The old man whispered, but the whisper was like a roar: *"You will be taken and damned to eternity in Hell. Do you comprehend eternity? Look beyond the virgin girls. The answer is there!"*

And in that instant of terror and pain, Father Nicholas Rosetti believed that he did understand something.

He was with the legions now, and they were Hell, and they had come up from the abyss of fire to Earth.

Monsignor Stingley was screaming at the top of his voice. "Get them off me! Please, please! They're eating me alive!"

Chapter 53

KATHLEEN FELT TOTALLY SPOOKED. That was the right word for it.

Even though nothing had actually happened, she felt an intense pressure building up inside her. She had the intuitive feeling that something really bad was creeping up on Sun Cottage and on everyone who lived there, especially anyone who tried to help her.

Anxious and fearful, Kathleen threw back the chintz curtains of her bedroom window. At first, all she saw was the reflection of her own face in the black windowpane.

Then, through the film her breath made on the glass, she saw gold lights pricking through the dark; the carriage lamps along the driveway cast a fuzzy glow along Ocean Avenue.

A couple of private security guards in dark fur-collared parkas were standing at the front gate. For some reason, their presence didn't make her feel at all secure.

A sudden movement caught her eye.

Directly below her window, a car door opened and a man got out.

He looked ominous: a black suit, a black hat with the brim severely pointed down, a bulging black satchel under his arm.

He looked *spooky.*

Even from above, Kathleen could see how stoop-shouldered he was, as if he were carrying a mountain of stone on his back.

And she had a very odd thought: They *are here for me.* Plural. They *are here.*

Suddenly, voices boomed out as the front door to the house opened and Father O'Carroll came out onto the veranda. He extended his hand warmly to the dark figure. That was how Kathleen knew with certainty who the man was.

He was the other investigator.

The priest from Rome.

Just before he entered Sun Cottage, he looked up.

Kathleen thought with a shudder, *He looked right into my eyes. He already knows the truth, but he hasn't the faith to believe it. This priest hasn't the faith.*

Chapter 54

FATHER ROSETTI HAD FINALLY ARRIVED. Now, I guessed, there were three of us watching over Kathy, trying to get at the truth. Was his presence a sign that I had failed?

Had I?

A meeting of the minds had already been called. I took my place in a straight-backed chair in one of the handsome double parlors on the first floor of Sun Cottage. I was only an observer. That was my job in this meeting. But my heart was thumping in panicky double time for Kathleen.

She sat beside me in an armchair, her protruding stomach looking as if it were about to burst open any minute. I hoped she wouldn't be too afraid, wouldn't be too affected by stress.

Charles Beavier offered drinks all around and, when he got no takers, poured himself a stiff scotch. Carolyn looked faint as she sagged into a chair on the other side of her daughter. Justin sat closest to the sliding oak doors.

The assemblage quieted down immediately. We were all waiting to hear what the priest from Rome had to say. He knew things that we didn't, and he *looked* so damned mysterious.

He was a formidable presence. Alien, downright strange. A black monolith with an unknown agenda. I watched him anxiously clasp and unclasp his large workman's hands.

He finally smiled, but it didn't look genuine.

There was no way Father Rosetti was as in control as he'd have us believe. He greeted us in a sibilant voice colored with the musical tones of his native tongue.

Then he strode to the center of the room and took a wide-legged stance in front of Kathleen.

"Kathleen, I have been sent here by the Vatican," Rosetti said. "For what it is worth, my official title is Chief Investigator for the Congregation of Sacred Rites. This Congregation of Sacred Rites is the body within the Church that investigates miracles, all varieties of supernatural phenomena, claims of sainthood."

"I guess you've come to the right place," Kathleen said.

The broad-faced priest smiled. "Nevertheless, please don't be afraid of me, Kathleen. I'm something of a pushover. In spite of the theatrical title, I'm simply a bureaucrat. I'm like a tax investigator of the supernatural."

Kathleen shook her head. "I'm not afraid of you, Father."

I was glad to hear her say this, but I was concerned for her. She looked pale and tired. I was afraid she might go into labor at any moment.

Father Rosetti seemed not to notice. He was definitely no pushover. "Kathleen, is the Blessed Virgin Mary here with us tonight?" He asked the strange leading question as if he were requesting the time of day. As if it were an afterthought.

Kathleen took a deep breath and pushed back a wisp of silken-blond hair.

"She's here. Yes," she said in a soft voice.

"Inside the house? In this very room with us?"

"Yes. *Right inside* this room, Father. Are you surprised? Don't you believe in the Blessed Mother?"

"I'm sorry, Kathleen," said Rosetti. His hands were working again, clenching and unclenching. "I'm just not used to having Our Blessed Mother around. Is she quite beautiful? Is she standing, Kathleen? Or is she sitting over on that blue chair, perhaps?"

"Father Rosetti," Kathleen said. "I know what you're doing, but please don't try to play tricks. They're quite beneath you. Our Lady is here with us. In appearance she is like a beautiful gentlewoman. You do believe in her, don't you?"

"Kathleen, I'm concerned only with what you believe," the Vatican priest said with an edge in his voice. I heard it. And I saw his facial muscles twitch.

There was no longer any doubt in my mind. The Vatican priest was absolutely terrified of Kathleen Beavier.

Why was he afraid of Kathleen?

What did he know that we didn't?

What was he here to investigate?

Chapter 55

I WAS MESMERIZED by Father Rosetti as he paced in a tight circle at the center of the long room. The atmosphere inside Sun Cottage was charged with anxiety, but especially with energy. And from the twitching and fidgeting I saw around me, things were clearly uncomfortable for everyone.

Rosetti himself was behaving like a caged panther. He seemed possessed. He had the confidence that comes only with absolute power.

"I have some extraordinary news," he said at last. It was apparent to me that he'd dismissed all of us but Kathleen. He fastened his eyes on her.

"One of the things I have uncovered thus far, one of the few things I'm truly sure about," the chief investigator said, "is that there are *two* virgins. Kathleen is not alone."

I gasped and shook my head in disbelief. But Kathleen's eyelids didn't flutter. In fact, by contrast to the rest of us, Kathleen was as serene as the calm before a storm.

"I sensed that there were two of us. *At least two,*" Kathleen said so quietly that I had to strain to hear her. She looked almost in a trance. "Everything is happening in great numbers right now. Plagues, deaths, illnesses, even virgins. It's the scariest time ever on the earth."

The Vatican priest's brown eyes narrowed. "How do you know that, Kathleen? You must tell me everything that you know. *Tell me now.*"

It was as if a volcano had erupted on the far side of the room. "Don't ever talk that way to my daughter!" Charles Beavier, who had been silently simmering, boiled over in rage. In two paces he was on the bulky Vatican priest.

I yelled "Stop" as Justin tried to drag him off Father Rosetti's flailing body. There was a struggle, Charles thrashing, threatening to throw the priest out of the house. A dam had broken. His daughter was being harassed again and he wouldn't tolerate it.

With his wife and daughter hovering over him, he shook himself off and settled down to half a roar. They returned to their seats.

"Enough with the third degree," Charles Beavier said in a sharp, angry voice. "How about answering a question for me? Let's cut the investigator crap. What's your business here, Father Rosetti? Why are you in our house trying to scare us to death?"

I shot a startled glance at Justin, who returned my look of alarm.

Kathleen leaned forward in her chair. Her wide blue eyes went from me to the priest to her father.

"I can answer that, Daddy. Father Rosetti has come here to find out which of the two girls is the true virgin."

Chapter 56

I WENT TO SLEEP that night trying to comprehend the startling news that there were two virgins and what it could possibly mean to the Church. It was half past four in the morning when I was awakened from a deep sleep by a persistent knocking on my bedroom door.

Twelve kinds of emergencies jumped into my mind as I scrambled out of bed, only to find a tidied-up and smiling version of Father Rosetti standing outside my room.

"What's happened? Is Kathleen all right?" I asked.

"Good morning. Sorry to get you up so early," he apologized without seeming to mean it. "Kathleen is still sleeping like a baby."

He was, he said, calling a meeting.

By five o'clock I had joined Justin and the Vatican priest in the library. From the look of things, it seemed the two of them had been up talking for a while.

Justin summed up what he knew so far. "The so-called second virgin is a young girl in Ireland. Her name is

Colleen. Sort of rhymes with Kathleen. The Church is struggling to keep her situation secret. That's easier there than over here. Father Rosetti has questioned her —"

"And I would very much like another opinion," Rosetti broke in. "Unquestionably, you are the two people most qualified to give it. You know Kathleen and can make a comparison. Cardinal Rooney and the Vatican agree. They also think it wise to keep our circle small."

That certainly woke me up. What was he saying? That we were to fly off to Ireland to meet this girl? But what about Kathleen? And Jamie Jordan? What about the night in question at Sachuest Point? My investigation was in Newport, not Ireland.

As if the priest had read my mind, he said, "I've already spoken to the cardinal in Boston. I'll stay here with Kathleen and wait for your return. Go quickly. You will be back in plenty of time."

Justin and I exchanged glances. I was thinking that I didn't particularly like this priest from Rome. I didn't trust him. And I cared about Kathleen. I also had a lot of work to do here in Newport.

Then Rosetti did something that surprised me. He completely humbled himself. "Please. I truly need your help," he said. "There is so very much at stake . . . for so many people around the world. And I cannot do this job alone. Please? *You have to help me.*"

My heart turned over in that instant.

"Of course we'll go," I said.

Rosetti's relief was tangible. He smiled again, and I realized with a visceral shock that he wasn't nearly as old as I'd thought. He was in his late thirties; forty, tops. What had aged this man so? What had he seen before he came to Newport? What did he know? What were Justin and I about to see in Ireland? Would we be in danger? Should I pack my gun?

"I think you will find Colleen Galaher extremely interesting. She has many of the same qualities you see in Kathleen," Rosetti said. "Go and you will see. Please, go. They could be sisters."

Chapter 57

LESS THAN TWELVE HOURS later, we were in Ireland, and I was trying my best to focus on a whole new set of problems.

I had said good-bye to Kathleen and her parents, and I also spoke to Cardinal Rooney, who asked me to cooperate with Rome as much as I could. So here I was . . . about to meet the second virgin, wondering what it all could possibly mean. And I was carrying my gun.

We scooted down a country lane in a tinny little car on the wrong side of the road. Justin seemed more at ease on his home ground and apparently was enjoying it to some extent.

I took comfort in his joy, and also marveled at the solemn beauty of the countryside. But mostly, I couldn't help feeling concerned and afraid. Too many bad things had happened already.

After nearly two hours of driving through low, striking hills colored a hundred different shades of green, we came to a gray wooden road marker for the town. Next to the town's name, GOD'S COUNTRY was printed in bold black letters. At another time, the irony of the words might have made me smile, but not now.

Turning down a narrow paved lane, we passed a drove of villagers: twenty men all dressed in earthy brown suits, plaid caps, and black boots that were obviously the work of the same cobbler.

Twenty pairs of eyes casting suspicious stares at our car as we drove by.

"What an odd group of men," I commented. "They make me think of the Druids."

"The last real peasantry in all of Western Europe," Justin said with a thin smile that expressed either pride or moderate embarrassment. "We've officially entered Maam Cross."

"I feel like we've stepped into a medieval hamlet," I told him.

"We have," he answered.

There were a few one-room stores on the main street of the village. Soot-stained advertising posters were stuck up on the walls: *Player's Please, Guinness for Greatness.* A livery stable and garage housed in one building. A row of stone cottages, freshly tiled and painted.

Justin explained that inside each of the cottages there would be a ten-by-ten-foot family room filled with souvenirs, a television, and numerous religious pictures. The bedrooms would all be cramped and tiny. The interiors would be badly lit and perfumed with the heavy smell of a turf fire.

I knew the real estate review was nervous chatter on Justin's part. The chatter abruptly stopped when we saw the graffiti on the fast-food hamburger joint that looked so out of place in the center of town.

The letters were angry, red brushstrokes high up against a freshly whitewashed wall: *Colleen sucks fairie dicks!*

"Aahh, that explains everything," Justin said and smirked as we zoomed on ahead.

Chapter 58

THE GALAHER HOUSE was about a mile and a half east of town. Justin and I went directly to it, almost as if we'd been there before.

I kept getting the feeling that none of this was in our control, and it frightened me in ways I'd never experienced. That morning, the *Herald Tribune* had carried stories of a terrible famine in India, a plague in Mexico, the polio outbreak in the United States. The stories reminded me of a scary book I had read years before called *The Hot Zone*. Ebola had almost seemed the work of devils.

As we pulled into the graveled car park, clouds snuffed out the sunshine, casting the tiny thatched and whitewashed cottage into gloom. There was nothing welcoming about the house, the yard, even the walkway.

"That's a peat fire you smell," Justin said as we climbed out of our rented car. "The smoke can be stifling. You won't forget that smell."

What I wouldn't forget was how I felt as we started to

walk toward the cottage. We were in Ireland, by God. We were about to meet the second virgin, and our opinion was important to solving a great mystery.

"Colleen's father died a year or so ago. A regular Finn McCool sort of man," Justin said. "Her mother was felled by a stroke. She's nearly senile as well — at forty. She's in her bed most days. The doctors out here are not terribly sophisticated. It's not the best situation for the girl. Not like life with the Beaviers."

"Kathleen's life isn't an easy one," I said, feeling a little defensive for some reason. "Not anymore it isn't."

"I know that, Anne," Justin said. "I like Kathleen very much. Now we have to find out some things about Colleen."

"Like how the Church in Ireland has been able to keep this a secret?" I said.

Justin shrugged. "That's no surprise to me. But I know the Irish Church. If Jesus Christ had been born on this island, the word still might not be out."

There was a rusting iron gate in the stone wall surrounding the cottage and it creaked as it opened under Justin's hand.

At that exact moment, the blue-painted cottage door swung open as well. A nun, a large, severe-looking woman, her black habit blowing in the soft breeze, stood there before us.

"I'm Sister Katherine Dominica," she announced curtly. "Who might you be?"

We introduced ourselves, and the nun nodded her head. She said she was expecting us. Dun-colored hairs peeked out from under her stiff white cap. She eyed us distrustfully but showed us inside.

The sister looked as forbidding as a crow and that was a fact. But I forgot her as soon as my eyes adjusted to the low light in the cottage.

There was a movement at the fireplace. A girl stood up from a low stool to greet us.

She wore a printed housedress under a frayed lace apron and had a striking mass of dark red hair curling down her back.

"Hello!" she said with obvious delight and surprise. "I'm so glad you're here. It means the Church believes in me."

The sunshine that had been obliterated by the clouds overhead had materialized right here. The smile on that girl actually illuminated the dim and dreary interior of the cottage.

I stared at her, not meaning to be rude. But she would have drawn stares anywhere she went.

Colleen Galaher had that coloring we think of as stereotypically Irish: transparent white skin, apple cheeks, clear green eyes, and, of course, her marvelous titian hair. But her radiant features transcended the stereotype.

I'll call it as I saw it. She was an exceptionally lovely girl — an exceptionally lovely girl who was hugely pregnant.

Fourteen years old, I couldn't help thinking. *The exact age of Mary of Nazareth when Jesus was born.* Father Rosetti had impressed that point on both of us. Did he believe this girl was the true virgin?

"Could I get tea for anyone?" the girl asked in a sweet, shy voice. "Some homemade soda bread after your long journey from America?"

I found that I liked Colleen Galaher instantly. Who

wouldn't? And that made me feel as if I were betraying Kathleen.

No wonder Father Rosetti needed help, I thought. This was an impossible problem.

Both girls seemed perfect.

Chapter 59

COLLEEN IMMEDIATELY IMPRESSED on us that she wanted to cooperate in any way she could. She had been hoping and praying that the Church would send someone.

We walked single file with her down a solitary mud path that twisted along behind the Galaher cottage. She said it was a good place to talk, and *listen.*

"It's very pretty out here," I said to the girl.

"Thank you," she said and seemed proud of the land. "I think it is, too. People around here say that it's God's country."

Colleen was taking the lead. I followed, and Justin brought up the rear of our march along this dull, uneven seam sewn into the otherwise bright green countryside.

I concentrated on Colleen, and what she was telling us. She definitely wanted us to hear her story.

"What do you want to know?" she turned and asked in the softest, sweetest voice.

Is she a little too good to be true? I wondered. But wasn't that true of Kathleen as well?

Two perfect girls — a perfect puzzle.

"Why don't you just start at the beginning," I suggested. "What's the very first thing that you remember pertaining to the pregnancy?"

"I can tell you that one. It was probably too late to be out alone," she said, "but I often come to Liffey Glade by myself. That's what happened on the night it all began."

Fields became sparse woodland, then dense thicket. When the gloom was thick around us, we came suddenly to a clearing within the trees.

Colleen pointed to a flat rock jutting out over the edge of a small stream. "I was right over there," she said, "watching the moonlight glinting on the water, when I heard their voices."

"Who did you hear, Colleen?" Justin asked. "What voices?"

A shadow crossed the young girl's face, as if her peace of mind had been breached by an ugly memory.

"It was two men and a boy around that bend," she said. "I thought they were trapping rabbits. Or perhaps fishing in the stream. I called out — and startled them. They were doing something wrong," said the young girl, her voice catching in her throat, coming out so ragged that it was hard to understand her. "They didn't want me to see."

"What kind of wrong?" I asked. "Did you see? What were the men doing?"

Colleen coughed, then cleared her throat. Her voice became a nervous whisper. "They had their pants down to the ground and one of them — a man as big as a bear — had his mouth on the boy . . . down there. The boy is in my school. The other man was someone I knew. A priest from another town. And he was touching himself."

Colleen suddenly started to cry. Big tears raced down her cheeks. She pushed them away with the back of her small hand. The tears seemed genuine.

"The priest recognized me and began to come at me. So I started to run. They did too. I could hear them breathing. I could smell them. I ran as fast as I could.

"The bigger man grabbed me by the waist and he pulled me down. I hurt myself. The priest covered my mouth and nose so that I couldn't scream — there was no air to breathe! Then it seemed like there were so many of them, not just the two men and the boy. It seemed like there were twenty or thirty, more than I could count.

"Then there was a loud cracking, louder than the loudest thunder. Big daggers of light turned the sky yellow and white!

"The men vanished. However many there were. Just scrambled up the scree, leaving me lying alone, scraped up and bleeding in the rain that came up suddenly and fell in the glade."

Colleen pointed across the clearing. An enormous oak was split in two. The damage looked recent. Half of the tree still stood, while the other half lay on the ground. I could see the fire marks that had scorched the length of the trunk.

"They didn't get me," said the young girl fervently. "The stories about me are all false, all lies. I got away from them untouched. I am a virgin, I swear it," Colleen said, cupping her belly with both hands.

"So how did this happen to me? How could it be?" she asked us.

As we stood in the gloaming in this fairy glen, I noticed the same pinkish glow that I'd sometimes seen emanating from Kathleen now shining faintly around this child. Could Justin see it? Could it be a nimbus?

I turned to him and saw to my shock that tears were flowing down his face. He could see the glow too. My God, what did it mean? What was the strange light?

"If you don't believe me, please ask my doctor," Colleen said. "He's right here in Maam Cross. He'll tell you the truth."

I believed her. I believed every word. And so did Justin.

And we didn't need the testimony of Dr. Murphy.

Early yesterday morning, Father Rosetti had pressed Colleen's dossier into my hands. It included the medical report from Trinity Hospital in Cork. At the Vatican's behest, they had sent a doctor to examine Colleen.

I'd read the report myself. So had Justin.

Colleen Galaher was eight and a half months pregnant.

And she was definitely a virgin.

"Please help me," she whispered. "I'm a good girl."

Chapter 60

Portsmouth, Rhode Island.

IT WAS HALF PAST nine, and the three friends were having a round or two of cocktails at Neely's infamous Lawn Bar. Jamie Jordan returned from the head, and he sauntered up to the crowded bar where Chris Raleigh and Peter Thompson were hunched over cold, foaming drafts of Samuel Adams, Boston's finest brew, or so the ads proclaimed. On the color television overhead, the blue-and-red-clad Rangers were pulverizing the local-favorite Boston Bruins.

Jamie knew from the slippery looks they gave him that his dear pals had been talking about the night at Sachuest Point. What else? That royally pissed him off. He pushed his hand back through his long blond hair.

"I told you that we don't talk about that night. That means we *don't talk about it.* That means you two dick-heads *don't talk about it* while I'm in the head."

Chris Raleigh rolled his dark eyes. "Paranoid asshole.

You're loaded, too. You're drunk. Do you believe him?" Raleigh turned to Peter Thompson.

Jamie Jordan's face turned bright red. "Thompson, were you talking about that night or what? If you weren't I'll buy the next round."

"Shots or beers?" Thompson said, trying to relieve the potentially bad scene the best way he could.

The three of them had been inseparable since their grammar-school days in Newport. That's why the friends were worried. They knew Jamie. Nothing had ever gotten to him like this. And now *everything* got to him.

"Were you talking or not?" Jamie asked again. The veins in his forehead bulged out against bone and seemed to throb.

"We *need* to talk about it, buddy. This whole thing has gotten out of hand. In case you haven't fucking noticed," Thompson said and pointed an index finger at his friend. "Do you know how out of hand this has gotten? We need to do something. We need a plan."

Without thought or warning, Jamie Jordan hit his friend hard in the chest with a closed fist. The dark-haired boy reeled off his chair and slipped down onto the puckered linoleum floor.

Hizzoner Tom Neely, proprietor, grabbed an old hardwood walking stick and waved it high over his bar. "You petty hoodlums cut the crap here or I'll brain the lot of ya!"

Neely's went dead quiet. The older workingmen glared down toward the corner where the ruckus had erupted. The three young friends were tall and muscular and looked to be in their early twenties. Each of them carried false IDs, which got them into most area bars.

Jamie Jordan spun away from his friends and lunged toward the front door. He bumped into a few ossified regulars, who did nothing. Jordan was six foot two and close to two hundred pounds. His friends were just as big.

Outside, with the sea breeze whipping across his face, Jamie Jordan thought about going right back in and wiping the floor with Thompson and Raleigh. Oh, Christ! He smacked his palm hard. Kathleen Beavier was the one he ought to wipe out.

He remembered how he'd had to practically get down on his knees and beg the Ice Queen for a date. He'd driven over to Salve Regina to meet the Catholic schoolgirl getting out of class on four different afternoons. He'd even worn his best Nautica sweater and ironed his black cords.

There was something different and special about Kathleen Beavier, he had to admit. Jamie had wanted her more than he'd ever wanted any girl. Not just for the sex, either, though the blond bitch *was* sexy. Jamie had just wanted to be around Kathleen. She had *it.* He had thought that he loved her.

Until that night at Sachuest Point.

Where something bad had happened.

Chapter 61

JAMIE JORDAN FIRED up the motor of his expensive Mercedes SLK. He twisted the radio to full volume and jerked the neat yellow sports car out of Neely's half-full parking lot. He yelled out the words of a Smashing Pumpkins song. His friends were right about one thing — he was bombed out of his mind.

As he motored up the steep cobblestoned hill behind Neely's, he angrily thought back to the night of January 23, when he'd taken Kathleen to the Salve Regina dance. Jamie's own parents were pretty wealthy, but he'd still felt intimidated as he drove up to the Beavier house that night. He'd worn a black tux and knew he looked great, but he was still unsure of himself. Charles Beavier had answered the front door and invited him in. He'd been preoccupied, rude actually, talking on his cell phone and barely giving Jamie a nod.

Jamie had cooled his jets in the living room and tried not to take the slight personally. A few minutes later, Kathleen appeared. Not half an hour late, the way a lot of girls liked to make you wait around for them. He appreciated that and his mood softened.

Actually, the sight of Kathleen had taken Jamie's breath away. She wasn't just another pretty schoolgirl — she was drop-dead gorgeous.

She had on a sleek, pale-green dress instead of one of those puffy gowns that made girls look so ridiculous on prom night. She wore a silver headband in her long blond hair. She looked like some kind of royalty, Jamie thought.

Unfortunately, the dance at Salve Regina was even worse than he had imagined it would be. The band was a stiff, middle-aged quartet that played at all of the pitiful Newport club and debutante teas. Besides that, there was an old-fashioned wooden running track that circled the gym one story above the dance floor. From there, flocks of Carmelite nuns watched over the dance like hawks from beginning to end. The nuns seemed to have a knack for laughing and tapping their feet at all the wrong times.

He'd been desperate to leave the dance after the first five minutes. Still, maybe Kathleen was worth all this torture.

There was supposed to be a fancy party after the dance — engraved invitations had been sent out: *Come to a great bash at Elaine Scaparella's house.* Kathleen had been pressing against him all night, tantalizing him with her CK perfume and the delicious hint of cleavage showing below her neckline.

When Kathleen put her head on his shoulder during the last dance, he could almost taste her. Jamie knew she wanted him too. There was no doubt about it.

He could hardly believe how easy it had been to talk

Kathleen into skipping the dumb party and going for a ride down near Second Beach and Sachuest Point. Now he wished to God that they had never gone there. He wished he had never laid eyes, or especially hands, on Kathleen Beavier.

Chapter 62

AS JAMIE HEADED OUT past Second Beach now, the high beams of his Mercedes stabbed through the thick, dreamy fog like glowing swords. He was pretty woozy, but his driving was okay. This wasn't the first time he'd been shit-faced behind the wheel of a car.

He was driving back to Sachuest Point — where he had taken Kathleen almost nine months before, the night that changed both of their lives.

Something bad *had* happened out there. Something insane.

He knew it.

So did Thompson and Raleigh.

And so did Kathleen, that phony bitch. That goddamn liar.

The funny thing was, Jamie wasn't exactly sure why he was going back. It seemed as if it was out of his hands. He *had* to go there tonight.

As he banked the sports car around a soft S-curve, he

noticed that his vision was tunneling. Strange as hell. And a dull, muzzy ache behind his left ear was moving up behind his eye.

Oh, Jesus, not again, Jamie thought to himself.

He looked down at the Mercedes dashboard. The car's glowing clock read 9:54. The speedometer was at 60-plus. And the ringing was starting. That meant that soon there would be a painful pounding at the top of his skull. Simultaneous noise and pain.

Memorial Boulevard slimmed down into a ruler-straight two-lane blacktop as it approached Sachuest Point. In his rearview mirror Jaime could see the receding lights of southeastern Newport and the glittery mansions on the coast.

He had a sudden desire to take the car over the point. It would be so easy — like flying.

He frowned, then shook his head painfully. That was a really stupid-ass thought. He *was* bulletproof, though. He was ten feet tall. He was Teflon J.J., but he knew the car couldn't fly.

Another unwanted thought circled, then intruded. *Kathleen.* And with the thought of her name, a shrill banshee wail started up in his brain.

Just remembering made him hurt so bad. But he couldn't turn back the clock — the day after the dance telling everyone that he'd made it with Kathleen. "I broke a vagina from Salve Regina." He'd strutted and bragged like the asshole he could be sometimes.

Jamie reached up and touched his head. The pain was so piercing it was making him nauseated.

That was why he wanted to cut the wheel — cut it now — cut it into the concrete retaining wall!

Wheels screamed. Rubber fused to asphalt.

He put both hands on the steering wheel and forced the car back to the center of the road. He was going crazy, that was it. The top of his head wanted to blow off. The incredible pain.

Then stop the pain, he heard. *You can do it, you know. You're in control. Besides, you know that you deserve to die. You know what you did.*

The yellow Mercedes swerved to the left and crossed the double yellow stripes again. The steering wheel didn't feel real. He couldn't grip it. Jamie's hands flew off the wheel and covered his ears.

See, you can do it! You can fly. YOU CAN FLY!

The sports car shot out of control, just missing an oncoming Jeep with fishing tackle waving wildly from the roof, missing it by ten inches or so. *God, that was close.*

Chrome yellow headlights blinded him for a second. An angry car horn trailed off into the thickening fog.

He held on tightly as his car continued its irresistible skid on the slick black road. Suddenly he *was* flying up into the thick gray fog. The front wheels left the ground and shot straight out with the pull of centrifugal force.

The car's headlamps trained vainly on the constellation of Orion before illuminating the downward curve of the car's trajectory.

Jamie Jordan screamed high above the rock music playing on the radio: "I'm sorry, Kathy! Oh, God, I'm so sorry for what I did! I'm so sorrrr-eeeee!"

Chapter 63

SOMETHING WAS WRONG; something felt terribly wrong to Kathleen.

The digital clock on her night table announced that it was 11:24, then 11:25, then 11:26. The numbers clicked forward inexorably. But Kathleen couldn't sleep.

I don't want you to sleep, she heard the Voice say. *You'll never sleep again. And that's not good for the babeee!*

The phone beside her bed rang.

Her hand slid slowly out from under the warm covers that sloped down the mound of her stomach. She reached for the ringing telephone. She'd *known* it was going to ring. How had she known? Was she psychic? How could she be?

"Uhm . . . hello? It's Kathleen."

She heard the uncertain distant-sounding voice of her friend Sara Petrie, who'd been mostly absent from her life lately.

"Oh, Kathy, I'm sorry to call this late. I wouldn't have, but it's godawful important. Something terrible happened."

"Sara, what is it? What's going on?"

"It's horrible, Kathy. Jamie Jordan cracked up his car at Sachuest Point. I just heard it on WPRO." Sara began to cry. She completely lost control. Then she hung up the phone.

Dazed, crying herself, Kathleen put down the phone.

She tugged on her jeans with the elastic front panel and struggled into a flannel shirt without opening the buttons. Bending over to put on her socks and boots made her want to heave. She was so sick. Sick to her stomach and, worse, heartsick beyond any feeling of loss she had ever felt.

A cup of dim yellow light shimmered at the far end of the upstairs hallway. Kathleen walked down toward the inviting light, the house creaking like an old ship under her feet.

She passed through a small, dimly lit anteroom that led to her father's bedroom. His door was ajar and she could hear him snoring gently. His keys were in the leather case on his desk.

She plucked them up, and as quietly as she could, Kathleen ran carefully down the stairs. She grabbed her navy blue parka off the coat hook.

She had to go out and see about Jamie.

She had an awful feeling that somehow this was her fault.

Chapter 64

KATHLEEN DROVE HER FATHER'S Lincoln down a gravel road that ran parallel to the beach, then twisted out of the beach bramble half a mile south of the main house.

She was throbbing inside; her eyes blurred with tears as she took Ocean Avenue, now slick with rain. The beachside road was like a twisting ribbon of shiny black glass. She was doing everything she could not to become a car crash herself, but the desire to make everything go away was so incredibly intense.

But she had more at stake here than her own life. She had the baby to think of. She had to keep the baby safe.

So Kathleen kept both hands rigidly clasped on the steering wheel and her eyes fastened to the bold yellow center stripe of the road.

As she drove, she began to remember what had happened that night in January.

It was finally coming back to her. She was close to the truth. . . .

But then she lost it again.

Damn it! Damn it! Damn!

She arrived at Sachuest Point a little past 11:45.

"Oh, my God," she whispered as she took in the scene of the accident.

The bleak, bald hillside that marked the beginning of the wildlife preserve was indirectly illuminated by the headlights of a long procession of cars that had come from town. City of Newport and Portsmouth police vehicles were parked helter-skelter all over the hill. Two shiny red fire engine pumpers were balanced on the bluff down near the accident scene.

She didn't need the emergency lights to tell her where to park the car. She knew exactly where to go. This was where it happened! This was where it all started in January!

She could almost remember — but it kept fading away.

She was blocking it. She knew she was.

Why? Why? Why?

There was a freezing wet wind slicing up from the ocean. Waves were crashing like thunder on the rocks just beyond the roadside.

A thick bluish gray fog lay over the entire area.

At least a hundred people were loitering outside their cars, trying to get a better look at the accident, trying to grasp the newest twist in the story of Kathleen Beavier. She was elbowing her way past the knot of onlookers to the automobile wreck when the Newport city police chief recognized her. He shook his head no, sadly.

"I have to go down there," Kathleen said. "I must. I'm going."

Captain Walker Depew took off his black-visored cap and nervously thumped it against his leg.

"It's not a good idea, Ms. Beavier. It's a terrible scene down there. He's gone. James Jordan is dead. I'm sorry. Don't go down there."

Kathleen began to sob at the final news about Jamie. She pushed past the flustered, red-faced police chief as if he weren't there. Peering through the fog, she could see where the yellow Mercedes had awkwardly struck the rocks, grille first.

Hypnotically, she put one foot in front of the other and, balancing her awkward body, began her rocky descent.

Your lover is dead! She heard a voice screech inside her head. *It's time to admit the truth about you and Jamie. Tell the truth, you bitch!*

Kathleen wanted to do it — but she couldn't remember what had happened.

"I don't know what happened!" she whispered through gritted teeth. *"I don't remember."*

A murmur rose and spread back among the crowd that was gathering on the road.

"It's her! The virgin."

"Hail Mary, full of grace!" A woman's voice rang out in the fog and drizzle. It almost seemed a sacrilege to Kathleen.

"No, please," she said and waved for the prayers to stop. "Go away. Please, just go away."

She walked on toward the harsh blue glow coming from two police emergency lamps set beside the overturned car.

A Newport policeman, a young trooper in a black leather jacket, held out his bulky arm to stop her.

"No farther there, miss."

She brushed past without even glancing at his face. There was no way any of them was going to stop her. Kathleen was less than thirty feet from Jamie Jordan now. She saw the whipped foam bubbling on the car's engine, a precaution against an explosion.

She couldn't help thinking: *Whatever happened back in January . . . it was bad. Really bad.*

Chapter 65

LES PORTER OF the *New York Daily News* sat in his rented car on a hillside in the frigid New England night, and he couldn't fully comprehend what was happening; he couldn't believe he was here to witness it. The battery on his cell phone was low, his coffee was cold, and he was seething with unanswered questions.

He wasn't alone in this regard. Word had exploded from the epicenter, where the yellow Mercedes embraced the rocks, to the fringes of the crowds in microseconds. Within minutes everyone knew the up-to-the-instant details. Before you could say "Live from Newport," television reporters and fanatics and run-of-the-mill rubberneckers with nothing better to do hied themselves to the fogged-in scene of the fatal accident.

Then Kathleen Beavier had arrived. Porter had rarely witnessed a more dramatic scene in his years as a reporter. She approached the still-smoldering automobile wreck where the boy lay dead.

She knelt to pray, and then a bright light suddenly appeared over the crowd. Someone in the crowd that was gathered on the shoreline began to scream, "Miracle. It's a miracle."

Fanatic, Porter thought to himself. But the strange light seemed to take on a halo effect. It kept coming closer and closer, directly toward Kathleen Beavier.

Porter switched on his radio and searched for the news — the competition. Andrew Klauk, of station WNPO in Newport, was reporting from Second Beach Road. Loud, interfering static preceded his report.

Finally, a crisp, young male voice came on in the unmistakably self-conscious style of local radio reportage.

"Kathleen Beavier is kneeling at the scene of James Jordan's tragic accident. It seems a touching and moving gesture to most of us in the crowd. The young girl is approximately fifteen yards from the twisted wreckage. The Sachuest Point area is blanketed with a kind of graveyard fog, which contributes to the general eeriness of the scene.

"A couple of people have actually begun to pray out loud with Kathleen Beavier. One can't help thinking of the power and glory of the ancient Church, of the role religion once played in so many lives.

"A bright light is moving right in toward the Beavier girl. Some of the people are becoming hysterical now. They seem to believe the light represents something mystical or divine.

"But wait. It's something else. There's an explanation for it. . . . The light is coming from a boat out on the water. The Castle Hill Coast Guard station's search-and-rescue boat, the *Forty-one,* has been drawn to shore by the noise and car lights. The fog covered her hull until she was up close. The lights we all saw were the twin revolving searchlights on the starboard side of the *Forty-one*'s cabin.

"There was *no miracle* at Sachuest Point tonight. The light was just a boat."

Les Porter stared down the hill and watched Kathleen Beavier walk slowly away from the smoldering wreck of the boy's car. *Was all this a hoax?* he thought. Of course it was; it had to be.

Chapter 66

I SAW KATHLEEN'S GIRLFRIENDS as we arrived at the accident scene near the ocean. Francesca, Sara, and Chuck looked grief-stricken as well as petrified. Once again, they were caught behind police barricades and couldn't get anywhere near Kathleen.

I walked past the girls on my way down to see about Kathy. I was sure she would be destroyed by what had happened to Jamie Jordan.

"You guys all right?" I asked the girls.

"This is so awful!" Francesca said, and tears filled her eyes. Car accidents involving young people were the saddest tragedies. It always seemed so pointless and absurd, especially this one.

"I'll tell Kathy you're here," I said.

"He'd never kill himself," Chuck told me. "He loved his ass too much. He'd never do this."

I continued down the steep hill toward the wreck. What

was Chuck intimating to me? Was it that Jamie Jordan had somehow been murdered?

"I'm Kathleen's guardian," I said before anyone tried to stop me on the way down. I felt that I had a right to be here.

Behind me on the path, Justin kept close; his story was that he was with the Archdiocese of Boston and staying with the Beaviers.

Kathleen saw us coming and she climbed the rocks toward me. I was suddenly afraid for her. The two of us hugged tightly and I could feel how upset she was. She was shivering. Her eyes were red-rimmed and she looked as if she'd been crying for hours.

"Something really bad happened here, Anne. Not just tonight — back in January. I *can't* remember! I'm trying with all my might, but I can't. It's why Jamie died, though. Oh, Anne, Anne, it's all my fault. I'm not a holy person. I'm a little whore! What is happening to me?"

Chapter 67

AS IF IT WERE a large ferocious dog, dread took Kathleen Beavier in its teeth and shook her out of the deepest sleep the next morning. She nearly always woke up with a sense that she had done something wrong and that she was going to be punished for it. But today, she *knew* it was true.

Jamie Jordan was dead. She still couldn't accept it, couldn't believe it, but she knew it was so. She'd felt Jamie's sagging weight in the body bag almost as if she were part of the EMS crew that staggered up the rocks with him. And she felt drained by the certainty that he was gone.

Outside Kathleen's window, the air shifted in the aftermath of the previous night's blustering storm. Leaves had been stripped from the trees and the tossing ocean had been disturbed.

There was a faint and dirty odor under everything which was hard to describe. Like a refrigerator that needed cleaning. Or old laundry left in a car trunk over the summer.

Like something was rotting.

Kathleen wondered if the odor was coming from her. She felt hopelessly displaced and confused.

Climbing stiff-legged and lopsided from her bed, she went to her bathroom.

She used the toilet, brushed her teeth; and while staring at her sleep-swollen face in the mirror, Kathleen was assailed by a recurring, guilt-ridden vision.

She imagined her baby with a grotesque and twisted body, a misshapen skull. When it cried, its voice would be like a calf's being torn from its mother, being dragged off to slaughter. It was a cruel fantasy, and Kathleen believed it was just that; but because the thoughts came regularly, it was a hard fantasy to shake.

Kathleen had other doubts, too, practical concerns about what she would do after her baby was born, about what her life would be like once she had her child.

The crowds of leering onlookers last night! They acted as if they owned her. They had jeered at her when the lights had turned out to be a Coast Guard cutter. Some had called her names.

How could she live a normal life ever again? She hadn't asked for this. She hadn't done anything to deserve it.

She wanted to tell everything about that night — the twenty-third of January. Just put it out there. *If only she could remember.*

Last night was the first time some things had begun to come back to her. There was an image of herself in the prom dress. A lot of men were gathering around her out at Sachuest Point. It didn't seem likely, but that was what she remembered. *A lot of men circling her,* not letting her get away. And then what had happened?

Kathleen heard the pine floorboards creak sharply across her bedroom.

"Oh, dear." She cupped her fist to her chest. "You scared me. Whew! Hello."

Kathleen smiled up into the stormy green eyes of the housekeeper, Mrs. Walsh. There was no cheery "Good morning" from her, though. Not a word. *What was wrong with Mrs. Walsh?*

Chapter 68

EVERYTHING WAS GOING as bad as it possibly could. Worse! Now Mrs. Walsh was against her too.

Kathleen's heart was thumping hard. She shot her eyes away from Mrs. Walsh. She was scared and she didn't want the housekeeper to know it.

She sat on the bench in front of her vanity mirror. Fumbling with her woolen socks, she began the exceedingly awkward job of getting her feet into them.

She welcomed the diversion. Was it all her imagination? Or had Ida been acting really weird around her lately? Had the housekeeper come to talk it out now? Maybe to explain what was wrong between the two of them?

The upstairs part of the house was particularly quiet and still. It made things even more uncomfortable between them, Kathleen thought. The woolen sock resisted her, tangling and frustrating her efforts, refusing to be a sock.

"I'll be out of here in just a minute. Two seconds," she said.

Why didn't Ida speak to her? Kathleen thought and began to perspire.

God, what could I have done to her? Mrs. Walsh has always been a dear friend, more of a mother to me than my own mother could ever be.

A flicker in the mirror caught her attention.

Kathleen looked up again at the older woman. It took a long, extended second to understand what she saw.

Ida held a double-edged knife in her right hand. It was a nasty-looking fillet knife, one used to slice and gut fish in the Beavier kitchen.

The housekeeper let out a harsh guttural rasp and shouted, "In the name of the Holy Father, I chase out Satan and his fiendish child!"

Then she slashed down hard at the bulging mound of Kathleen's stomach.

Pure shock and reflex made Kathleen twist away from the flashing, razor-sharp knife. The long blade drove deeply into the wooden vanity, missing her by inches.

Kathleen jerked herself away from Ida Walsh even as the crazed housekeeper furiously struggled to pull the knife free.

Kathleen slid by into her bedroom.

"Ida, stop! It's me, Kathleen. What are you doing?"

"You're not one of God's! *You're not even Kathleen!*" Ida Walsh screamed at the top of her voice. "You *are* Satan."

Her face was screwed up, livid, her eyes blazing with hate. The muscles of her arms were tense and bulged.

Kathleen barely recognized the woman she had known since childhood.

"Ida, no. Please. I *am* Kathleen! See, look, it's Kathleen. It's me. And my baby!"

The girl's screams echoed off the pink walls of the bedroom.

"Someone please help me! Oh, God. Please help me."

Kathleen ran awkwardly for the stairs, ricocheting off the doorjamb as she passed through. She caught the finial of the banister flanking the staircase.

She had gotten one foot firmly onto the tread when she felt a mighty shove at her back. Then came the awful, terrifying feeling of weightlessness.

Kathleen screamed again, a long looping wail, a sound she barely recognized.

She reached for the banister, but her falling weight was too much for her tenuous grasp. Her arm wrenched in the socket, and she had to let go.

Oh, God, no. The baby.

She fell forward, her shoulder slamming solidly into the banister. Wood cracked, then gravity dragged her down. The pain in her arm was excruciating.

The steep stairs were like a chute filled with boulders. Kathleen began to roll. She cracked against every step, feeling every sharp dig. Shooting pains went through her elbows and shins.

The wind went out of her as she took a powerful blow to the stomach. She feared for the baby.

Dear God! Oh, please, don't let it end like this.

Lancing pain radiated from a blow to her right ear.

Kathleen was aware of everything. She wouldn't let

herself black out. The landing rose up and smacked her hard across her swollen breasts. She didn't care. She couldn't let Ida get to her again. Levering herself up painfully, she got to her knees.

Kathleen knew it without looking. Ida Walsh was breathing hard, lumbering down the stairs, coming fast behind her. She still held the murderous knife.

"Satan!" she screeched. "He is inside you! It's Satan himself. You can't deny it any longer."

Chapter 69

I HAD DUG MYSELF a snug windbreak among the small hunchbacked dunes rising and falling along the beach behind Sun Cottage. I was flat on my back on a plaid wool blanket, feeling the brief and sudden appearance of autumn sun on my face.

I breathed in the clean, crisp October air that lashed at the grasses and the dark blue water and listened to the distant scream of a seagull.

Glorious, just glorious.

That oddly plaintive cry made by laughing gulls.

I was pondering how perfect the moment was, how perfect nature could be. Then I was thinking about Justin and those thoughts warmed me.

I didn't have the foggiest idea where the two of us were headed — if anywhere — but I felt that we were doing it the right way this time. I had to admit that the more I saw of him, the more irresistible he became. I wondered what he was thinking. Was he in love with me? Was Justin questioning his vows as a priest? Or were we fated always to be apart?

I reveled in the luxury of just plopping down here for a few moments, sunbathing in my clothes, letting the ocean breeze refresh me. It was still very early, but soon I was going to town. I had meetings set up with two of Jamie Jordan's best friends.

I listened to the distant crying seagull again and heard the blast of a horn from a ship.

But something about that gull was wrong. With a jolt of unwelcome cognition, I got to my feet.

I looked around, suddenly nervous and afraid.

The cry came again.

A piercing cry that seemed to be coming from Sun Cottage. It increased in intensity, then cut off abruptly.

And a chill snuffed out all the warmth for miles around.

The cry hadn't come from a bird.

It was Kathleen!

Then I saw her. She was climbing out on a side roof of Sun Cottage.

Chapter 70

KATHLEEN RAN BAREFOOT, bruised and bleeding from her fall, into a second-floor bedroom. She pushed the rattling window wide open. There was no time to think about this. Ida Walsh was close behind her with the knife and the strangest, scariest inhuman gleam in her eyes. She had gone mad.

Kathleen stepped down hard on the steep roof jutting out over the main dining room.

"You are not one of God's!" She heard the shout behind her. "You are Satan! I see through your tricks. Your disguise!"

"Go back!" Kathleen screamed back at her. "Leave me alone. I *am* Kathleen. Ida, please, it's me!"

She tottered above the flagstone patio that seemed to pulsate with her own heartbeat. Her bare feet clung tenuously to the cold roof shingles.

"Help! Somebody please help," she called into the fierce, cold wind.

Her voice trailed away from the roof like smoke from a chimney. Nobody seemed to hear her. Where was everybody?

She heard sounds behind her; she swung her head around and saw what was happening.

Ida Walsh had squeezed through the bedroom window and now crab-walked along the steeply slanting roof, trying to grab Kathleen. Her arms and legs and hands seemed oddly powerful and strong.

"You are not Kathleen!" she bellowed, her voice sounding almost like a man's.

Two groundsmen working below stared up at the roof in terrified disbelief.

"Please help me!" Kathleen screamed to them. "She's crazy. She has a knife!"

Protect the child became Kathleen's only thought. *Protect the child. Nothing matters but the child. Not Satan's child either. My baby!*

She stared back at the woman who had once loved her, braided her hair, said prayers with her, sang her to sleep. Where had that sweet woman gone?

"You are not Kathleen! I know Kathleen! I loved Kathleen!"

She inched across the tile even as Kathleen, injured and ungainly, moved away from her.

Ida Walsh's eyes were wide and blank and incredibly shiny. Her white hair fanned out in the wind in thick ropes.

Kathleen finally saw Anne racing up from the beach, screaming, waving her arms wildly.

"I'm here, Anne. Please help me," she called down over

the edge of the roof. She could easily fall now. She was so close.

She saw her mother leaning out another window, not believing, trying to get outside too. Poor Carolyn. Curious and concerned, but never any real help. They would all be too late. There was no escape from Mrs. Walsh and her knife.

Kathleen went out as far as she could, out to where the half-roof made a 90-degree turn around a corner of the house. She couldn't take another step without falling. Tiles slid and rattled underfoot.

She suddenly screamed at the housekeeper, "I command you to stop! I command you!"

Ida Walsh's bare white arm stretched out for Kathleen. Her hand scratched at the roof. The woman's eyes were fixed in a hateful stare. The knife gleamed in the sunlight. "I know the truth about you. I know your dirty secret!"

A figure suddenly ran down below the roof in the driveway. Kathleen was afraid to look away from Mrs. Walsh and the knife. She thought it might be Anne down there. How could she help, though? How could anyone?

A loud noise cracked, then thundered away from Sun Cottage.

Kathleen's mouth opened wide in disbelief and horror.

Blood sheeted from Ida Walsh's neck. The woman moaned, her face frozen in hatred. Then her body dropped like a heavy stone from the roof. The woman's body bounced once on the flagstone patio and lay motionless.

It was quiet, except for the distant crash and roll of the sea.

Kathleen's eyes fell to where Anne stood. Her legs were spread in a shooter's stance. She held a pistol in front of her.

Anne had saved her life, and the baby's.

Chapter 71

I WOULDN'T LET MYSELF go into shock; I couldn't. I thought that I finally understood why I was at Sun Cottage. I understood, the way a soldier must finally understand when he or she fights in a war, that killing simply can't be avoided.

I remembered John Rooney asking me if I had a license for a gun. I'd thought at the time he was making a joke. Now I knew better. This was no joke. I wasn't here just to investigate Kathleen; I was here to protect her.

It was getting harder and harder not to believe in something. In Kathleen? In Colleen? In good? In evil? What had happened that morning was very real. I had shot and killed someone, a sixty-two-year-old woman named Ida Walsh. It was horrifying, obscene; it was the essence of evil. And now I understood evil in a new way too.

Kathleen and I sat huddled together on the antique glider in the sunroom, staring blindly at the choppy sea.

I was rocking a still-tearful Kathleen in my arms when

I heard the phone ring downstairs. Now what? The Newport police had already been out here to question me. EMS workers had taken away the body of Mrs. Walsh.

I had killed her. How could it have happened?

Just before one o'clock, Father Rosetti called another of his famous meetings. The Beavier family, Justin, and I gathered in the library, where Rosetti revealed that he had received orders from Rome a short time ago. The shooting had apparently galvanized the Vatican. Or maybe there was something else we hadn't been told about? Kathleen, along with a small entourage, was to leave Newport immediately. Sun Cottage was no longer safe, which was hardly news for me. But was anywhere safe?

At one-thirty, three black Lincoln sedans skirted inside the elegant porte cochere at Sun Cottage. As the front gate swung open, a horde of shouting journalists stampeded up the long drive on foot.

On signal, seven of us were escorted out of the house and into the three waiting cars.

Windows up, doors locked, seatbelts tightly cinched, our small caravan shot toward the gate and streamed off the estate accompanied by the police escort's penetrating sirens. We sped right past the surprised reporters.

The ear-splitting noise and the speed summed up my mood perfectly.

We hit Route 140 and moments later were traveling at more than eighty miles per hour. I turned to look behind us.

Vans stuffed with frantic newspeople were already only a few carlengths away from our rear bumper.

I hung on to the armrest and prayed that Kathleen, who was in another car, would be safe. I was afraid that the bumps and twists in the road might make her go into labor. Or that a wrench of the wheel could send the car careening into a tree or stone wall.

There was an intersection of four roads up ahead. It looked dangerous at the speed we were going. The three drivers, who had been in constant radio communication, knew what to do. At least I hoped they did.

One car peeled off to the west, another to the east.

The third car, our car, headed north to Logan International Airport in Boston.

I settled back in my seat for the journey. I shut my eyes, and I kept seeing Mrs. Walsh as she fell from the roof.

"Kathleen, Kathleen," reporters yelled as they swamped our car at Logan, hemming us in to the curb.

I got out of the car and whisked off the black shawl covering my head. I tossed the pillow I'd stuffed under my dress into the backseat.

"No, I'm afraid not. I'm not Kathleen Beavier," I said and couldn't hold back a smile.

The furious and frustrated press howled their anger at this ruse. The disguise meant to throw them off Kathleen's trail had worked. They had no idea that she was boarding another plane at a different airport.

Justin and I were traveling together again. I wondered why. But then I gave in to sleep, which I badly needed. We arrived at Orly Airport in Paris at 10:45 A.M.

We'd barely set foot on the ground when I caught a glimpse of Kathleen's picture on the overhead televisions inside the main terminal.

I paused to see the CNN report.

Pictures flashed one after another on the overhead screen. Children stricken with aches and high fevers were streaming in droves to Broussair University Hospital in Paris. It was polio again. The epidemic had jumped the Atlantic Ocean and had launched itself against Western Europe.

I felt faint and had to sit down. I remembered what I had seen at Cedars-Sinai Medical Center in L.A.

Children were dying. There was no logical explanation. But it was happening. And it seemed mysteriously connected to Kathleen, or the child she carried.

Chapter 72

COLLEEN GALAHER AWOKE with a depression, or some kind of physical sickness that she couldn't explain. Each day, each hour, it was getting worse, much worse than she could ever have imagined.

She wanted to go to confession, to cleanse her soul. She needed absolution. *Now.*

A blessing. *Now.*

She wanted to do it for the child growing inside her. She wanted to do it to honor God. To show that her love and devotion were unwavering.

"I want to go to church. I want to pray. Please." She told this to Sister Katherine in a simple, powerful, indisputable way. The nun agreed.

It was morning, and the glorious hills surrounding the Irish village of Maam Cross were shining through a misty curtain of gentle rain. On a stone wall–bordered path twisting down out of the hills, the virgin and the black-cloaked nun walked, their heads bobbing against a sea of lush green. God's country.

After thirty minutes or more, they reached the spare, rocky crossroads into the village. There, five villagers, gross products of the arduous life in the region, waited for the city milk truck from Costelloe.

The men perked up when they saw the two women approaching.

"Is the father among us, Colleen?" One of the villagers called in his cruel odd-bird's voice.

"Won't ya at least tell us that, dearie? Who's the da for this kiddo?" asked the crinkled face under a bent Donegal cap.

"I'd say she's ready for the Abbey Theatre, with her fine actin' performance there."

"I'd say she's the Anti-God!" a huge, scary one shouted in a voice like a human bullhorn. *"Anti-God, I say!"*

As Colleen and Sister Katherine Dominica got a few paces down the cobbled road, a heavy stone thudded, kicking up a volley of dirt at their feet. The stone could easily have felled either of them.

"No harm intended," one of the men called and laughed. "Sticks and stones won't hurt ya."

"Yer little whore, yer!" came another shriek. "Colleen hussy!"

Colleen whirled about to face the gang of men. She cast a fierce, damning look back at them, her hands over her belly protectively.

"Yer all cowards!" she shouted. "Scoundrels and worse. I am a virgin! I am that! I am a good girl and always have been."

The Irish men continued to laugh loudly until one, then

two, then all of them began to look at the sky above their heads.

Everywhere, as far as they could see, there were large black birds coming together like a big, dark cloud, in a way they had never seen before.

It made the Irish men as silent as the dead.

Chapter 73

THE BIRDS HAD GONE away as quickly and mysteriously as they had gathered, and Colleen continued into the town without further incident. She felt better, though. She felt protected.

The Church of St. Joseph's was a dignified stone edifice enclosed by a neat fieldstone fence. It sat at the village center, its immaculate tidiness contrasting sharply with most of the other ruined buildings.

Colleen blessed herself with holy water at the entrance font, eagerly anticipating the Scripture readings and hymns that would connect her with the Father. She hoped the homily would transport her. She shivered and was parched for a benediction.

The church doors opened as they arrived, and Father Flannery, the young village priest, appeared in the heavy stone archway. He was new to the parish, here only a few months. The priest stared for long moments at the girl, and she stared back at him. His black hair, freshly washed, was combed neatly to the left. Colleen shivered. She had thought him the handsomest man she had ever seen. But the priest who had come from America, Father Justin O'Carroll, surpassed him. *Where was Father O'Carroll now?* she wondered. Where was help when she so badly needed it? Why was she being left alone in this poor, backward village? God had to have a good reason.

"Colleen Galaher, I'd like a word with you," the priest said in a tender tone. "Please. Come inside the rectory. It's important that I talk to you."

He turned and, with a nod, dismissed the nun. He showed the girl into the rectory, and he closed the heavy wooden door behind him.

"What is it, Father? Is it word from Rome? Has there been a decision?"

Colleen's heart beat faster as she entered the musty and darkened room. She lifted her face toward the priest, anxiously awaiting his instructions. She was wide-open, vulnerable, in love with God.

The priest reached out a long-fingered hand and grazed her cheek with it. *His touch seared her skin.*

"You've done nothing wrong, my child. You're a beautiful, beautiful woman now. There's nothing wrong in that."

Father Flannery reached out both hands and he cupped her breasts.

Colleen gasped and clasped herself across the chest. She stumbled backward against a hassock and barely caught herself from falling.

"No," she whispered. "Get away, get away! You're a priest. I'm pregnant."

"But I love you," Father Flannery said. He was quicker

than the awkward, gravid teenager. He reached for her, pulled her face toward his, pressed his lips against hers. Again her flesh burned at his touch, as if his lips were fiery irons.

"Nooooo!"

She pulled back and stared at him. Just *stared.* He stopped suddenly. The priest began to moan and whimper.

Colleen twisted free of his grasp. She whirled, burst through the narrow doorway, and out into the dusty soil of the village square.

Rude noises erupted again. Hoots and jibes fell around her like hailstones. A half-dozen or so villagers had already gathered outside. Word had gotten around that she was in town.

"She has no right to be inside the church!" a woman called out. Then they all joined in. "Not in our church! Not in our church."

A young boy picked up a stone and threw it at her.

Colleen tried to run, but she couldn't. It was too dangerous and she would never risk hurting the baby. She stumbled and lurched through the crooked streets.

This was so unfair, so unjust. She wondered if Mary of Nazareth had suffered the same insults and cruelty, and Colleen was sure that she had. Even Joseph, Mary's betrothed, didn't believe in her at first.

"I am what I say," she sobbed, "a virgin with child."

And on the way home, the birds were back in the sky again — protecting her.

Chapter 74

I SLUMPED INTO the deep leather backseat of the chauffeur-driven sedan. A tight fist of tension had burrowed into the small of my back, and my daylong headache was pounding furiously behind my eyes.

I found myself thinking of Colleen Galaher marking time in the hovel she called home. Kathleen — wherever she was with Father Rosetti — was counting down the hours as well. After the births — what?

As our car flashed through the dark, silent countryside toward the village of Chantilly, I replayed the falling, tumbling body of Ida Walsh. I could still hear her final screams. I had never killed anyone. I never believed that I would, not even when I was with the Boston police.

The image of Ida Walsh's broken body on the flagstone patio of Sun Cottage was a nightmare to me. I heard Father Rosetti's explanation. "The Devil," he told me, "is irresistibly drawn to Kathleen. Anne, I don't know why that is so. Not yet. *Satanas Luciferi excelsi.*"

What did he mean by "the Devil will be exalted"? Where? When? How did he know this? The Vatican was famous for its secrecy, and Rosetti was obviously a skilled practitioner of the art. What secrets did he know?

I looked away from the hypnotic smoky gray highway. Thick glass separated Justin and me from the driver, a silent, thick-necked man in the traditional peaked black hat. Who was *he?* How could we be sure that he could be trusted? It seemed appropriate to feel paranoid about everything. If Mrs. Walsh could suddenly become possessed, then it could happen to anyone . . . even to Justin or me.

Satanas Luciferi excelsi.

"I know what happened today." Justin came out of his reverie and spoke. "Emotionally, though, it's like action in a dream. It couldn't have happened, but I *saw it.*"

"Yes," I said. "Everything feels bizarre. I have that same thought fifty times a day. Continually. I was brought in to expose a hoax, to be a paid skeptic, but I find that I can't anymore. I can't deny what I've seen with my own eyes, what I've done with my own hands."

Justin rubbed his palm over a day-old beard that I kind of liked. He had dark pouches under his eyes, and I'm sure I looked no better. I couldn't imagine anyone whom I would rather be with now. We'd been together through the most terrifying times, and it had gotten us very close in a short period.

"What's happening reminds me of the way it was when we were children growing up in Cork. No one in authority would ever answer our questions. About anything. We were always kept in the dark."

I nodded my agreement. "Children often experience life as magical — but also threatening."

"Life is," Justin said, "both of those things."

I reached out, took his hand, and held it until we arrived.

And I thought to myself, *The hand of a priest.*

Chapter 75

I AWOKE WITH A start, wondering where I was, and then I remembered that we were in another of the Beavier cars. It was dark outside, and the fog had grown thick, obscuring everything beyond the car's headlights as we sped through the French countryside. What were we doing here? What was happening?

We were going very fast, too fast, and I dug my nails into Justin's arm. He was unresponsive, as if his mind was very far away. I took a moment to study his face and felt another swell of tenderness. I couldn't help wondering again how the two of us fit into the mystery.

We were headed to a safe house that had originally been chosen as the site of Kathleen's delivery. It was a gentleman's farm belonging to Henri Beavier, Charles's younger brother, who lived there with his wife and children. We were to wait for Father Rosetti's orders once we were there. Rosetti and the Vatican were in charge now; that much was clear.

The car slowed as it approached a row of high dark hedges, then stopped just outside the looming black iron gates. I was relieved that we'd finally arrived, but even that small burst of joy was tainted by anxiety. The large villa seemed forbidding at this hour.

Electronic gates swung open, and as they did, a white van materialized out of the fog, brakes screeching. Then the grinding metallic sound of sliding doors.

I saw electric blue lettering on the van's side: GDZ-TV.

It was an ambush and I felt outraged by it.

Cameramen with minipacks strapped to their backs rushed headlong out of the van. At the same time, a disjointed squad of waiting reporters sprang at us from beneath a copse of shadowy evergreens.

"They're here! They're here," someone called out in French.

There was a loud thump on the car's carapace.

A face pressed against my window; it was shaggy-bearded, distorted. Another face peeped into the rear window.

"Why have you come to France? No, no, you are not Kathleen! Where is Kathleen Beavier?"

Lights blazed from headlights and from the security lights now coming from the courtyard within the gates. Over the commotion came the bleating, looping wail of a police siren.

The car lurched forward as our driver stepped hard on the accelerator. A reporter clinging to the hood was flung into the shrubbery.

My eyes darted everywhere, searching for some unknown enemy. I fixed on a man who was standing calmly in the shadows. He had long black hair and wire-rimmed glasses. He was wearing a khaki coat that looked glaringly bright in the headbeams.

I watched him flick a cigarette into the road. It made a slow, graceful arc. His calm, calculating expression was jarring. The insolent way he stared at us made me uncomfortable as well.

Who was he? Why was he watching the farm? I didn't like his being here. I felt in my heart that he shouldn't be here. The reporters shouldn't be here either. Who had leaked the information?

A minute later, our car was at the front door to the villa and we were being hustled inside.

Strangers took away our coats and led us into a huge and aromatic country kitchen. There we were joined by Charles and Carolyn Beavier, who had arrived before us. We embraced like long-lost friends; we took strength from one another. We were like family.

I wanted desperately to feel safe and warm and normal, and not to be afraid, not to be paranoid. It was a lapse of judgment — understandable, but a lapse all the same. I forgot about the darkness and the fog. I forgot about the menace outside.

I thought only about Kathleen and Colleen, and their babies.

Chapter 76

FATHER ROSETTI LEANED in close to Kathleen. "Listen to me, Kathleen. Are you listening? You *must* listen closely now. Nothing in your life has prepared you for this. And nothing in my life has prepared me for this."

"That's comforting" was all Kathleen chose to say in reply.

"Well." Rosetti smiled thinly. "While your attitude is certainly understandable, it isn't very comforting to me."

"I'm sorry," Kathleen finally said. "I don't know where we are, or *why* we're here. I'm upset."

"Understood. We are where we're least expected to be, where, hopefully, no one is looking for you. We're here together because it's essential that I spend some time with you."

"You're investigating me, testing me?"

"Yes, I suppose I am. I *will* tell you that we're on our way to Rome."

Kathleen and Father Rosetti were sitting in a second-class compartment of a train leaving France, heading for Italy. So far his strategy was working — no one had spotted them. The railway was run by the Société National des Chemins de Fer Français, the SNCF. As the train bore down a blurred tunnel, the overhead lights flickered and died.

Rosetti's speech was uninterrupted by the dark. He didn't even seem to notice, and Kathleen wondered if he could see perfectly in the dark. He was trying to communicate an important point, she could tell, but she was so tired and so afraid.

Kathleen felt her homesickness as grief. She was away from home and at the same time homeless. Where did she live now? Where did she belong? And what of the baby?

"Kathleen, please allow me to tell you one thing," Rosetti said. "It's something I believe, something the Church in Rome believes, something which I will ask you to try to accept on faith also."

"What is it, Father? I'm so tired," Kathleen said faintly. She had to pay close attention, since his accent made some of the words difficult to follow.

"I believe that evil is a powerful and tangible force on earth. Evil is as real as you and I are real. Even today, the Devil exists. The Devil is a brilliant imitator, Kathleen. A master of perverse mimicry. He can seem not to be anywhere, but he is *everywhere!*

"Those who would deny the existence of evil — supposedly on a rational basis — are denying what they see in the world, what they hear about, what they think and feel almost every day of their lives. They are denying what they read in newspapers. Believe me, Kathleen, evil is all around us right now. I know this to be true."

"You're really scaring me badly," she said, "and I'm already so scared. I can't bear it. I can't listen anymore."

"Yes, I know." He nodded. "But not for the right reasons, Kathleen. You must fear the Devil, not a little harmless darkness, not the *words* I'm saying."

The ceiling lights came on with a whine as the power regenerated. Kathleen stared into the priest's dark eyes. She did believe him. She'd seen it, smelled it, felt it in the air. She was never far from evil now. Not for a minute. And she felt at the mercy of whatever or whomever laid claim to her.

For the first time in her life, Kathleen was afraid of the Devil. She knew he was close, right there on the train. *He didn't want her to have the baby.*

Chapter 77

COLLEEN HEARD THE DOGS barking and she struggled out of the rocking chair, where she was studying a history textbook. She had maintained straight A's since she'd first entered school, and she saw no reason to let her grades slip, not even now. If anything, Colleen found that she learned more from her own close study of the texts than she did with the interference of her teachers' opinions.

It took her a moment to get to the front door, but when she did, her mouth dropped open.

A bright orange school bus that read DUBLIN TOURS was parked in the driveway.

People, mostly women but a few men and children, were climbing off the bus.

One woman, blond, in a green oilskin coat, came forward while the others hung back.

Colleen tentatively stepped onto the stone stoop.

"Yes? Can I help you?"

The blond woman smiled pleasantly. "Please excuse us if we're intruding."

Colleen didn't understand what was happening. "I'm sorry? Why are you here?"

The blond woman suddenly looked embarrassed. "Oh, dear, dear. We tried to call ahead. We discovered you don't have a phone."

Colleen shrugged, then she finally smiled. "Actually, we do have a phone. What we don't have is money to pay a monthly service charge."

The blond woman's smile was restored. "We've traveled all the way from Dublin to see Colleen Galaher. You're Colleen?"

"I am. None other. And why would you be coming all the way from Dublin to see me?" she asked.

Another woman broke forward from the group standing near the bus. "My mother and my sister live in the village. They told me about your special situation. Sister Eleanor" — she indicated the blond woman — "talked to a friend of hers at your school. We're here, well, because we believe there might be a very special birth here. In Ireland. We understand that a priest from the Vatican was at your school."

Colleen shook her head from side to side, but she couldn't get angry at the very pleasant people from Dublin. Besides, she craved their company, and maybe even the attention they were giving her.

"I'd invite you inside, but —" She gestured toward the small house.

Sister Eleanor shook her head. "There's no need of

that. Just seeing you is enough, Colleen. This is worth our entire trip. Seeing you, hearing your voice, is our reward."

Suddenly tears came into Colleen's eyes; she started to weep.

Someone believed in her — someone finally believed.

Chapter 78

I WOKE FROM A deep sleep but found that I was still exhausted and could hardly move my arms and legs.

I lay in a comfortable bed in a house in the French countryside. I thought about Kathleen and Colleen and hoped they had gotten through the night all right.

The time was close for both of them, and I wondered if they might deliver their babies on the same day, the same hour, perhaps the same moment. I truly believed anything could happen now.

My God, I thought to myself, *I do believe. I believe.*

And at that very instant I heard a voice, not in the room but somewhere inside my head. I recognized it from a long time ago, when I'd been younger, and believed, and prayed frequently.

It was a voice that I talked to and carried on a dialogue with in my prayers. Sometimes it seemed male, at other times female, but it was always understanding, kind, lov-ing.

I need your help. I spoke to this presence inside my mind. *Please help all of us on this earth, but especially those two poor girls.*

Then I heard the simplest message: *You must be brave and so strong now, Anne. That's why you're here. You are the bravest of all. You've been put here for a purpose.*

I listened to the words and I took comfort in them, even though I didn't understand completely what they meant.

For the first time in so long, I believed, and I loved the feeling.

And, I think, I was loved.

Chapter 79

Rome.

A BURLY OLD MAN in a beret and navy greatcoat walked slowly down a greasy, cobbled alley off the Viale dell' Università. The Termini, named for the train station nearby, was a restless maze of streets and alleyways. It was a wasteland of cheap rooms furnished with cots, filled with penniless immigrants.

Feral cats were everywhere, their unblinking eyes watching from under parked cars and from the ruins of the Baths of Diocletian. They were as wily and as alert as survivors of a scourge or a war. They watched the stooped old man.

The surrounding buildings were ponderous and depressing, as was the ugly cement cemetery filled with modern mausoleums. It was difficult to believe that anyone actually lived in this section by choice.

The stranger stopped in front of one of the gray buildings, his eyes roaming up the soot-covered windows. He noticed a bent television antenna on the roof and a faded billboard for Cynar. He noticed the cats. The old man stiffly climbed the crumbling front steps and pulled a dangling bell.

A stout middle-aged woman with a dragging limp finally came to the door. She held a cat in her arms.

"Buon giorno, signora. Per favore, desidero una camera tranquilla." ("Good day, madam. Please, I need a quiet room.")

Signora Ducci quickly took in the large, poorly dressed man. He was in his late fifties or sixties, she guessed. Still strong-looking. A workman, no doubt. Not likely to die during the winter, at least, thought the Italian housewife.

"I have a room — I must have one month in advance." The woman stiffened her lower jaw to show her intransigence on that point. Her cat uttered a soft hiss.

"I only wish to stay a week or two, *signora.* I don't have much money."

"One month in advance. That is my rule. There are many other rooms in Rome." Sighing, the man said, "I will pay what you wish."

An hour later, Signora Ducci saw the man climbing the front stairs with a young girl by his side. The girl wore baggy clothes, but she seemed pretty at a quick glance. She didn't appear to be resisting the man, Signora Ducci noticed.

She smiled. The words *child bride* tumbled through her mind. She had seen something strange and fearful in the man's eyes, but now she knew what it was — lust.

Upstairs in the old building Nicholas Rosetti first closed the dirty curtains and then opened his greatcoat.

He locked the door.

He thought that he had found a perfect hideaway for himself and Kathleen. He was here to test her, to investigate — but also to protect the girl if he possibly could.

Chapter 80

THREE STORIES ABOVE the dark, steaming street, a bright yellow square of light shone brightly, like an oblong star, over the derelict Roman district.

Kathleen sat behind the window. She was hugging her throbbing stomach, feeling the baby's heartbeat racing inside her. She hadn't been this frightened since her visit to the abortion clinic, but this was far worse.

Anything can happen to me now. People have died, been murdered. Plagues and sickness have broken out like nothing since ancient times. I feel as if I have stepped into the pages of the Bible.

She tried to put those thoughts out of her mind.

I am going to be a mother very soon. Nothing else matters but my child. I won't let it. I love this baby. My baby will make everything right.

Across the small room littered with newspapers and food containers from lunch and dinner, Rosetti prayed in a barely audible whisper. The priest was so intense, so focused on the unseen and unknowable that he frightened her.

She turned to the cheap, blinking black-and-white television set on top of a packing crate. A reporter spoke in Italian while video clips depicted the ongoing hunt for her through Western Europe. A report came in that she had been spotted in France. Another that she was back in America.

"You said to tell you when I was ready, Father," Kathleen finally said in a tremulous voice. "I think I'm ready," she whispered.

Last year at this time she'd been playing field hockey, sailing on Easton Bay, crewing for the Newport Newts. Now she sat hunched over her big belly in a small, dingy room in Rome. There was no way for her to believe her own life.

Rosetti snapped open his black duffel bag and took out several items: a cross, a stole, a silver rosary, a small bottle of holy water, and two thick black books. Shadows seemed to flit in the corners of Kathleen's vision. Was someone else there?

"I'll tell you what's going to happen, Kathleen. First, I will read from this." Rosetti held up a cloth book with a blood red cross on its cover. "It's called the Roman Ritual. Some of the most powerful prayers ever written are contained in this book."

"Tell me the truth, Father. Please stop with the mumbo jumbo. Is this an exorcism?" she finally asked.

"No. Not an exorcism. But, Kathleen, I do believe that the Devil is here in this room. The Devil is definitely nearby. Something is keeping us safe from him."

"So far," Kathleen said.

"Yes. So far. Let's keep it that way. We will defeat Satan. He can be beaten. He is, after all, only a fallen angel."

Rosetti solemnly kissed a violet stole, then dropped it over the slope of his broad shoulders. Kathleen could see that his large hands were shaking.

There was a tremor in his voice. "The Evil Presence is sometimes called Moloch. Did you know that, Kathleen? Or Mormo — which means King of the Ghouls. Or Beelzebub — which means Lord of Flies. In parts of Africa people still call him Damballa, the Beast. But in Europe, in America, he no longer has a name. That is because so many Westerners no longer believe in Satan. He seems invisible, but is *everywhere*."

Rosetti solemnly blessed himself. Then the broad-shouldered man began to sweep across the room toward Kathleen. His eyes never left her face. She wanted to run from him, but didn't, couldn't. Her body seemed pegged to the chair.

The trembling girl began praying in a loud voice. "Lord God, my Father, protect the child inside of me. Please protect my baby."

Chapter 81

FATHER ROSETTI MOANED, then he paused, as if he didn't want to begin the holy ritual yet. *He knew what to expect.* First, the sense of the dreaded, all-pervasive Presence. Then the chilling, unforgettable *Voice.* Then perhaps an appearance by the Evil One himself.

He vividly remembered when he had been struck down inside the Vatican gates. It had proven to him that the Devil was everywhere, even in the Holy See. He remembered that he had seen a multitude of devils, not just one. He felt them surrounding him in the small room. They were like a sea of vermin.

"Dear Lord, please give us a sign." Rosetti began the most important prayer of his life. He felt such hopelessness in the face of the abyss. He believed with all his heart that he was taking the first step into eternal Hell.

He held a silver pocket watch in his hand. His parents in Milan had given him the watch on the day of his ordination. Now he let Kathleen see the face of the antique watch. "Quarter to twelve," he told her.

"Which virgin will bear our Holy Savior? Which virgin will bear the hateful Beast of this age?" he said in a strange voice that almost sounded like someone else's to Kathleen.

Almost at once, she could feel the dreaded Presence herself. She saw the lovers from her dreams, only now they were with her in the small room. She had the thought that none of this was possible, but the dream lovers were definitely here.

"Can you see them, Father?" she asked. "Please say you can."

"Leave us now!" he suddenly shouted, and sprinkled holy water at the lovers.

At the touch of the water, they turned quickly into animals — fierce dogs and howling wolves and bears standing tall on their hind legs. Kathleen stared in disbelief as they metamorphosed into birds and then into cats, just like the ones outside in the Termini.

And then they were back to the lovers from her dreams. They smiled smugly at Kathleen and the priest.

"They're devils, aren't they?" she asked. "Are these the fallen angels?"

Rosetti didn't speak — only listened, watched. A few of the lovers were naked, but some wore tight pants, or tight underwear, and they all stared at the girl with the same terrible *possessiveness.* They watched her intently.

They watched her stomach, never blinking. They looked hungry, ravenous. Would they try to eat the child?

"Can you still see them?" Kathleen asked Rosetti.

"I can see whatever you see, Kathleen. Who are they? Do you know them?"

"No," she said. "Well, yes. But only in dreams. They're not real. They can't be."

"What happens in the dreams?" Father Rosetti asked. "You must tell me everything you can. Hold nothing back."

Kathleen trembled. She wanted to kill herself again, to get away from here. The way the lovers looked at her was so vulgar and awful. No one had ever looked at her with such hatred and disdain. Even when they transformed into animals they had that vile look.

"They come to me almost every night . . . and they make love to me," she finally confessed. "Sometimes they do it *as animals.*"

"How do you feel when they do that to you?"

"I hate it! No, that's not completely true, Father. Sometimes, I feel the most amazing physical pleasure. It confuses me."

As the priest spoke, the lovers continued to watch and to slowly circle around her. Kathleen strongly sensed that they would hurt her if they could. Why didn't they attack? It was so eerie, and also disgusting. They kept eyeing her stomach, wouldn't look away.

Then finally, the leader spoke and she recognized the Voice that had been inside her head for so many months.

"I only want what is mine, what the Father *promised* to me, cheating, lying bastard that he is. I want the child. My child."

"Tell me how you feel when they come to you." Father Rosetti continued with his questions to Kathleen.

"Violated," Kathleen said. "But, oh, Father, I did feel pleasure, too. And then the worst shame," she said.

"Because?"

"I'm no longer a virgin . . . and I'm pregnant."

"Kathleen," the priest asked, "have you ever *known* a man? Have you known these men?"

At that moment, they all rushed at her, every one of the lovers. They were growling, moaning, making grotesque animal sounds and a kind of group hissing that sounded like the word *yessss. Yesssss. Yessssss!* She retched. They entered her — everywhere they could. Their penises were like knives piercing her skin in dozens of places.

She felt such shame and guilt again. She didn't want the priest to see this. She knew they were here to hurt the baby.

"This is our child!" the Voice screamed. "We fucked you and you conceived. Tell the priest! Confess. Tell God! Tell the truth!"

Kathleen screamed, and it was an unearthly sound. Her arms beat the air. Her legs thrashed about furiously. Her head shook back and forth. Her eyes rolled up into her head.

Then they were gone. Just like that.

The room was silent.

Kathleen was blinking her eyes rapidly, not comprehending what had just happened to her.

There was only Rosetti. And his silver pocket watch.

"What happened?" she whispered, looking around the empty room, her eyes wide with terror.

"I hypnotized you," he said. "Perhaps it was all in your mind, Kathleen."

Chapter 82

SISTER KATHERINE DOMINICA came to Colleen's house that same night, after the bus from Dublin had departed. The elderly nun sat across from Colleen in the small living room that was heated by a peat fire.

"Your mother? She's sleeping already?" the nun asked.

"She's awake. But you almost wouldn't know it. Most of the time she doesn't know who I am."

The nun nodded. "That must be very hard for you, Colleen."

"We get along fine," the girl said. "We make do."

"We haven't heard any more from that priest from Rome, have we?"

Colleen couldn't help frowning. "I haven't, have you?"

"Mmm," the old nun said. "There was a bus in town today. Do you know anything about it?"

So that was it. Now Colleen understood why the nun had come to visit. She wanted to lie to her and say she *hadn't* seen the bus, but she couldn't do it, couldn't lie. Not even to nosy Sister Katherine.

"The bus stopped here, yes. There were nuns on board, lay brothers, too. A retired priest. They came to see me, Sister. They heard about my special situation."

The nun clucked her tongue softly. "Was that all?"

Colleen thought about her answer. "They said — that they believed the Savior would be born in Ireland. Isn't that a wondrous thing? They believe in a virgin birth, Sister. Do you?"

Chapter 83

I HEARD A LOUD *gong* and my eyes swung to the marble and dark wood mantel. The clock had struck midnight. It was October 11. Two days before the feast of the mysterious appearance of the Gentlewoman of Fatima. Two days before the babies were due to be born.

Kathleen's.

Colleen's.

Justin and I hadn't left the villa since breakfast. We had spread newspapers over the carpets, over the tables, making a wreck of the place in our fervent need to know. What was happening in the world? Where was Kathleen? The press throughout Europe and the United States knew nothing of her whereabouts. The Vatican had refused to issue a statement. And they wouldn't put us in touch with Father Rosetti or Kathleen.

Justin snatched up the *International Herald Tribune* and stared at the stories one more time.

"I feel so helpless, Anne, and I'm not used to it. Are we

expected to just sit here and wait for the birth — the births? Was there *anything* that Father Rosetti might have said? Anything Kathleen said at any time? Where in hell could they be?"

I looked up from the sprawl of newspapers and shook my head. We'd been over this mess so many times it seemed like a wrinkled road map in my mind.

When I wasn't thinking of the horror going on outside the four walls, I was thinking about being here with Justin. I couldn't help it. There had to be a reason for that too. There was a plan — we just didn't know what it was yet.

"I'm going for a walk. I need some air," I said. "Do you want to come with me?"

In the last hour the fog had turned to rain, a soft dense sheet of it. Outside the walled compound, speeding cars made a sound like giant tape being ripped off the ruler-straight highway. The press continued to wait outside the gates. They were as frustrated and mystified as we were by Kathleen's disappearance.

There was a large umbrella outside the door, and Justin unfurled it. He opened the door. A fresh, clean smell swept the night air and I inhaled deeply.

We stepped out onto a graveled path between barbered boxwood hedges. Our footsteps crunched in unison.

But I couldn't make myself relax. I hadn't been completely honest with Justin and that thought was making me sad. I wondered how much longer we had together.

I had to say something to him, to tell the truth. What was the popular game — Truth or Dare?

"I can't stop thinking about you," I finally admitted. I thought those were probably the bravest words I'd ever said in my life. I had guarded myself from feelings of affection and love for so long, but now they engulfed me. *Why now?*

Justin's footsteps slowed, but I pressed his arm and propelled him forward.

"I've been protecting myself from you ever since the day I met you. But it hasn't done much good, has it? My life lately seems to be a blur of nervous moments, with you in the middle of them."

I laughed at myself; I couldn't help it. At least I had that left — good, honest self-deprecating laughter. Justin smiled too.

"It isn't funny," I said, continuing to smile.

The two of us walked on, arm in arm. I liked the feeling. The crushed-stone path led to a *potager,* a beautiful kitchen garden.

Espaliered fruit trees hugged the walls. Rows of winter crops, including kale, leeks, and Brussels sprouts, sprang up lustily in the neat rows. It looked like a tapestry of the Garden of Eden. Rain dripped from the rib tips of the umbrella onto my shoes.

I gazed upward and looked directly into Justin's eyes. His pupils were so large and beautiful, so honest and fine, that I felt that I could see right into his soul.

My voice quavered. "Next week we'll be apart again. And I just want to tell you — I *need* to tell you — that I do love you more than I ever imagined was possible. I don't know why I'm saying —"

His kiss was so gentle I wanted to cry. I gave everything I had to the moment. I lingered over the feel of his lips, trying to memorize every sensation. I was using my own lips to convey the strength of my feelings, to apologize for all the times I'd rebuffed him, to learn what it felt like to kiss another person with my whole heart.

I felt the umbrella fall to the ground. Heard it blow down the rocky path. I didn't chase after it.

Justin swept me up in his powerful embrace and we kissed again. This time it was a more demanding kiss that made me want to surrender completely. I went with it, feeling so wonderful, so alive. For a long, long time I had wanted someone to love me like this. I realized suddenly why it had never happened. It was because I had been unable to give love back to anyone. Now I could.

I had closed my eyes during the kiss and now, as I opened them, I saw someone watching us. *What in hell?* I thought. Who's there?

At first I felt a twinge of shame. But then I remembered how glad I was that I had kissed Justin, and it was something else about the watcher that bothered me.

I realized who was spying on us. It was the dark-haired man in the khaki raincoat from the night before — the one who had frightened me when we were just arriving.

"Justin, someone's there. He's behind you. I saw him last night too."

Justin turned and called out in a sharp voice, "What are you doing here? Hey, *you!*"

The man started to back away, but we wouldn't let him go so easily. I suppose that we were hungry for answers — any answers at all.

Justin and I started to run. We chased the man back into the groves of apple trees directly behind the garden house. We were gaining on him. We were going to get our answer after all.

The man realized it too, because he stopped moving

away. He stopped and waited for us. He stared at us, watched us coming through the rain, and he began to laugh in the most contemptuous manner.

"You *know* me," he finally said when we were only yards away. "You know exactly who I am. I am your desires."

And then, right before our eyes, he was no longer there. He had vanished.

"Did I see that?" I asked Justin.

"We both did. We saw it. He was right *there.* And now he's gone."

An intrusive voice called out as we stood staring in disbelief at the spot where the man had been just an instant before.

"Justin, Anne! Are you out there? Anne? Where are you two?"

It was Carolyn Beavier. She had a flashlight and a cell phone clutched in her hands.

"It's Kathleen," she announced. "God, it's Kathleen calling. She's safe."

I reached for the telephone and pressed it against my ear. I strained to hear her words.

"Anne — will you please come get me? Will you come *now?*" Kathleen sobbed. "I'm ready to have my baby."

Chapter 84

JUSTIN AND I FLEW to Rome as early as possible the following morning to meet Kathleen and Father Rosetti. We were so close to the births now that I was anxious all the time. Rosetti's mysterious games didn't help.

The Italian national police and soldiers from the Italian army succeeded in diverting the paparazzi away from our arrival gate. We found a queue of chunky little Fiat taxis. Parked on one side of the taxis was our limousine.

I held Justin's hand as the limo sped along the rain-slicked Via Cristoforo Columbo, then into the center of Rome. The driver then plunged us into the shadows of the ancient buildings of the Termini, one of Rome's seedier districts.

"Why are they staying here and not at the Vatican?" I verbalized my thoughts, knowing Justin wouldn't have an answer. "This whole thing makes me think of scary horror movies. Rosetti is a total control freak."

Justin's eyes surveyed the dismal city streets. "The image I've been having lately is the battle between the Archangel Michael and Lucifer with his legions, an epic battle between good and evil."

I looked over at him. "Are you Michael?" I asked. I was only half-joking.

Justin smiled. "Not even close."

"Well, we need Michael and all his angels. We seem to be badly outnumbered. The powers of darkness are winning."

Our car braked at the curb of a particularly disreputable-looking street in the Termini. We got out and hurriedly climbed the steep front steps of a crumbling old building.

The front door was unlocked. Inside, stairs corkscrewed darkly upward.

Justin and I quickly mounted splintered flights to a top-floor hallway that terminated at three dirty gray doors and a wired-over skylight, dim with soot. A black cat jumped out of a dark corner and scared both of us.

Justin turned to me and said, "It gets stranger and stranger."

"This is the part where the movie audience always screams, 'Don't go up there!'"

"So of course we continue up the stairs," he said.

One of the hallway doors opened suddenly, and my heart jumped. Nicholas Rosetti stood in the white light that flooded the hall and stairs.

"Justin and Anne, thank God. Please, come in. Thank you for coming."

Rosetti attempted a smile, but his face was incredibly haggard and drained. I couldn't believe how thin he was. The Vatican investigator seemed to have lost nearly twenty pounds in less than a week. The skin on his face was sallow, sagging on his cheeks and around his dark eyes. Father Rosetti looked as if he was dying before our eyes.

"Are you all right?" I asked him.

"Of course, of course." He patted my shoulder and led the way inside. "I'm tougher than I look, and I look tough."

Across the small, bare room, Kathleen was propped on a sagging two-seat sofa. She pushed herself up and waddled awkwardly to us. She also looked ashen and exhausted.

She got her arms around me and began to cry. "I'm so glad to see you," she sobbed. "I'm so afraid. This is so awful. Being pregnant, being *here.* We have to talk, Anne."

"What's going on?" I turned and shouted angrily at Rosetti. "What have you done to her? Why are you here? Kathleen needs to be around doctors."

He waved away my concern as if it were too trivial to respond to. "I simply don't have time to explain everything to you!" He spoke to me in a sharp tone that matched mine. "Kathleen would have been unsafe anywhere except with me. If you don't understand that, so be it. And now I have to move her again. To the holy sanctuary of the Vatican where the baby must be born."

Chapter 85

JUSTIN WAS TALL and strongly built, and he moved toward Rosetti like a great column of fury. Once upon a time he'd been a rough-and-tumble Irish footballer, and he certainly looked it now. "You risked *her life* — and the child's," he shouted.

"No, I did no such thing. I would never put a life in jeopardy. You just don't understand the facts of the situation."

"Tell us something *factual*. Tell us something," Justin shouted, the veins bulging out in his neck. He still looked ready to punch out Father Rosetti. "What do you know? *Tell us!*"

I put my hand on Justin's arm, felt his tension and strength. "I feel the same way, Father Rosetti. We're sick of being in the dark," I said. "You say you need help, but you never give us a reason. *Believe,* you say. Believe what?"

"I'm sorry," Rosetti said, his voice ragged with fatigue.

"I do trust both of you. It is a very difficult thing for me, but I do. I know how you care for Kathleen. I know you are both good. That's why you're here. But I can't. I promised. Oh, God . . ."

Father Rosetti began to speak of an intensely frightened Holy Father who knew a terrifying secret. "And then," said Rosetti, "the pope was struck dead in his sleep! I had already accepted my mission. Before then, I had been an ordinary priest in the Congregation of Sacred Rites. My qualifications for the job were that I was a thorough investigator and a good priest. I am a detective for the Church.

"*If* you help me now," Father Rosetti said, "you will know everything soon. Every last twist and infernal turn and trick of the abominable Beast! Are you sure you want to know what I must do? Are you prepared to confront the Evil One? Are you both in a state of grace?"

"Are *you?*" I challenged Rosetti. "You look like a mad person. You expect us to do as you say because you come from the high-and-mighty Vatican, the Holy See. Tell us the truth. *Tell us now!*"

Rosetti sighed, shook his head, and then gave in, or at least seemed to. He whispered so that only we could hear.

"The Devil is to be born as a human child very soon. Only then can the legions multiply and take over the earth. But a savior is to be born as well. A savior will be born to one of the two virgins. Anne, Justin, I still don't know which girl it is. You must help me find out."

Chapter 86

EARLY THE FOLLOWING MORNING, we waited for Kathleen and Rosetti in a small, dreary café in the Termini. I was so jumpy I couldn't keep my hands still, or my mind on the indescribable moment.

Did I really want to know what Rosetti claimed to know? Did I want to play by his rules?

Was I prepared to confront evil, whatever that might turn out to be?

The questions seemed completely absurd and melodramatic, and yet I had to know the answers. I realized that I had changed so much since the day I arrived in Newport. I believed that something monumental was going to happen, I just didn't know what.

Our tiny metal table was jammed in between a radiator, a pistachio green wall hung with music scores, and a large man feeding tidbits to his schnauzer. It was hard to talk over the breakfast-hour din, but in a way the noise and the smells were reassuring. It seemed *normal.* The real world still existed.

We had just spent the night on the floor of the room Rosetti had obtained for himself and Kathleen. He had been in constant prayer throughout the night, his features contorted as if he was in terrible pain.

In the gloom, illuminated only by the faint glow of a streetlight, I imagined that Rosetti was standing watch. A lone sentry listening for the approach of . . . *what?* Another plague? Demons? His own death?

And then he talked to us, and it took him the better part of an hour. He told us what we had to do and why. He said we had two choices: walk away, or take our chances that he was right.

Justin looked into my eyes. "We don't have to do what Rosetti has asked of us, Anne."

I nodded. I knew Justin was questioning his faith, but perversely, mine had solidified. "Justin, I do. Rosetti *is* from the Congregation of Sacred Rites. He's for real. And so are Kathleen and Colleen. We have to help him."

We were both upset and frightened and very, very tired. We were to be separated in a few minutes. One of us was to go with Kathleen to Vatican City. The other had to go to Ireland, to be with Colleen. One of us might be in terrible danger. Maybe both of us.

And this wasn't just about everyday, run-of-the-mill pain and suffering — it was about eternal pain and suffering.

Without being aware, I'd crumbled my *papassino* to powder. Justin pushed his plate aside and dropped some coins onto the table. We stood and awkwardly negotiated our way out of the café and onto the street.

I stopped just beyond the doorway and reached out for him. I felt someone brush past me on the narrow sidewalk, muttering *"Scusi,"* but I didn't look up. This was so strange and weird and it kept getting worse, more and more intense, more and more incomprehensible.

I pressed my face into Justin's sweater and felt his arms come around me. Tears flowed down my cheeks. I couldn't stop them. I'd changed so much recently that I hardly knew myself. Once I'd finally allowed myself to feel, I couldn't contain my emotions. Feelings were rushing through me in such great, dizzying waves. I wondered if I had any control over myself.

"I love you," I sobbed into Justin's chest. "Why couldn't I have told you such a simple thing?"

"Maybe because it isn't so simple," he answered.

He held me tightly, resting his cheek on the top of my head, swaying with me gently while Italian pedestrians parted around us. He was so strong, so good. How had I ever given him up? What was going to happen to us now?

"I'll be back," he said. "I promise."

Two dark blue sedans arrived at the curb outside the dismal building where we'd spent the past twenty-four hours. Kathleen and Rosetti finally appeared. I stared at her face. She still looked pale and stricken. She would go into labor soon.

Then what?

Last night she'd fallen asleep so quickly and slept so soundly that we'd never had a chance to talk. Then this morning, it almost seemed that Rosetti was keeping Kathleen away from me.

It was time to go, time for Justin and me to part.

I would go with Kathleen.

And Justin would go to Colleen.

We hugged one final time and I was struck with the awful thought that I would never see Justin O'Carroll again.

Chapter 87

AFTER JUSTIN LEFT, Father Rosetti and I stood in an anxious knot on the sidewalk. The priest took both my hands in his and the touch was surprisingly gentle. He seemed almost human.

He whispered, "Anne, what I'm about to ask will horrify you, repulse you. It will go against everything you stand for. But I have to get your promise."

My mouth was dry as I listened. I prayed for strength. I had no idea where he was going with this, but I knew that I wouldn't like it one bit.

Rosetti continued, "I hope that I'll soon know the final truth about the two young virgins. The message of Fatima has provided a trail to be followed. The Bible has provided clues in the apocalyptic writings."

Rosetti's eyes scrunched up as if he'd suddenly received a blow. "But, Anne, I'm not certain. Ultimately, this will be a matter of faith. It will not be simple. Nothing ever is."

Rosetti's voice intensified. "You must watch for a clear sign. A sign at the moment of the birth was promised. We will know which child is the Beast and which is the Savior. *You* will know."

I felt as if I were watching myself in a dream; everything seemed so unreal.

"I hear what you're saying, Father. But then what do I do?"

He was resolute, unwavering. "Anne, the Beast must be killed. The child of the Devil must be destroyed. And the child of God must be protected at any cost to us. *Any* cost."

Reading my shock, Rosetti made the sign of the cross. "You will know what to do when the time comes," he whispered. "That's why you're here."

I had faith; but trusting in God was one thing, killing a newborn infant was another. Could I do it? I didn't think I could ever kill again.

"I d-don't know, Father," I stammered.

"I believe in you, Anne," Rosetti said. "You are a good person. You are the strongest of all of us. You can defeat the Beast."

Chapter 88

WAS THAT WHY I was going with Kathleen? Because I was supposedly a strong person? And why were both Justin and Rosetti going to Ireland? Why was Colleen suddenly getting the most attention?

I entered the cool interior of the waiting car. Kathleen reached for me and I hugged her. At the same time I felt sick at heart. Would I have to betray her and her child? Would I have to do much worse than that?

The car had been sent by the Vatican. It was a specially made Fiat with an official license plate. Two Swiss Guards sat in the car. One man drove while one rode shotgun. It made me wonder about Rosetti and Kathleen's escapades the past few days, but as I had always known, the Church works in strange and mysterious ways.

As we pulled away from the curb, I was startled by a swarm of uniformed police on motorcycles. They appeared suddenly and flanked our car. In minutes, I understood why the extra security was needed. Kathleen's whereabouts had apparently gotten out.

The sidewalks were a solid mass of pushing, screaming people — all trying to get a look at the young American virgin. Thousands of the faithful, but also curiosity seekers, were packed on both sides of the narrow roadways. They were hanging off the heavy stone overpasses.

Kathleen gripped my arm so tightly she nearly cut off the circulation. I could hardly breathe as we approached the gates of the Vatican.

"My God, Kathleen," I whispered. "This is all for you."

"No, Anne," she said. "It's not for me at all. None of it is. It's for him. It's for the child inside me."

We cast glances at the great Vatican towers, the stucco palaces, and the gold crosses blazing everywhere against the vast blue skies. Banked deep in front of the small shops and trattorias on the Via Merulana, a two-mile-long column of worshipers greeted the virgin.

Our driver spoke in broken English. "They saying two hundred thousand people, and it just starting."

Flowers bombarded the car as we drove past the huge crowd. Joyful cries washed over us in an undulating wave of emotion.

The part of me that was still a good Christian understood completely. These people wanted desperately to believe in something. The majestic, awe-inspiring scene spread before us was profoundly moving. The magnitude of the crowd, the devotion and the honest love in the eyes of the people were humbling. It gave me chills to think what effect a miracle would have in this supposedly rational but oddly susceptible age. I was tingling all over and felt light-headed.

I was entering the Vatican for the first time in my life, sitting with a young girl who supposedly would give birth to the Messiah.

Gone was my doubt, all of it.

I believed once again, and it was the best feeling I could imagine.

Chapter 89

I FELT TRANSFORMED as we looked out at the sea of faces. It was a strange, prickling feeling spreading through my body. I looked over at Kathleen.

"You wanted to talk, Kathy," I said.

"I do, Anne. I remembered something when I was with Father Rosetti these past few days. Wait until we're in the hospital, and settled in. I'll tell you then. There's still time."

"Is there?" I asked. "Are you sure?"

"Yes, I am. There's time." Her eyes turned back to the street. "My God, look at all of these people."

Kathleen undoubtedly had no idea why she'd been chosen for this, but she did know one thing: She knew her purpose. She knew why she'd been put on Earth. I was as moved as she was. Tears filled my eyes.

When the car came to a stop outside the hospital where she would deliver, I saw a colorful wall of the Swiss Guard awaiting our arrival. They quickly drew a protective circle around the car. They held back the mob of people waving handkerchiefs and jumping and bobbing to get a glimpse of Kathleen.

Rows of priests in white surplices and flowing black cassocks knelt and crossed themselves. They seemed swept up in ecstasy. I felt their love as a physical force, and it was overwhelming.

I got out of the car and gave Kathleen a hand. As she climbed out and touched her feet to the ground, a loud, thunderous roar swept up the avenue.

Tears suddenly slipped down Kathleen's cheeks. I didn't cry, but I was close. I remembered Rosetti's words: *You are the strongest of all of us.* Why did I need to be strong?

My eyes drifted over the surging, brightly colored mass. I saw a crack in the wall of guards and police. A quick movement.

Then I saw him! My heart fell.

It was the watcher.

Over the din, I shouted as loud as I could, "Over there! Stop him!"

I was pointing to a man in a khaki-colored raincoat, slick black hair, wire-rimmed glasses. He was the man from the French countryside — the one who had disappeared before my eyes. The Devil? One of the fallen angels? An assassin?

He was pushing through the opening, moving swiftly toward Kathleen. Something in his hand sparkled in the sunlight.

"Gun!" I shouted. "Gun!" I wasn't the only one who saw it.

My heart jumped. I didn't have my gun — it was still packed away. The man was bent low. Coming even faster now. Then he was running toward us with his right arm extended.

"He has a gun!" I screamed again.

Then I hurled myself between the onrushing man and Kathleen. I didn't even give it a thought.

Time elongated. My neck twisted sharply to the right. My chest bucked as it received a terrific jolting blow.

I felt the crush of falling soldiers and police. It was as if I had been sucked into a deep, dark hole.

There was a bright, white, loud explosion at the center of the thick wall of people. Kathleen screamed high and long. I screamed.

The pile of frightened policemen thrashed wildly, their batons rising and falling.

I could hear Kathleen, but I couldn't see her. "Anne," she wailed. "Anne!"

I was lying on the ground. I could see the man in the raincoat was bleeding from head and neck wounds. As he was dragged toward a police van, he pinned me with his eyes. He spoke in English, his mouth spewing hate.

"Kathleen Beavier is not of God! You must destroy her. *You* must destroy the child. *You* must do it."

Suddenly I wasn't sure if he was the same man we'd seen in France. My vision blurred and spun. Everything was happening so quickly. I forced myself to my feet against the urging and advice of Italian policemen.

"Kathleen!" I shouted as I saw her being taken into the hospital. She called out my name and waited for me. Then the two of us hurried inside the heavy doors. We hugged each other tightly.

"I thought you were dead. Shot," she sobbed. "Oh, Anne, I was so afraid for you."

"I'm fine, I'm just fine," I murmured as we held on tight. I kept thinking that this was a good girl. The Devil couldn't be inside this young woman. Not inside Kathleen. Colleen Galaher had to be the one.

And yet, she had seemed such a good girl too.

Book Three

NATIVITY

Chapter 90

COLLEEN FELT SURPRISINGLY GOOD, considering how close she was to term. *I'm going to be a real mother soon! A wee tiny baby is going to come out of me,* she thought. It was still astonishing to her. It brought hope and joy that kept her going most days and then through the long nights at the cottage.

Colleen was making herb tea for herself, her mother, and Sister Katherine. She cut into a dark loaf of soda bread marked with the traditional cross.

The simple act of tea-making kept her mind off all the things that were happening now, things that didn't make any sense to her, things that possibly never would.

How will I take care of my mother and the little one? Will I be able to go back to school? "I'm only fourteen years old," the young girl finally whispered. Her small, freckled hands trembled so hard the lid rattled on the teapot. "Somebody please help me. I'm a good girl."

Colleen brought the tea and steaming bread out into

the tiny living room. Where was Sister Katherine? She had been sitting there only moments before.

Colleen called out inside the house. No answer. Her mother had fallen asleep again. She wouldn't wake for hours. Colleen unlatched the front door and went outside.

Sister Katherine was nowhere to be found.

But a dark shape was making its way up the path. Colleen could see that it was a priest. Oh, God, it was Father Flannery from town. How dare he come?

Colleen crouched behind a clump of gorse, its wiry branches forming a thick barricade. *Had he seen her?* She thought not.

She couldn't bear to be anywhere around him. There was something wrong with the parish priest. There had to be. Why else would he have touched and kissed her inside the rectory?

Colleen pushed herself to walk as quickly as she could the twenty or so paces to the barn. She pressed her weight against the sliding door.

Panting heavily, she slipped inside. Suddenly, she felt tired and breathless. And so, so afraid.

She heard the pathetic priest calling to her: "Colleen, I've come to bless you, child."

"God help me, you won't," she whispered.

Colleen cast her eyes around in the gloom of the barn. The straw on the floor seemed to eddy around her feet, and a warm draft brushed her cheek. Gray Lady whickered a greeting. She felt protected by something unseen, something or someone who loved her.

There was a stall at the very back of the barn. It was dark and pungent with the scent of lanolin, occupied now by an old ewe that was kept for wool.

"Hush, Bridey," Colleen spoke to the sheep, pushing her aside. Then Colleen squirreled herself into the farthest corner and covered herself with hay. The smell of it was thick in her nostrils and she nearly sneezed.

Outside, Father Flannery's voice became a wheedle, a whine. "*Colleeeen.* Come to me, now. I am your priest."

Then his voice sharpened with anger. "Come out, Colleen. I'm here on God's business."

No, I don't believe it. God doesn't fondle and kiss young girls. God isn't a pig!

Colleen shut her eyes as tight as she could. Eventually, the only sounds she heard were those of the animals, stamping and chewing in the barn. It was fragrant and peaceful here. A stream of sunshine came through the hayloft, a long bright shaft of light.

It dawned on her, then. It was so fitting; it was perfect. This was where she would give birth to the child.

As it had been in Bethlehem, God had led her to a manger.

Chapter 91

NICHOLAS ROSETTI HAD ARRIVED in Maam Cross, and still the dreaded, damnable Voice was constantly with him, trying to distract him from the end of his mission, trying to drive him insane. He was here ahead of Justin O'Carroll, who'd gone to meet with a doctor who had examined Colleen in Dublin.

No one has the right to ask this of you. You will damn yourself to an eternity in Hell, the Voice said into his ear. *Eternity is a long, long time, Nicholas. You have no idea, but I do!*

Father Rosetti struggled into the small hotel room. He noisily dropped his bag onto the sticky, thinly carpeted floor. He didn't bother to switch on the overhead lights.

Yes, get used to the dark. You see, there are dark fires in Hell. You didn't know that, did you? But I do.

He walked over to a water-streaked window and stood there, observing the cool, silent Irish village. He had to be close to the truth about the two virgins. And yet he feared that he was committing the sin of pride to believe so.

His night sweats were with him during the day now. His big heart seemed to seize up without warning and dance erratic cadences in his chest. But his mind was still sharp. The Beast had made use of artifice, illusion, imitation, disruption, misdirection. Nicholas Rosetti could see through it; at least he thought he could.

He was still alive, wasn't he? He hadn't been condemned to Hell yet.

Soon, Nick, the Voice taunted. *You're so very close to the eternal gates of doom. Be careful where you step. Careful, Nick. It's a long, long drop.*

In his briefcase were the documents revealing what he knew. Before he left to see Colleen Galaher, the papers would go into the hotel safe.

No place is safe from me, Nick. Don't you know that yet?

A rapping sound shattered his troubled reverie. A knock at the door. It should be Justin, thank God.

But it wasn't Justin O'Carroll standing in the hallway. There stood a gaunt man, not much more than five and a half feet in height, wearing a suit of good-quality tweed. He seemed in his mid-forties and had a professional air about him.

"I'm Dennis Murphy. Deirdre downstairs said you had arrived," said the man at the door. "*Dr.* Dennis Murphy," he added. "Fourteen years ago I brought little Colleen Galaher into the world. I've been thinking you should see this." He spoke in a heavy brogue.

Rosetti stood mute in the doorway as Dr. Murphy

shoved forward an aged manila envelope. It was marked in the upper-right-hand corner with a name, written in pencil, in the careful script born of a Catholic-school education.

Rosetti took the envelope and read the name written on it. *Colleen Galaher.*

Then he ripped open the envelope and read what was inside.

A great ringing sounded in his ears and there was a suffocating constriction in his chest. His whole world narrowed. His skin became as cold as ice. This was what he needed to know, wasn't it? This was the sign he'd been searching for. This *had* to be the sign.

He looked up, but Dr. Murphy was no longer there. Rosetti ran out into the hall, but there was no one there either. He phoned downstairs, and there *was* a Deirdre at the front desk.

"Father, I don't understand," she said. "Dennis Murphy died at least ten years ago. Dr. Murphy is dead."

Rosetti hung up the phone and heard a roar of laughter in his ears.

So where is your precious sign, Nicholas? How will you know the truth? The answer is so simple — you won't.

Chapter 92

THAT NIGHT, ARMED GUARDS stood outside Kathleen's door. They watched the hallway, but I scrutinized everyone who came into the room.

There were so many strange new faces at the hospital, and every stranger was a possible threat to the baby.

There were supposedly legions of devils, so why couldn't they simply overtake us? What was holding the Evil One at bay? There had to be a reason I didn't understand.

I sat on a hard-backed chair beside Kathleen's bed and we watched the news. The assassination attempt led off the newscast. A grim-faced reporter said that Kathleen Beavier had entered Salvatore Mundi Hospital, an exclusive private hospital where cardinals and even the pope went for the best medical care in Italy. A team of Italian and American doctors would be assisting the birth, which could come at any moment.

The first official report out of Salvatore Mundi came

from the Italian chief surgeon himself. We watched the announcement on CNN.

Dr. Leonardo Annunziata was an elegant, dark-haired man in his early forties. He carried authority easily in his meeting with reporters in a pristine-white conference room.

"Ms. Kathleen Beavier is in excellent condition." The doctor spoke English in a gracious tone. "The birth of the child can be anticipated in the next twelve to twenty-four hours. We are expecting no complications whatsoever."

Kathleen and I looked at each other — and we began to laugh for the first time in days.

"Dr. Annunziata could be in for a surprise," she said.

The news was all bad that night on CNN. The natural disasters around the globe continued and actually seemed to be getting worse.

Kathleen and I held hands as we watched. There was no way to connect the plagues and sickness and famines to events occurring in Rome and Maam Cross, Ireland, but all my instincts told me there had to be a link, and that we would soon know what it was.

"Maybe the world is going to end," Kathleen mused. "Or maybe my baby can stop it."

Or Colleen's baby, I couldn't help thinking.

Chapter 93

EACH HOUR SEEMED TO take our paranoia to a new and previously unimaginable height. I was feeling time as both too fast and too slow. The excruciating wait was almost over — but I was still unprepared for the unknown.

Kathleen had at last nodded off and I needed to take a break, to clear my head if I could. I could hardly be her Rock of Gibraltar when I was feeling so unsure and wobbly myself.

Take a little walk, I heard. *You deserve it.*

Had I said that? I must have.

I told the guard outside the door what I was doing. Then I walked down the deserted marble-and-stone hallway, which reeked of disinfectant. Standing within a neat line of religious statues, a young Italian policeman with a rifle watched me approach.

"Signorina," he said. He tipped his visored hat, knowing that I was the virgin's companion. "Is she all right? The young girl, Kathleena?"

"Yes, everything's fine," I reassured him. "She's sleeping right now."

My shoes squeaked on the spotless floor as I walked, echoing loudly in the early-morning silence. I wondered what Justin and Rosetti were doing. They would probably be at Colleen Galaher's cottage by now.

I thought of Colleen often, and with fondness. She was younger than Kathleen and, if anything, even more innocent. I remembered her nearly transparent white skin and the pink aura that seemed to emanate from her.

Both girls seemed so perfect for the role one was destined to play. Which girl was the actor, then? Which one might be a liar?

Turning another dark stone corner, I found that I'd reached the far end of the hospital building. I'd gone too far.

Struck with sudden anxiety, I turned and practically ran back to the room where Kathleen was sleeping. Was she safe? How could I have gone so far? What was I thinking?

I burst into the small room. Kathleen was sleeping peacefully. Breathless, I stared down at her, then watched her sleep gently for a good long time.

I had read a couple of books on the subject of childbirth recently. Inside Kathleen, I thought, was an infant hanging upside down in her womb, like a circus acrobat. The baby was lightly holding the umbilical cord with one hand.

The head was wedged against her cervix. The limbs, fingers, toes, nails, eyebrows, and eyelashes were all fully developed. The heartbeat was steady and fine. The senses of sight, hearing, and touch were undeveloped but ready to blossom quickly once exposed to stimuli.

The baby was probably around twenty inches long, a little over seven pounds — quite average in that way. In each tiny brain cell there was all the love and goodness, the capacity for both happiness and sadness, the genius, the wit, the love of beauty, and the will for survival within the human race.

In all of those ways, this was a child like any other.

I prayed that Kathleen's baby had drawn the lucky straw, because I doubted with my whole heart that even if it emerged with horns and a tail I'd be strong enough to take away its precious breath.

How could I kill an infant? Any infant? How could anyone do such a thing? But especially, how could a woman?

I sat in my chair, tipped it slightly back. I gazed out through the window in Kathleen's room and watched a burnt-orange and crimson sun rising up above the Trastèvere.

It was a beautiful sunrise.

It was surely a sign.

Chapter 94

I MUST HAVE DOZED in my chair near her bed. Kathleen groaned loudly in pain, waking me instantly.

"It's time, Anne," she whispered urgently.

It was after five in the morning. We were alone together in suite 401 of Salvatore Mundi International Hospital, both of us terrified and pretending to each other that we believed all the assurances that we had nothing to worry about.

The hospital building was four stories high, plain straw-colored brick and large churchlike windows. It was enclosed by a high brick wall and shaded by tall umbrella pines.

I'd heard that outside that wall eighty thousand people had gathered. Hundreds of thousands more were said to be collecting in St. Peter's Square.

I couldn't help wondering what was happening in tiny Maam Cross, Ireland.

Beside me, in the soothing, pale blue hospital suite, Kathleen grabbed her belly. She let out a sound that was a cross between a shriek and a moan. Then she relaxed again.

"Don't push, Kathy," I said. "Don't push yet." In a way, I almost felt as if I were giving birth myself. "That's it, breathe . . . and now, rest."

"God, this hurts so much," Kathleen grunted. Her long blond hair was wet and stringy. Her face was already flushed from exertion. We both knew she wasn't ready to give birth yet. But she was getting closer.

As I placed a damp cloth on her brow I noticed that Kathleen was looking past me. I followed her gaze and saw that we were no longer alone. It scared the hell out of me.

A man was standing in the stone archway leading into the hospital room. A solemn elderly man whom I recognized immediately.

Pope Benedict XVI himself had come to see Kathleen.

The slanting rays of morning sunlight streaming through the window engulfed his narrow shoulders, making him seem as if he were an icon of pure gold. Not like a man at all.

We all stared at one another. Finally, he spoke. "Have you anything to say, Kathleen? Anything to confess?" the pope asked Kathleen in a forceful voice. "I'm here to help you."

Kathleen paled.

Then she was struck as if by a fierce seizure. Her eyes rolled back. Her nostrils flared. She opened her mouth wider than I would have thought possible. She began to scream and scream. I had never been more surprised or more frightened at any time in my life. Suddenly, I had the feeling that I didn't know Kathleen at all.

When I looked back to the doorway, I saw that Pope Benedict was walking away. He never looked back.

Chapter 95

A YOUNG AND HANDSOME dark-haired priest stood lookout on the grand stone terrazzo of the Apostolic Palace. More than four hundred thousand people were spread out before him, completely blanketing the majestic piazza of St. Peter's Square, stretching as far as his eyes could see.

He spoke into a hand-held microphone. His rich baritone voice boomed out over the great sea of heads in St. Peter's Square. *This* was why he had entered the priesthood — this glorious power, this majesty.

The crowd in Rome answered his prayer in a thunderous roar.

In Mexico City, nearly three-quarters of a million of the faithful attended an equally emotional Mass in and around the Basilica of Guadalupe, the site where the Blessed Virgin had appeared to a local Indian in the sixteenth century.

All through Spain and Holland, throughout France and

Belgium, in Poland, in Germany, Ireland, and England, the great old cathedrals were beginning to fill to capacity once again. The people of Europe wanted something to believe in. Now they had it.

At sunup, long lines flowed into the churches in Amsterdam, Munich, Paris, Brussels, Frankfurt, London, Madrid, Hamburg, Warsaw, and Berlin. The strains of "Ave Maria" swelled majestically into the fall air.

In the United States, a television satellite provided instant participation from New York across the Midwest to California. Every person who was able to do so tuned in to news of the birth on television.

In Los Angeles, an emotional gathering was held in Frank Lloyd Wright's Hollywood Bowl amphitheater. Sprawling out over fifty acres, the amphitheater accommodated more than seventy thousand people. Another fifty thousand crowded outside. Natural acoustics were supplied by the surrounding hills, making microphones unnecessary for the celebrity and religious hosts.

The service that morning was for an immense gathering of families and friends of those stricken with polio. Together they recited the rosary; they prayed for a great miracle. They prayed to the Virgin to mercifully cure their loved ones.

At St. Peter's Basilica, the young priest's voice continued to echo out in the colonnades and towering, ancient columns. "Pray for us sinners, now and at the hour of our death. Amen."

"We trust in the will of God!" The people cried together in a deafening chorus.

All over the world, after all the years of difficulty,

decades of diminishing spirituality, so many people still believed.

But the plagues, the famines, the unexplained sicknesses, especially of children, continued unabated. Everywhere, people talked of the Apocalypse, perhaps the end of the world.

Which explained why so many were suddenly going to church.

Chapter 96

JUSTIN AND ROSETTI were nearly at the Galaher house and neither of them had ever seen so many birds. The woods were filled with them and so was the darkening sky.

As the English Ford hummed along the undulating country roads, Justin felt the weight of the heavy metallic sky looming overhead. He was being tested now. There was a powerful voice in his head.

You know that you shouldn't be here. Your faith isn't strong enough. You don't even want to be a priest anymore.

You want to be with her. It's the only thing that matters to you now. You love Anne Fitzgerald more than you love God. Leave this place.

Go to Anne.

Or die!

He couldn't stop the troubling thoughts. He wondered if Father Rosetti sensed his inner torment. He turned the wheel of the car into the driveway that cut through an open field.

They had finally arrived at the Galaher house outside Maam Cross. But it was strange, Justin thought, staring at the unfamiliar stucco bungalow and barn that had appeared in the Cortina's dusty windshield.

It isn't as it was before. Something has changed.

"Something's wrong," he muttered as he stopped the sedan in front of the house.

Rosetti said nothing. He'd been silent for nearly the entire ride.

Justin studied the small house. There was an unremembered television antenna. It looked like a snarled branch caught on the thatched roof. It was hanging loose, as if blown down by a storm. The grass was pale now, no longer a lush loden green. The cottage seemed to be listing to one side.

It was all wrong, and he was almost certain his imagination wasn't playing tricks. Everything looked different — or *was* it his imagination?

Tricks! he thought. *The Devil plays tricks. Is the Devil here in Maam Cross?*

As they arrived at the door, he saw Rosetti become highly agitated. He threw open the heavy wooden door without knocking. He searched the house in seconds, then burst back out. His eyes were wide with fear.

"The girl's mother is dead, Justin. She's hanging from the ceiling upstairs. So is the nun from the convent school! We have to find Colleen. Help me, Father."

As they walked to the barn, a burly young priest appeared. A mop of red hair blew around his face. The priest blocked the entrance to the barn. His fists were clenched; his eyes were wide.

"Colleen is in here," said the priest forcefully. "I'm Father Flannery from the parish. I'm taking care of her now. We care for our own."

"Be gone, Satan!" Rosetti bellowed at the priest. "You have no power over me! You have no power over Father O'Carroll. You have no power here on earth! Not yet, anyway."

Rosetti shoved the redheaded priest aside with a powerful motion of his arm. Flannery quickly regained his balance. He rushed at Rosetti and again threw himself between the priest and the doorway.

"You can't go in! This doesn't concern you! This girl is one of ours!"

"No!" Rosetti screamed at the top of his voice. "Never! You have no power over this poor innocent girl."

As Justin watched, Rosetti grabbed a pitchfork that was leaning against the barn. *"Move,"* he warned, his voice thrumming with danger. "Move or I will pierce your infernal heart."

"It's my child," the priest suddenly hissed, his face twisting with rage. "I'm the father of that bairn. I'm *one* of the child's fathers!" he said, then laughed out loud.

"You are not the father!" Rosetti said. He held the pitchfork with both hands, leveled at Flannery's chest. "You are from Hell — and to there you will return!"

With a powerful thrust, Nicholas Rosetti drove the pitchfork into the red-haired priest's chest. He fell over backward and lay in the dirt of the front yard.

His blank eyes stared up at the heavens.

"Go straight to Hell!" Rosetti said.

Chapter 97

NICHOLAS ROSETTI CARRIED the young girl out of the barn. Colleen tucked her face under the crook of his chin. She seemed to turn herself completely over to his protection. She was so young, and so very close to giving birth.

"He was lying," said Colleen. "I don't know why. But he was lying. He's not the father of this child. I swear it. You have to believe me."

"I know that, Colleen. Don't trouble yourself. You must be strong for the baby's sake."

Rosetti directed his next comments to Justin, who was following close behind him. "Sister Katherine wasn't strong enough!" he said as they crossed the barnyard. "We have to be strong, Justin. Yesterday I told you I trusted you. I do trust you. I trust no one but you and my-self. Watch the body of Father Flannery. If it's necessary, *kill Father Flannery again!*"

Entering the cottage, Justin had a feeling of vertigo.

The whole world seemed to be spinning out of control. The living room looked different. A big mahogany grandfather clock that reached to the beams was ticking somberly. It wasn't there before.

My God, he had just watched the murder of a priest. He'd done nothing to stop it. Why?

Because he believed in evil? Because he was surrounded by it? Because Hell was right here on earth?

"The Beavier child should be born quietly too. Out of the public eye, just like this one," Rosetti complained. "The crowds in Rome — a terrible mistake."

"Why are we here?" Justin asked. "Why Colleen?"

"I have the same question, Father. We'll see very soon."

Bending low to avoid the heavy ceiling beams, Rosetti and Justin entered the small room off the kitchen. Justin turned back the threadbare bed coverings. He helped ease the pregnant girl onto the bed.

"*Oooh,* the pain is terrible," Colleen cried. She clutched at the crucifix that hung from a chain around her neck.

Rosetti looked at Justin. "Will you please get me my stole, Justin? Also the manual."

Colleen was having severe contractions and labor pains. Her small freckled face looked almost anemic. It was covered with perspiration. Justin could see movement in the swell of her belly beneath the blankets.

"Where is the doctor?" he asked suddenly. "Why isn't the doctor here yet?"

Rosetti's eyes narrowed. "We are going to deliver the child," he whispered.

Chapter 98

THE SKIES OVER ROME had never been so dark and foreboding. Streaks of lightning stabbed the city. Rain fell in torrents.

The delivery room inside Rome's Salvatore Mundi Hospital was calm and vast and sparkling white. It must have seemed as scary as a morgue to Kathleen, though. It certainly did to me.

Kathleen seemed fine again. She had screamed and lost control when the pope had entered her room, but now she was herself again, and she had no memory of his visit or her terrified, violent reaction to him.

A nervous group of Salvatorian Sisters in immaculate white uniforms and starched, veil-like headdresses were busily at work assisting the special team of doctors. Kathleen's mother and father visited, but neither seemed comfortable in the birthing room. Nor did Kathleen appear to want them there.

"You're staying, Anne?" she asked me as soon as they left.

"Of course. As long as you want me here."

As two of the nuns effortlessly transferred her from the gurney to the sterile white delivery table, Kathleen closed her eyes. The nurses gently placed her feet in cold metal obstetric stirrups. This was it.

They swiveled down a mirror so that she could watch herself. She looked into her own eyes, and I wondered what she saw there.

"No! Please!" Kathleen suddenly shouted in the bustling delivery room.

"It's all right, Kathleen. Everything is fine so far," she heard a calming male voice tell her.

We both turned to where the voice had come from.

A good-looking man in loose-fitting white scrubs stood there, his dark brown eyes sparkling with amusement. A harsh light was glinting behind him. It almost seemed to be winking out of the doctor's right eye.

"I am Dr. Annunziata. You remember me? We met last night in your room. I would like to give you something to help with the delivery, Kathleen. What we call an epidural. Okay?"

Kathleen answered with a gut-wrenching moan. "I don't feel well. I think something's wrong. It feels odd in my stomach. It feels really bad. Almost as if there are more babies than one."

Dr. Annunziata nodded sympathetically. "Just one baby, I promise. Believe it or not, everything is absolutely perfect so far. You are in glowing health, wonderful condition to have a beautiful baby today."

"I hope so," Kathleen mumbled.

A second doctor pierced a long sharp needle into her back. It hurt me just to watch the needle go into Kathleen.

Then Kathleen saw that I was looking on from behind a white gauze mask. "You won't leave? No matter what?"

"No matter what," I promised and gently patted her. I couldn't leave if I wanted to. I had a job to do here.

"You're going to have a beautiful baby, Kathleen," Dr. Annunziata said. "This is my four thousand three hundred sixty-fourth baby. Did you know that? Absolutely true.

"Nothing to it," the doctor whispered beguilingly to Kathleen. "Nothing can possibly go wrong."

Chapter 99

NO ONE COULD POSSIBLY understand how she felt. Kathleen still couldn't believe any of this was happening to her. In that regard, nothing had changed since the abortion clinic in Boston. She squeezed her eyes shut real hard.

It was brighter and more vivid behind her eyelids than in the hospital delivery room. She felt as if she were being lifted, then carried far away from Salvatore Mundi. Her baby was insignificant in the sweep of the universe and infinite time.

I am in so far over my head. This is so horrible. It must be a nightmare.

What is happening? Oh, my God, am I dying? she thought. *Please, let me wake up from this.*

"Push," she heard Anne say, and that brought her back to the present for an instant. Father Rosetti had told her to trust Anne, no matter what happened. She did. Anne was the only one she trusted. Anne was the best person here, the most solid, maybe the holiest.

Through eyes opened only a slit, a scene came to Kathleen in a rush. *It was nine months ago. It was the night of the dance, January 23.*

She remembered everything as if it were happening all over again.

Her dress, the pale green satin Vera Wang that she had begged her mother to buy for her in Boston, was crumpled up underneath her breasts. There was a terrible weight on her chest. She could hardly breathe.

She saw herself in the speedy yellow Mercedes. Yes, she remembered that. Jamie was driving, and he looked drop-dead gorgeous. She could see every detail of his face and hair, and the way he looked at her. His good looks scared her but pleased her too.

The car had a dark, shiny interior and a gleaming instrument panel. The radio was blaring loud rock and roll, one group after another — Matchbox 20, Silverchain, Green Day, 'N Sync.

Then everything had changed — just like that.

They stopped to park, and he wanted to go all the way. He expected it. Jamie began yelling at her over the rhythm-heavy rock music. He was using words that were so sexual, so crude and suggestive. Kathleen held both her hands over her ears.

They were at gloomy, pitch-black Sachuest Point and it was late at night. No one was around but the two of them.

"I told you *no!*" she finally yelled back at him. "No means *no.* Please, Jamie. Please listen to what I'm saying. Don't you dare touch me! Take me home. Is that clear enough?"

Then Jamie went really wild and berserk and nuclear. Kathleen felt a rough hand mauling her chest, grabbing at her between her legs. Jamie's voice was suddenly much deeper, scarier. He outweighed her by a hundred pounds and he was strong.

She was terribly afraid of him now. So helpless in the dark, deserted park.

She didn't know what to do, or how to stop him. She bit down hard into the back of his outstretched hand. Jamie screamed in pain.

He threw the door open on her side, then pushed at her roughly. Jamie was yelling obscenities at her, the worst she'd ever heard, even at school. His face was beet red.

"Walk home, Ice Queen! Walk, you cunt!"

Suddenly, another car pulled up in the lovers' lane. Two boys got out. They staggered, looking drunk or stoned or both. She knew them. It was Peter Thompson and Chris Raleigh. Had they been following behind the Mercedes?

Kathleen stumbled out onto the crunching, frozen roadside. The raw smell of freezing cold ocean filled her nose. Her body tingled from the biting cold.

Jamie and the two other boys came up from behind. Jamie lunged at her. She had never seen anyone so out of control and angry in her life. The other two boys were almost as bad.

She didn't want to remember any more of this.

She didn't want to remember Jamie Jordan and what had really happened at Sachuest Point.

"Push, Kathleen," she heard.

Chapter 100

SWEAT DRIPPED OFF JUSTIN'S forehead and ran down the sides of his face in rivulets. It was hot and dank and close in the small bedroom. It was also the most intimate experience Justin had ever had — to be present at a human birth, to watch this young girl deliver her baby.

He kept hearing the words over and over in his mind: *If you can't believe there can be a miracle now, a divine birth, how can you say that you ever believed?*

Colleen Galaher was fully dilated and she was working hard to deliver the child. He was right there with her.

Justin wondered if the fourteen-year-old girl had been in any way prepared for the intense pain. He now understood a little of what it was like for a woman to have a baby. He felt humbled by the experience. He also felt tender and loving toward the patiently suffering girl. Most of all, he felt blessed.

If you can't believe there can be a miracle now.

But he could, by God, he did believe!

Once or twice, his mind left the cottage room in Maam Cross. He wondered what was happening in Rome. He was terribly afraid for Kathleen and Anne. If anything happened to them he could never forgive himself.

In the last few minutes a profound change had come over him. He was starting to believe that Colleen was the true virgin, that hers was the true holy child. If that was so, what would happen in Rome? What *was* happening? Had Anne been put in danger by Father Rosetti?

In the small bed with the tattered blankets, the Irish girl cried softly and tried to be brave. She was much prettier than he had thought. The birth of her child was tense and scary, but it was also the most beautiful thing Justin had ever witnessed in his life.

"Be prepared for anything," he heard Rosetti warn from the other side of the bed. "You're drifting. Stay with us, Justin."

"I'm right here, Father. I'm ready."

"Are you ready for *this?*" Rosetti asked.

As he looked on, a tiny head began to slide from between Colleen's thin legs. Suddenly, he was seeing life in a way he never had before. He understood something about marriage and love and sex that he had never understood before.

Justin reached out and gently placed his hand under the child's tiny head. It had thick dark hair like Jesus' as a man. He was rapt with awe.

"He's here!" Colleen announced in a soft, reverent voice. "He has come."

Chapter 101

"PUSH," KATHLEEN HEARD.

She *pushed.* God, how she *pushed.* She *pushed* Jamie Jordan away and tried to run as fast as she could for the road out of Sachuest Point.

The skirt of her satin dress was slim and restricting. She pulled it up around her waist and ran. Jamie was insane about not getting what he wanted. What was he thinking? What was he doing? What about the other boys? Why were they here?

Behind her, both cars accelerated, shooting up sprays of gravel, white smoke, sand, and dirt. Jamie and the other boys were heading back to Newport without her?

Oh, my God, it's freezing, Kathleen realized, and began to panic. *He can't just leave me out here. How can he be so mad? I don't belong to him. He has no right. I didn't lead him on. I didn't promise him anything.*

Tears blinded Kathleen. The harsh, strong wind coming off the ocean blew right through her clothing, blew her beautiful silver headband off her head. Dervishes of powdery snow swirled around her thin-soled shoes.

He has to come back for me. I'll freeze out here. I could die. I will die!

Kathleen slowed to a walk on the crusty dirt road. She had no other choice. This was the only way back to town, and it was miles.

She pointed herself toward the distant pocket of lights that were the city of Newport. Everywhere she looked there was a faint, eerie ground glow. All around her, the ocean was roaring like a squadron of low-flying airplanes. No one would hear her screams for help.

One of her feet struck a sharp, protruding rock. She fell, striking the ground hard. She groaned and sobbed loudly. She had twisted her leg. Kathleen curled herself into a small, safe ball on the ground. That felt better — better than facing the freezing cold.

She wondered if she could sleep right here. Be all right in the morning — just sleep. No, she would be dead. She'd freeze to death.

How could Jamie and the others leave her out here?

Then Kathleen heard cars speeding back down the long stretch of park road. The bright lights were flashing through the bare-limbed trees and up the deserted, pitch-black road. Afterimages danced before Kathleen's eyes, looping red and violet rings, waving streaks of silver, like in a dreamy dance hall.

Kathleen pushed herself up to a kneeling position. Sharp stones stuck into her hands. She brushed off her crushed, stained gown, once so beautiful.

Then a terrible blow from behind came crashing down on her skull.

It had to be Jamie. He'd hit her incredibly hard.

She was falling, falling, falling into darkness. Where was she?

"She's coming to," she heard. It was Chris Raleigh. He was crouched over her. They all were.

Peter Thompson was running his hands roughly over her breasts. Then he slid both breasts out of her dress. His hands were freezing cold.

"No, please," she whispered. "Please don't touch me. Please."

Through haze and fog Kathleen saw Jamie's face looming above her. He was holding something in his hand. His face was red; he was blowing with exertion.

Something white spurted from his hand!

Kathleen knew what it was. She saw his swollen penis. Jamie Jordan was ejaculating all over her. It was so horrible, unspeakable, unbelievable to feel his warm sperm raining down on her.

"Push," she heard. *"You have to push, Kathy!"*

Kathleen screamed. She wasn't in Newport! She realized she was in the delivery room in Rome. White masks leaned in closer. Doctors and nurses. Hovering over her.

"It's all right, Kathleen. Just push again. Push."

What was happening? She was going back and forth between two realities — the hospital in Rome and the beach outside Newport. She had no control over the sequence of the scenes.

"Get off me! Get off me! Get away with that thing!" she screamed.

Her panties were pulled down around her knees. Jamie was rubbing his cum between her legs. She was all sticky and wet down there.

Jamie! Jamie had done it. Now she knew. She finally remembered! She remembered everything as if it had just happened. Jamie had gotten her pregnant at the beach that night.

She *was* a virgin, but the birth of her child couldn't be divine. Could it? Jamie Jordan had gotten her pregnant. She was absolutely sure of it.

There was a cry!

Whose cry was it?

Where was she?

Kathleen's eyes suddenly opened wide. Of course. She was in the hospital in Rome. Her body felt a rude shock, a jolting sensation like a punch. Her pelvis tightened. She was as exhausted as she had ever been in her life.

She saw blazing kettledrum lights whirling over her head. Then the swarming doctors and nurses, and Anne standing right beside the delivery table.

In the mirror she saw the baby's head emerging. She saw a face, and Kathleen Beavier fainted.

Chapter 102

COLLEEN GALAHER SOBBED LOUDLY as she watched sharp sewing scissors floating over her quivering stomach.

What were the two priests doing to her now? She watched as the umbilical cord was carefully tied by Father O'Carroll. Then the exhausted, sweating priest cut the cord. Father Rosetti held her baby.

The young girl felt vindicated. She was a true virgin, and here was the child. Now what would happen to them?

The infant was being held up high like a beautiful little lamb, like a chalice at the Celebration of the Holy Eucharist, in the priest's strong hands.

She wanted to see his face. She smiled at the thought of it.

She reached out her arms and saw that they were shaking badly. She was incredibly weak; she'd never felt like this before. Of course not; she had never been a mother before.

"Please, Father, let me see?"

Colleen thought that the light slanting in the bedroom window was making a golden robe around the child's shoulders.

Tears were in her eyes. *I am a mother.*

"I want to see. My baby? May I?"

"In a minute, Colleen."

Father Rosetti began to rub the baby's throat in an upward motion with his thumb. He then wiped away mucus with a swab of disinfected linen. He gently flicked the sole of the baby's foot, to ensure it was breathing.

"He's alive, healthy," he said softly to the young girl. "He's just fine."

"Let me see him," she pleaded again. "I want to hold my baby."

But Father Rosetti carried the child out of the bedroom. He didn't let the mother touch the infant. He never allowed Colleen Galaher to see her little son's face.

He left Colleen crying, still not understanding any of what had happened to her.

"Please, my baby. Why won't you let me see my baby?"

Chapter 103

THE TWO PRIESTS HURRIED from the lonely cottage to their car. *We must look like kidnappers,* Justin thought. Perhaps they were.

"Father, wait," he called ahead. "What about the girl? Poor Colleen?"

But Rosetti was already running with the child wrapped in his arms. He hurried into the backseat of the car.

"You drive, Father. Woodbine Seminary. Just go straight."

"The girl? Colleen?" Justin insisted.

"We'll get help for her at Woodbine. *Drive!* Do as I tell you."

The car accelerated down the rocky dirt road twisting away from the forlorn cottage. It carried Father Justin O'Carroll; it carried the chief investigator for the Congregation of Sacred Rites, who was gently cradling the infant.

Justin was seething with questions. He had the feeling

that this was so wrong. What were they to do with the child? What plan did Father Rosetti have?

What was the whole truth about Colleen Galaher's baby? And Kathleen's in Rome? He had a bad feeling about this, a terrible feeling.

Justin drove the car in stunned silence. He felt numb. He was living a nightmare that wouldn't end. Why was he here in this car? Why him? He was kidnapping a young girl's baby. He had left the poor girl alone moments after she gave birth.

"*Father Rosetti!* I can't do this."

"Drive, damn you! You are under orders from the Holy Father in Rome. Obey them. Obey me. *Drive!*"

They rode past eerie, broken-down farms on the road toward Costelloe. Past vast stubbled fields of barley and potatoes. Past a clique of frowning redheaded men in a crippled donkey cart and a young woman in a mackintosh and plastic bonnet — a girl who reminded Justin of poor Colleen.

He turned toward the backseat. "Father?" he asked again. "What about the poor girl?"

Rosetti refused to answer. He was off in his own world, and he wouldn't take his eyes off the face of the baby.

They rose up a curving road onto a wild moor that was parched and dry. Smoking fog began to curl from the ground, shredding as the speeding car blew through it. The sky was dark and threatening.

Terrible fear crowded in on Justin. He couldn't catch his breath. He turned, trying to peek inside the blanket at the same time. He saw nothing except the baby's dark curls.

"Where exactly is this Woodbine Seminary that we're headed to?" Justin asked.

"Straight ahead. Close. I told you. Drive, and please shut up."

Just then the road turned in toward the Irish Sea and past a small wooden sign: WOODBINE 7 KM.

"Woodbine," he said, relieved that there was such a place.

As Justin nervously steered the sedan along limestone cliffs over the sea, he clearly heard Rosetti praying in Latin. *"Requiem aeternam dona eis."*

Justin's hands locked tightly on the steering wheel.

He froze. The hairs on his neck stood.

He recognized the holy prayers of the Anointing of the Sick.

The Roman Catholic prayers for the seriously ill or just deceased.

Prayers for those in danger of death.

Justin stepped down hard on the brakes.

The small gray car fishtailed to the left with grand plowing slowness. The front grille effortlessly sheared away a row of baby scrub pines. The tires screamed like banshees.

The car continued its full 360-degree turn, rolling over gnarled bushes and rocks, finally smacking hard into a full-grown fir tree.

Justin's forehead smashed against the windshield. His head rolled to one side and then slumped down onto his chest.

Out of the corner of a bloodied eye, Justin saw a quick, bounding movement.

Rosetti was plunging out of the car's back door. A small bundle of pink blanket was clutched in one of his arms. The baby was wailing and Justin had to save it.

Chapter 104

JUSTIN REELED FROM THE car and stumbled after Rosetti and Colleen Galaher's baby. The whipping cold sea air slapped harshly at his body and his face. The sky was getting darker and darker. The wind made a shrill, high-pitched wail. "Father! Father, please stop! Where are you going? Father Rosetti!" Justin screamed. "Stop, you son of a bitch. You murderer!"

He ran forward, straining his muscles and clutching his burning chest. Up ahead, the baby continued to cry.

The Irish Sea came into view as he made it to the top of a bare promontory, a pointing finger of black rocks and boulders. The height and the sheerness of the dark cliff took Justin's breath away.

It was at least three hundred feet straight down to where great rollers were thundering over jagged rocks that looked like tombstones.

There were birds all over the sea, thousands of birds screeching louder than he'd ever heard.

"Dear God!" he shouted. "What is happening here?"

Justin tottered across a foot-wide ledge to the next plateau of rock that was spotted with lichens. The harsh winds sliced right through his clothes. He painfully hoisted himself over a loose molar of shale slanting into the cliffs at a 60-degree angle.

A sheen of cold sweat coated his forehead. He felt as if his lungs were going to burst. *God, make me strong.*

Thirty feet above him, the black-clad figure of Rosetti stood perched on another weathered rock face. High over his head the sky was filled with birds. Everything was becoming dark beneath them. It was like night, but it was the middle of the day.

Justin saw a flash of the pink blanket. The child. The poor baby continued to cry.

"Father, please, stop — please. You can't be sure. Are you sure?"

"You don't *believe* anymore." Rosetti's powerful voice echoed down the steep cliffside. "None of you believe! Not in Our Lord! Not in Satan! Not in anything that matters!"

Rosetti was holding the child loosely in one powerful arm. They were both hanging out over the edge of the rocks.

Justin had a blinding thought. It made him ill. *Rosetti could be Satan himself. How do I know otherwise? Satan could right now be holding the Savior of mankind.*

He had to see the child's face for himself. That was his mission. It was why he was here, wasn't it?

Horrified, he saw Rosetti lift the infant high in the air with both huge hands. The priest's eyes were like empty black holes as he stared down on Justin.

Above the cliff, the birds were swooping in. Thousands of birds were flying wildly in every direction. The noise of their screeches and calls was deafening. The winds were nearly as loud.

Justin was so afraid that he could scarcely breathe. Something unearthly was happening. His ears were ringing and starting to ache.

Nicholas Rosetti's voice was harsh and barely recognizable.

"This is the Beast! Have no doubt of it, Justin. All the signs in the prediction of Fatima have been met. The Virgin has guided me to this very spot, with this child. This is the Beast! Satan is so wise, so clever, the girl herself never knew. Do you find that so difficult to believe? Is it not possible for you to believe anything on faith? Do you believe in your God, Father? Only your faith will save you now, for you are in grave danger. All of these foul, black birds — they are devils. Fallen angels. The *child* commands them. The *child* has called them here."

Justin couldn't take his eyes away from the poor helpless infant. He couldn't just believe. He had to *see.*

"Who are you?" he shouted at Rosetti.

"Suppose I told you I was Michael the Archangel? Would that satisfy you? Fine then, I'm *Michael!* I am Michael. Believe it if you must."

"Let me see the child. You said you trusted me. Let me see, Father."

Above them, the mountainside rose another two hundred feet. The uppermost rocks seemed to pierce the clouds. More black birds slowly circled, screeching angrily. Screaming down at Rosetti. Were they the legions?

Was Rosetti telling the truth about the devils? And the child who commanded them?

Justin shielded his eyes and called up to Rosetti again. "How can you be sure? How do you know that you aren't holding an innocent baby? Father? I see no sign."

"You are like doubting Thomas. Must you always *see* to believe? How can you be sure that Jesus Christ became man?" Rosetti's voice rang out angrily. "How can you be sure that Jesus has redeemed our souls from the eternal fires of Hell?"

"Has he?" Justin called back. "Has he redeemed us from Hell? It seems that the gates of Hell are wide open right now."

"It's their time, their turn. Unless we stop them. They don't have power on Earth yet. They can act only through humans. This child is human."

The idea was monstrous, and it was consistent with everything Justin had ever read about the fallen angels.

He was seized with vertigo. Great waves of nausea washed over him. Was he engaged in a dialogue with the Devil? Or was he siding with Satan against everything good and holy in the world? What did Father Rosetti know? What had he seen? What was he holding in his arms?

He knew he couldn't look down at the spinning vortex tempting him, trying to pull him off the cliffs.

Once again he hollered above the crashing sea, above the piercing cries of gulls and crows and gannets clouding over the cliffside. He screamed above the cries of the devils, "We can go to the Woodbine Seminary! We can perform an exorcism. Father! We can talk. You know what I'm saying is best!"

As Justin gazed skyward, he saw Rosetti's broad shoulders sag forward. The priest carefully moved a step back, away from the edge of the rocks. Dark yellow bile began dripping from the corners of his mouth. Blood ran from his nose. Was he dying?

"Come up here, Father," the Vatican priest said in an oddly quiet voice. "If you must, come to me. Come see the child for yourself."

Justin took a single step forward on the loose, shifting rocks. The sea winds flogged his face. Something warned him not to go any higher. *No closer to Rosetti and the child. No higher on the dark, slippery rocks.*

But he took step after step on the steep rocks. His arms felt like blocks of stone. He was afraid he wouldn't be able to hold the baby if he reached Rosetti. He was afraid that he was about to die, not ever knowing the truth of the virgin births.

Justin's leaden feet moved upward, as if against his will.

When he finally looked up again, he was staring into the burning eyes of Nicholas Rosetti.

"You want to see? Then look, Justin O'Carroll. Feast your eyes. Look at the child! Look! *Look!*"

Chapter 105

KATHLEEN UTTERED THE WORDS in a soft, barely audible whisper. "My baby's all right? Is my baby all right? Doctor?"

It was the voice of a frightened and very emotional sixteen-year-old girl. The voice of a new mother.

Kathleen stared up at the dark and shriveled child. The doctor was holding the baby at the far end of the birthing table. She strained to see its face.

"Is anything the matter?" I asked Dr. Annunziata in a low whisper that Kathleen couldn't hear.

"No, no. Of course not," he muttered, but I wasn't sure whether to believe him. He was behaving oddly.

Meanwhile, the other doctors and nurses from Salvatore Mundi were watching the mother and child in awed, almost reverent silence. The Swiss Guards were watching, and waiting.

The guards still seemed tense. What had they been expecting? What were their orders? I couldn't help noticing that they were armed. Were they present to protect Kathleen and the child? Or was there another reason why they were here?

The chief obstetrician lightly slapped the baby's bottom. The tiny infant obligingly began to scream, an unmistakable, anguished, and perturbed *human* sound.

Dr. Annunziata finally smiled. The roomful of medical and Church people smiled at the naturalness of the child's response. Even some of the Swiss Guards loosened up and grinned.

I tried to think positively as well. The baby was like us. The baby was human. The baby was beautiful and good. A new life had come into the world, and that was always a miracle.

But was this birth a *sign* as well? Had it been promised more than eighty years before at Fatima?

I moved closer to Dr. Annunziata. "*Is* there a problem, Doctor?"

He looked at me. "No, not really a problem. But there is a . . . a situation."

Chapter 106

NICHOLAS ROSETTI FELT A sudden calm and he wondered if it was another trick being played on him. Soon he would be relieved of his great burden for the first time since his meeting with Pope Pius. He had done his job, his investigation. He believed he had found out the truth.

"I need to know." Justin O'Carroll was calling above the howling winds and the eerie cries of the seabirds. "I'm coming up there with you, Father."

Only love and pity made Rosetti address the young priest. "If you have no faith, then believe this," he said. "Believe *medicine.* Believe *science.* Listen to me. Colleen Galaher was christened *Colin* Galaher. The child was born with two sets of sexual organs. Her doctor in town did what he could."

"I don't understand," Justin said, waving his hand toward the child. "What are you saying?"

"Colleen Galaher has *no ovaries,*" Rosetti said hoarsely. "They were removed."

Rosetti held the baby aloft. He spoke in an agonized voice, nearly incomprehensible. "This baby is the Devil's own. This baby will change the world."

A muffled cry rose out of the pink blanket, startling Justin. A *baby's* cry.

Doubt flooded his mind. Who could he believe now? The Devil was clever, and he was everywhere.

The wind quickly swallowed the baby's cry as the birds hovered everywhere around Father Rosetti. They looked as if they wanted to swoop down and carry away the infant.

Justin heard a tortured cry from above. "Pray for me, Father O'Carroll."

With trembling hands, the Vatican priest slowly opened the woolen blanket. His lips moved in prayer as he crossed the baby's forehead with the side of his thumb. The infant howled in pain and struggled fiercely.

Then Father Rosetti opened the blanket and showed the head and face to Justin.

Justin stared into the child's eyes — and thousands of eyes stared back. He could clearly see countless eyes inside those of the child's. The legions were right there.

Justin stumbled backward, almost losing his footing on the rock. His heart thundered. At first he had seen a child's face, but then it changed before his eyes. What he saw was grotesque. It became the face of the fiercest animal, then several animals in one, and it roared angrily at him. It tried to scare him away, and nearly succeeded.

The sound was hideous and unearthly. The animal shook furiously, with great strength, and then bit into

Rosetti's cheek with long, sharp teeth when the priest wouldn't release his grip. The animal, the Beast, screamed and screamed. All of the devils inside the infant seemed to scream at once.

The priest didn't pull away. Nicholas Rosetti held the Beast right up to his face.

"You saw it, Justin. The eyes, the legions. You know. Now go back to Rome. The true virgin is there. Please pray for me, Father."

Rosetti stepped right off the high cliff. The priest and infant fell together. They seemed suspended by an invisible cord for a few seconds. The infant continued to struggle, to cling with its teeth to Rosetti's lower face.

The birds flew all around the falling priest. Their wings whirred like thousands of rotor blades. Shrieking, they seemed to be trying to catch Father Rosetti, to break his fall.

At last Rosetti and the child clapped the cold, choppy water and disappeared beneath the dark and turbulent waves. A thick column of smoke rose from the sea. The water hissed loudly.

The birds all over the mountain shrieked louder than ever as they swooped in enormous numbers to the sea below. They changed shapes — became flying wolves. They dived into the waves and never reappeared, never resurfaced.

Justin finally dropped to the rocks of the high cliffside, and he sobbed uncontrollably. *"Requiem aeternam dona eis."* He prayed for the eternal soul of Nicholas Rosetti, and for his own soul as well.

He had seen the face of Satan.

Chapter 107

I WAS KEENLY AWARE of the almost unnatural quiet that had fallen over the hospital room. First the silence, then the laughter, and then . . . silence again.

The doctors, the Salvatore Mundi nurses, and the technicians stood still, staring with awed faces as they watched the infant's first awkward moves. They looked as if they were experiencing the most important and beautiful moment of their lives.

No one could have been affected more than I. I had begun trembling as if the room were very cold, while in fact the room was quite warm.

You are here for a reason. You are the bravest of us all. Over and over, I heard the words of Father Rosetti the last time we'd spoken.

Anne, I hope and pray that I know the truth about the two young virgins now. But the Beast must be killed.

I was dizzy and on the verge of panic when I suddenly

heard my name spoken. The voice was deep and resonant. What was I supposed to do?

I looked up at a doctor nearby. *He hadn't spoken my name.*

I turned toward a dark-haired technician monitoring the EKG machine. *The voice wasn't his either.*

The voice came again. Louder. Surer. Nearer.

Anne, it called to me. *It must die — or we will. An eternity of suffering for mankind. Kill the Beast, Anne! Kill the child now!*

I moved closer to the doctor. Closer to the child. My body was quivering.

In the name of the Father, kill the child of evil!

We were promised a clear sign at the moment of the divine birth, Father Rosetti had said. He said it was a matter of faith. Did I have faith? Why me? Why had I been chosen to be in Rome?

I recited simple prayers from my childhood. The Hail Mary. Glory be to the Father. I felt terribly alone in the hospital room.

I heard the deep voice again.

In the name of the Father, and of the Son, and of the Holy Spirit — KILL THE CHILD!

My hands were trembling and my legs were weak. I could barely stand, but I took another step closer to the infant.

My eyes checked a table of sharp metal instruments used during the delivery. There was a scalpel I could use.

I nearly fainted at the thought. It repulsed me.

You must, Anne. That's why you're here.

"Give him to me." I finally spoke, hearing my own voice

as if it were someone else's. "Let me hold the child. Let me give him to Kathleen."

As I reached out my arms, Dr. Annunziata suddenly turned and handed the child over to a nurse.

Something in the doctor's eyes gave me pause.

Was I imagining it, or had Annunziata observed something about Kathleen? Something that I needed to know?

He spoke quietly to me, confidentially. I heard the regret in the doctor's voice. "This is not a holy child. But he is still a child of God."

The voice in my head stopped abruptly. This infant wasn't the Savior. But it was an innocent, human baby.

The nurse holding the baby wrapped it with a clean blanket in a few deft movements. Then she presented the baby to Kathleen.

Kathleen took the child into her arms. Her eyes immediately filled with tears. I saw that the baby had the same blue eyes as Kathleen.

She looked into the baby's sweet face and I could see a mother's love wash over her. "My son," she said. "My baby boy."

I believed that. I believed in the mother and her child. And I believed that my investigation was finished.

Chapter 108

IT WAS FINALLY OVER for me. The suffering was apparently over for countless others.

That night, word arrived that rain had come to parts of India where there had been nothing but punishing heat and sun for months; children with polio stopped arriving at hospitals in Boston, Los Angeles, and elsewhere; the plagues that had run rampant in Asia and Mexico suddenly, miraculously ended. It would be someone else's job to decode and demystify everything that had happened.

Not mine.

I still didn't know what had occurred in Ireland. I couldn't reach Justin. No one had called Rome from there, at least not to my knowledge.

A room had been reserved for me at a nearby hotel and I decided to walk there from the hospital. I was bone-tired, but I didn't think I could sleep.

I tried to stay off the main streets for fear I might be

recognized. I didn't even know the name of the narrow, cobblestone alley where I was walking, but it didn't really matter. I wanted to be alone, and I was.

Suddenly, I was driven to my knees by a hard blow to the center of my back. The pain was terrible. I looked around but saw no one.

My body began to shake and wouldn't stop.

A deep voice spoke to me and I could feel and smell hot stinking breath.

You failed your Church, Anne. You failed again.

"I don't think I did," I protested. "I didn't fail!"

I was struck again, even harder than the first time. Then I was pressed facedown into the dusky cobblestones of the street. I tasted dirt and then my own blood. I was petrified.

You're willful and disobedient. And now it's your turn to die. You can join Father Rosetti and Father O'Carroll. They're already dead. They died horrible deaths in Ireland.

"No!" I yelled as loudly as I could with my nose and mouth jammed into stone. "They're not dead. Leave me alone."

I took another incredible blow; it was as if a bat had struck my head and neck.

I touched the place where I'd been struck. *No blood!*

"You can't hurt me!" I yelled, even louder this time.

Suddenly, I wasn't afraid. I picked myself up and I stared defiantly at where the Voice seemed to come.

"Where are you? Why don't you show yourself? *Coward!*" I yelled.

There was a flash of light. Nicholas Rosetti stood before me where no one had been a moment before.

He was on his feet, but I could tell that he was dead. His skin was waxy and pale and blue in places. His eyes showed no movement. But the Voice came from his mouth, like a cheap ventriloquist's trick.

I told you that Rosetti was dead. Now do you believe in my power? Still believe I can't hurt you?

I looked at poor Father Rosetti in sorrow and shock, and then Justin was standing where the priest had been. Justin looked more animated than Rosetti. Was he alive?

Still believe I can't hurt you, Anne? the Voice asked again

"Yes, yes. In the name of GOD, I do believe that," I yelled. "You can't!"

I walked toward Justin and tears were streaming from my eyes. I kept going, and when I got to him I slowly reached out my hand.

Justin was gone before I could touch him.

"You have no power over me!" I screamed like a wild woman on the deserted street. "Be gone! You can't hurt me. Go! Damn you, go!"

I stood my ground. I *was* strong. Father Rosetti was right about that.

And then I swooned. I dropped to the street like a sack of wet sand. But it was more than a faint. It was a powerful loss of consciousness, like nothing I had ever experienced.

I was afraid I was dying.

Chapter 109

I SEEMED TO ACTUALLY leave my body and then to arrive within an intricate, detailed vision. I tried to be a skeptic, an investigator, but I couldn't. The vision was too powerful, too overwhelming. I had no choice but to accept it.

I saw a plain clay house high over a busy marketplace. The air was hot and dry, and I knew I was in a town called Nazareth. I have no idea how I knew this, but I did. There was a young girl coming down the steps from the clay house where she lived.

And then she was walking right beside me. She looked at me with dazzling blue-green eyes. She was young, and she was very pregnant. I knew that this girl who smiled at me was the Virgin Mary. This was Christ's mother.

I looked deeply into Mary's eyes and saw a truth about all women there, a truth about myself. "You are right, Anne. He can't hurt you. Not here on Earth; only in Hell.

You are too strong. You're a special person. God bless you, and take care."

Then the scenes before my eyes began to change rapidly. They came and went in split seconds. I found that I could take in all the details with ease. It was almost as if I had known everything before and the vision was a memory.

In the distance, across a long stretch of sand, I saw Jesus as if he were here in the present time. He was nailed to a crude wooden cross, his limbs contorted grotesquely. Then I was with him, looking into his face above me, and crying as I watched him suffer in the most gruesome and obscene manner.

Jesus was a lovely, dark-faced man. His eyes were closed. His body was scourged and wounded in so many places. A hideous platted crown of thorns pierced his head. I had read the accounts of the Crucifixion in the Gospels. Now I understood it for the very first time.

The scene shifted. I had a flash of real-time cognition. I knew who I was, where I was. I wondered, *What is this vision? Am I insane?*

I thought of Justin again. Was he alive?

Then I thought of the cloister where I had taken my vows.

I remembered poor Father Rosetti and his intense questions, and I knew that he really was dead.

The tone of the fast-flying images changed. Something like a shattering earthquake shook me. As I watched in terror, a tidal wave covered the crowded streets of a major city. Buildings were crushed. Thousands were drowned in an instant of horror and evil. I felt the all-powerful, deep presence of the Beast. The Voice was calling my name again, and it was so real. I prayed. *I reject Evil with all of my strength. I reject Evil. I reject Evil.*

My eyes opened.

I felt a stirring inside my body. It was painful, but then I felt the deepest calm. I knew that a miracle had happened.

It had happened to me.

And I finally knew why I had been called into all this, why I was here.

I was pregnant, and I was a virgin.

Chapter 110

THE FOLLOWING MORNING I awoke early to the sound of a phone ringing beside the bed in my hotel room. I picked up and heard, "I'm here. Can I come up, Anne?"

Tears immediately filled my eyes. My body shook. "Yes. Come now," I told Justin.

He was alive and he was in Rome.

It took Justin a couple of minutes to get upstairs, time enough for me to splash water on my face and run a brush through my hair. My stomach felt funny, but I needed no reminder that I was pregnant. I was certain of it now. The night before I had bought and used a home pregnancy test and it was positive.

There was a knock and I hurried to the door, realizing that my feet were bare and I was wearing an old night-gown but not really caring.

I opened the hotel door and fell into Justin's arms. I let myself go. I burst into tears. We hugged, and then he kissed me, and if there had been even the smallest doubt in my mind that I loved him, it was gone.

I pulled away so I could see him better. I felt so good about him. I almost couldn't believe that I had gone thirty-four years without feeling what I did now. It was such a long time not to experience love. There had to be a reason, and now I thought I knew what it was.

"More than anything," Justin whispered, "I missed you. Anne, I was so afraid I would never see you again. I dreaded that more than dying in Ireland."

"Tell me everything," I said. "Kathleen's child isn't the Savior, Justin. Kathleen isn't the virgin mother."

"I know," he said. "Father Rosetti told me what he knew during our last few hours together. He's dead. He died horribly, and so did Colleen's child. The child was the Beast."

I told Justin what I had seen on the back street between my hotel and Salvatore Mundi Hospital. Then I told him about my condition.

Justin stared back into my eyes. "Rosetti said that the true virgin was here in Rome. He meant you, Anne. He said that the message of Fatima was that there would be more than one virgin mother, and that one woman would bear the Savior, one would bear the Beast."

"Colleen?" I asked. "She isn't dead? She's all right?"

"I brought Colleen to Woodbine Seminary. She's being cared for there. I saw Satan, Anne. The eyes of the legions of fallen angels were in the eyes of Colleen's child. Thousands of eyes, like tiny pinpricks. Such incredible hatred and evil in those eyes. Like nothing I've ever seen or imagined."

"Hold me," I whispered, and Justin did. I felt safe in his arms. I felt totally accepted and loved.

"I love you so much, Anne." He told me what I already felt so strongly.

"I love you, Justin. What do we do about it?"

He knelt before me and softly bowed his head. "I love you with my heart and soul. I know that I'll love you for eternity. I have to leave the priesthood. Then, please marry me?" he asked.

I knelt and faced Justin. I wanted to be as close to him as I possibly could be. I needed to stare directly into his beautiful eyes.

"Yes, I will marry you," I told him.

Chapter III

NINE MONTHS LATER. Brigham and Women's Hospital, Boston, Massachusetts.

Who can tell about the ways of God? Who can truly understand? I certainly can't.

The tiniest, most precious baby was in my arms. The child was only moments old, eyes open and staring directly into mine, actually holding my gaze. Not a thousand eyes, just two beautiful blue ones. It was a perfect child, but I didn't need the doctors to tell me that.

I knew. I just knew.

Dr. Maria Ruocco leaned in close to me. She was a lovely woman, but not commissioned by the Church to be here. Gently, she brushed the hair away from my face. I saw something in her eyes. This doctor, who had confidently delivered thousands of children, was confused.

She finally spoke to me. "Anne," she said, with hushed reverence. "You were still *intact.*"

"I know," I said.

The baby whimpered, cried, then pulled at me in a most glorious way. Tears of happiness rained down my cheeks. I let down the front of my gown and gave the infant my breast. I thanked God. I didn't completely understand, but I knew this was good, this was right. It was nine months since I had suddenly and mysteriously received the incredible gift. I had conceived without having sexual intercourse. And now I was delivered of a healthy child.

Justin stood close to me, his scrub mask hanging around his neck, his handsome face beaming. His eyes were filled with love for me, and love for the child. He had proved himself in a thousand ways while I was pregnant. I loved him even more now than I had that day in Rome.

And he believed — we both believed in this miracle before our eyes.

I didn't know what would happen after I left the hospital room, what the child's life would be like, or mine either. But I knew happiness on this day. I never wanted it to end.

I stared down at this child — this holy child — this baby girl, Noelle.

The Savior of us all was a girl.

Epilogue

NOELLE, NOELLE

Chapter 112

NOELLE WAS EIGHTEEN YEARS old when she witnessed the terrible car accident on Vandemeer Avenue. She was living with her brothers and sisters and her mother and father, the O'Carroll clan, in a small town in Maine.

She was a university student and wanted to become a doctor, to do as much good as she could. She had learned that from her parents, who were both good people. They taught at the University of Maine, but they also operated a home for wayward young women. They had always been loving, caring parents.

In her eighteen years, Noelle had never seen anything as horrible as the crash at the usually quiet Vandemeer Avenue intersection. It shocked and saddened her, forcing tears into her eyes. It made her feel vulnerable, feel mortal and afraid.

And suddenly, Noelle experienced tremendous doubt,

even anger, about the cross-purposes of God. Her eyes went back to the obscene, twisted wreckage.

The yellow Volvo station wagon had struck a chestnut tree. The unyielding tree had split open the vehicle, passing through the engine block, through the front and back seats.

The driver and his young wife died instantly. Three small children appeared to be dead. It was so needless, so tragic.

A fourth child, an adorable little girl in slipper-feet pajamas, had been thrown free of the car. She was lying, badly injured, on someone's lawn.

The girl was crying softly, being attended to by men and women from the neighborhood who had rushed to the accident scene.

Noelle could stand the terrible suffering no longer. It made her so angry that these people had died. She turned away from the unbearable sadness, the earsplitting wails of approaching police cars and ambulances.

She had never been affected like this before. Her head ached. She couldn't bear it. She had to do something to help the family.

She prayed with all her heart — to make the family whole again. She didn't know if she could do it. She *saw* them alive and well in her mind.

She looked at the girl on the lawn — and nothing had happened.

Let this family live. They deserve a second chance. Let them have it, she prayed. *Come back to life. Come to life, little children. Come back to life, mother and father.*

She heard cries coming from near the car. "They're alive. All of them. They're alive."

She had brought the family back to life, just as Jesus raised Lazarus out of love and compassion. It was the first of Noelle's miracles, and as she watched the children, the mother and father, her heart leapt with joy and purpose.

Noelle hurried away so as not to be noticed. She had no way of knowing that she was being watched.

The eyes hungrily followed Noelle up the pretty oak-lined street. All the way to her home. They were the fathomless eyes of a boy who'd been washed up cold and hungry on a beach nineteen years before. A boy who'd been thrown from the cold Irish Sea and survived.

There was a faint red mark on the young man's forehead, a cross made with the fingernail of a man of God.

The mark always burned, and it kept his hatred focused.

He'd waited all these years. He had been patient. But now, as he watched Noelle and her family, he meant to take what was rightfully his.

He watched her — with thousands of vengeful, bestial eyes.

More
James Patterson!

Please turn this page
for a
bonus excerpt from

1ST to Die

a new
Little, Brown book
available
wherever books are sold.

Prologue

INSPECTOR LINDSAY BOXER

It is an unusually warm night in August, but I'm shivering badly as I stand on the substantial gray stone terrace outside my apartment. I'm looking out over glorious San Francisco and I have my service revolver pressed against the side of my temple.

Goddamn you, God! I whisper. Quite a sentiment, but appropriate and just, I think to myself.

I hear Sweet Martha whimpering. I turn and see she is watching me through the glass doors that lead to the terrace. She knows that something is wrong. "It's okay," I call to her through the door. "I'm okay. Go lie down, girl."

Martha won't leave, though, won't look away. She's a good, loyal friend who's been nuzzling me good night every single night for the past six years.

As I stare into the Border collie's eyes, I think that maybe I should go inside and call the girls. Claire, Cindy, and Jill would be here almost before I hung up the phone. They would hold me, hug me, say all the right things. *You're special, Lindsay. Everybody loves you, Lindsay.*

Only I'm pretty sure that I'd be back out here tomorrow night, or the night after. I just don't see a way out of this mess. I have thought it all through a hundred times. I can be as logical as hell but I am also highly emotional, obviously. That was my strength as an inspector with the San Francisco Police Department. It is a rare combination, and I think it is why I was more successful than any of the males in Homicide. Of course, none of them are up here getting ready to blow their brains out with their own guns.

I lightly brush the barrel of the revolver down my cheek and then up to my temple again. Oh, God, oh, God, oh, God. I am reminded of *soft hands,* of Chris, and that starts me crying.

Lots of images are coming way too fast for me to handle.

The terrible, indelible honeymoon murders that have terrified our city mixed with close-ups of my mom and even a few flashes of my father. My best girls—Claire, Cindy, and Jill—our crazy club. I can even see myself, the way I used to be, anyway. Nobody ever, *ever* thought that I looked like an inspector, the only woman homicide inspector in the entire SFPD. My friends always said I was more like Helen Hunt married to Paul Reiser in *Mad About You.* I was married once. I was no Helen Hunt, he was sure no Paul Reiser.

This is so hard, so bad, so wrong. It's so unlike me. I keep seeing David and Melanie Brandt, the first couple, who were killed in the Mandarin Suite of the Grand Hyatt. I see that horrifying hotel room where they died senselessly and needlessly.

That was the beginning.

Book One

DAVID AND MELANIE

Chapter One

Beautiful long-stemmed red roses filled the hotel suite—the perfect gifts, really. *Everything* was perfect.

There might be a luckier man somewhere on the planet, David Brandt thought, as he wrapped his arms around Melanie, his new bride. Somewhere in Yemen, maybe—some Allah-praising farmer with a second goat. But certainly not in all of San Francisco.

The couple looked out from the living room of the Grand Hyatt's Mandarin Suite. They could see the lights of Berkeley off in the distance, Alcatraz, the graceful outline of the lit-up Golden Gate Bridge

"It's incredible." Melanie beamed. "I wouldn't change a single thing about today."

"Me, either," he whispered. "Well, maybe I wouldn't have invited my parents." They both laughed.

Only moments before, they had bid farewell to the last of the three hundred guests in the hotel's ballroom. The wedding was finally over. The toasts, the dancing, the schmoozing, the photographed kisses over the cake. Now it was just the two of them. Both were twenty-nine years old and had the rest of their lives ahead of them.

David reached for a pair of filled champagne glasses he had set on a lacquered table. "A toast," he declared, "to the second luckiest man alive."

"The second?" she said, and smiled in pretended shock. "Who's the first?"

They looped arms and took a long, luxurious sip from the refreshing crystal. "This farmer with two goats. I'll tell you later."

"I have something for you," David suddenly remembered. He had already given her the perfect five-carat diamond for her finger, which he knew she wore only to please his folks. He went to his tuxedo jacket, which was draped over a high-backed chair in the living room, and returned with a jewelry box from Bulgari.

"No, David," Melanie protested. "You're my gift."

"Open it, anyway," he said to her. "This, you'll like."

She lifted the top. Inside a suede pouch was a set of earrings, large silver rings around a pair of whimsical moons made from diamonds.

"They're how I think of you," he said.

Melanie held the moons against the lobes of her ears. They were perfect, and so was she.

"It's you who pulls my tides," David whispered.

They kissed, and he unfastened the zipper of her dress, letting the neckline fall just below her shoulders. He kissed her neck. Then the top of her breasts.

There was a knock of the door of the suite.

"Champagne," called a voice from outside.

For a moment, David thought of just yelling, "Leave it there!" All evening, he had longed to peel away the dress from his wife's soft, white shoulders.

"Oh, go get it," Melanie whispered, dangling the earrings in front of his eyes. "I'll put these on."

She wiggled out of his grasp, backing toward the Emperor's Master Bathroom, a smile in her liquid brown eyes. *God he loved those eyes.*

As he went to the door, David was thinking he wouldn't trade places with anybody in the world.

Not even for a second goat.

Chapter Two

Philip Campbell had imagined this moment, this exquisite scene, so many times in his head. He knew it would be the groom who opened the door. He stepped into the room.

"Congratulations," Campbell muttered, handing over the champagne. He stared at the man in the open tuxedo shirt with a black tie dangling around his neck.

David Brandt barely looked at him as he inspected the brightly ribboned box. Krug. Clos du Meynil. 1989.

What is the worst thing anyone has ever done? Campbell murmured to himself. Am I capable of doing it? Do I have what it takes?

"Any card?" the groom said, fumbling in his pants pockets for a tip.

"Only this, sir."

Campbell stepped forward and plunged a knife deeply into the groom's chest, between the third and fourth vertebrae, the closest route to the heart.

"For the man who has everything," Campbell said. He pushed his way into the room and slammed the door shut with a swift kick. He shoved David Brandt against the door and powered the blade in deeper.

The groom stiffened in a spasm of shock and pain. Guttural sounds escaped from his chest—tiny, gurgling, choking breaths. His eyes bulged in disbelief.

This is amazing, Campbell thought. He could actually feel the groom's strength leaking away. The man had just experienced one of the great moments of his life, and now, minutes later, he was dying.

Campbell stepped back and the groom's body crumpled to the floor. The room began to tilt like a listing boat. Then everything began to speed up and run together. He felt as if he were watching a flickering newsreel. Amazing. Nothing like he had expected.

Campbell heard the wife's voice and had the presence of mind to pull the blade out of David Brandt's chest.

He rushed to intercept her as she came from the bedroom, still in her long lacey gown.

"David?" she said, with an expectant smile that turned to shock at the sight of Campbell. "Where's David? Who are you?"

Her eyes traveled over him, terror-ridden, fixing on his face, the knife blade, then to her husband's body on the floor.

"Oh, my God! David!" she screamed. *"Oh, David, David!"*

Campbell wanted to remember her like this. The frozen, wide-eyed look. The promise and hope that just moments ago had shined so brightly were now shattered.

The words poured from his mouth. "You want to know why? Well, *so do I.*"

"What have you done?" Melanie screamed. She struggled to understand. Her terrified eyes darted back and forth, sweeping the room for a way out.

She made a sudden dash for the living room door. Campbell grabbed her wrist and brought the bloody knife up to her throat.

"Please," she whimpered, her eyes frozen. "Please don't kill me."

"The truth is, Melanie"—Campbell smiled into her quivering face as he stepped close—"I'm here to save you."

He lowered the blade and sliced into her. The slender body jolted up with a sudden cry. Her eyes flickered like a weak electric bulb. A deathly rattle shot through her. Why? her begging eyes pleaded. Why?

It took a full minute for him to regain his breath. The smell of Melanie Brandt's blood was deep in his nostrils. He almost couldn't believe what he had done.

He dragged the bride's body back into the bedroom and placed her on the bed.

She was beautiful. Delicate features. And so young. He remembered when he had first seen her and how he had been taken with her then. She had thought the whole world was in front of her.

He rubbed his hand against the smooth surface of her cheek and cupped one of her earrings—a smiling moon.

What is the worst thing anyone has ever done? Philip Campbell asked himself again, heart pounding in his chest.

Was this it? Had he just done it?

Not yet, a voice inside answered. Not quite yet.

Slowly, he lifted the bride's beautiful, white wedding dress.

Chapter Three

It was a little before eight-thirty on a Monday morning in June, one of those chilly, gray summer mornings San Francisco is famous for. I was starting the week off badly, flipping through old copies of the *New Yorker* while waiting for my GPE, Dr. Roy Orenthaler, to free up.

I'd been seeing Dr. Roy, as I still sometimes called him, ever since I was a sociology major at San Francisco University, and I obligingly came in once a year for my checkup. That was last Tuesday. To my surprise, he called at the end of the week and asked me to stop in today before work.

I had a busy day ahead of me: two open cases and a deposition to deliver at district court. I was hoping I could be at my desk by nine.

"Ms. Boxer," the receptionist finally called to me, "the doctor will see you now."

I followed her into the doctor's office.

Generally, Orenthaler greeted me with some well-intended stab at police humor, such as, "So if you're here, who's out on the street after *them*?" I was now thirty-four, and for the past two years, lead inspector on the homicide detail out of the Hall of Justice.

But today, he rose stiffly and uttered a solemn, *"Lindsay."* He motioned me to the chair across from his desk. Uh-oh.

Up until then, my philosophy on doctors was simple: When one of them gave you that deep, concerned look and told you to take a seat, three things could happen. Only one of them was bad. They were either asking you out, getting ready to lay on some bad news, or they'd just spent a fortune reupholstering the furniture.

"I want to show you something," Orenthaler began. He held an X-ray up against a light.

He pointed to splotches of tiny ghostlike spheres in a current of smaller pellets. "This is a blowup of the blood smear we took from you. The larger globules are erythrocytes. Red blood cells."

"They seem happy," I joked, nervously.

"Those are, Lindsay," the doctor said, without a trace of a smile. "Problem is, you don't have many."

I fixed on his eyes, hoping they would relax, and that we'd move on to something trivial like you better start cutting down those long hours, Lindsay.

"There's a condition, Lindsay," Orenthaler went on. "Negli's aplastic anemia. It's rare. Basically, the body no longer manufactures red blood cells." He held up an X-ray photo. "This is what a normal blood workup looks like."

On this one, the dark background looked like the intersection of Market and Powell at 5:00 P.M., a virtual traffic jam of compressed, energetic spheres. Speedy messengers all carrying oxygen to parts of someone else's body.

In contrast, mine looked about as densely packed as a political headquarters two hours after the candidate has conceded.

"This is treatable, right?" I asked him. More like, I was telling him.

"It's treatable, Lindsay," Orenthaler said, after a pause. "But it's serious."

A week ago, I had come in simply because my eyes were running and blotchy and I'd discovered some blood in my panties; and every day, by three, I was suddenly feeling like some iron-deficient gnome was inside me siphoning off my energy. Me, of the regular double shifts and fourteen-hour days. Six weeks accrued vacation.

"How serious are we talking about?" I asked, my voice catching.

"Red blood cells are vital to the body's process of oxygenation," Orenthaler began to explain. "Hemopoiesis, the formation of blood cells in the bone marrow."

"Dr. Roy, this isn't a medical conference. How serious are we talking about?"

"What is it you want to hear, Lindsay? Diagnosis or possibility?"

"I want to hear the truth."

Orenthaler nodded. He got up and came around the desk

and took my hand. "Then here's the truth, Lindsay. What you have is life threatening."

"Life threatening?" My heart stopped. My throat was as dry as parchment paper.

"Fatal, Lindsay."

Chapter Four

The cold, blunt sound of the word hit me like a hollow-point shell between the eyes.

Fatal.

I waited for Dr. Roy to tell me this was all some kind of sick joke. That he had my X-ray mixed up with someone else's.

"I want to send you to a hematologist, Lindsay," Orenthaler went on. "Like a lot of diseases, there are stages. Stage one is when there's a mild depletion of cells. It can be treated with monthly transfusions. Stage two is when there's a systemic shortage of red cells.

Stage three would require hospitalization. A bone marrow transplant. Potentially, the removal of your spleen."

"So where am I?" I asked, sucking in a cramped lungful of air.

"Your erythrocytic count is barely two hundred per cc of raw blood. That puts you on the cusp."

"The cusp?"

"The cusp," the doctor said, "between stages two and three."

There comes a point in everybody's life when you realize the stakes have suddenly changed. The carefree ride of your life slams into a stone wall; all those years of merely bouncing along, life taking you where you want to go, abruptly ends. In my job, I see this moment forced on people all the time.

Welcome to mine.

"So what does this mean?" I asked, weakly. The room was spinning a little now.

"What it means, Lindsay, is that you're going to have to undergo a prolonged regimen of intensive treatment."

I shook my head. "What does it mean for my job?"

I'd been in homicide for six years now, the past two as lead homicide inspector. With any luck, when my lieutenant was up for promotion, I'd be in line for his job. The department needed strong women. They could go far. Until that moment, I thought that I would go far.

"Right now," the doctor said, "I don't think it means anything. As long as you feel strong while you're undergoing treatment, you can continue work. In fact, it might even be good therapy."

Suddenly, I felt as if all the air had been sucked out of the room and I was suffocating.

"I want to give you the name of a hematologist," Orenthaler said.

He went on about the doctor's credentials, but I found myself no longer hearing him. I was thinking, Who was I going to tell? Mom had died eight years before, from breast cancer. Dad had been out of the picture since I was thirteen. I had a sister, Cat, but she was living a nice, neat life down in Newport Beach; and for her, just making a right turn on red brought on a moment of crisis.

The doctor pushed me the referral. "I know you, Lindsay. You'll pretend this is something you can fix by working harder. But you can't. This is deadly serious. I want you to call him *today.*"

Suddenly my beeper sounded. I fumbled for it in my bag and looked at the number. It was the office—Jacobi.

"I need a phone," I said.

Orenthaler shot me a reproving look, one that read, I told you, Lindsay.

"Like you said . . ." I forced a nervous smile. "Therapy."

He nodded to the phone on his desk and left the room. I went through the motions of dialing my partner. Jacobi's gruff voice came on the line. "Fun's over, Boxer. We got a double one-eight-oh. The Grand Hyatt."

My head was spinning with what the doctor had told me. In a fog, I must not have responded.

"You hear me, Boxer? Work time. You on the way?"

"Yeah," I finally said.

"And wear something nice," my partner grunted. "Like you would to a wedding.